Mistress to the Beast
By Eve Vaughn

Can this beauty tame the beast?

Her father's shop is more than just a family business. It's the place they lovingly call home. When a powerful property development company stoops to barely legal tactics to force them to sell, Lila's outrage spurs her straight to the source to fight the injustice.

A serious accident left Hunter Jamison's body scarred. A bitter split from his latest lover has left the former playboy without faith in the female sex. Yet, confronted with Lila's fiery beauty, he finds himself offering her a deal: If she'll be his mistress for three months, he'll allow her father to keep the shop.

A simple agreement? Hardly. It's a battle of wills that flares into much more than either of them bargained for—a consuming passion that could heal Hunter's soul-deep scars...or inflict new ones.

Warning: This title contains blackmail, vehicular sex, angry sex, light bondage and graphic language.

Head Over Heels: A Cinderella Story
By Lena Matthews

Sometimes you have to make your own happily ever after.

Working at the Glass Slipper is anything but a fairytale for Cyn Elder. After one especially long day, all she wants is to kick off her shoes and put her feet up, but she reluctantly lets her friends drag her out to a new club.

Movie mogul and fledgling club owner Parker Maguire is bored with the Hollywood scene and its plastic women, and the club scene isn't proving to be much better. Until he finds a sassy woman refusing to back down from his overzealous bouncer.

Cyn is a breath of fresh air, neither impressed by celebrity status nor bowled over by his charisma and wealth. She's honest, genuine—and arousing in more ways than he could have ever imagined. For once, Cyn puts herself before her shop and lets herself be swept off her feet by a man who pursues her with a delightful vengeance.

Her father's evil girlfriend and her two lazy daughters, however, see Cyn's new happiness as nothing more than a threat to their own comfortable lives. Their plot to break the two lovers up could turn Parker and Cyn's "once upon a time" into a "happily never after."

Unless Cyn's Fairy Drag Queen can pull something out of her pink-chiffon sleeve...

Warning: This title contains hot, dirty, workplace sex; hot, dirty, sauna sex; heck...just hot, dirty sex in general. As well as fairies of the non-magical variety, and dreams coming to life.

Ever After

A Samhain Publishing, Ltd. publication.

Samhain Publishing, Ltd.
577 Mulberry Street, Suite 1520
Macon, GA 31201
www.samhainpublishing.com

Editing by Angela James
Cover by Scott Carpenter

Mistress to the Beast, ISBN 1-60504-179-3
First Samhain Publishing, Ltd. electronic publication: June 2008
Head Over Heels, ISBN 1-60504-233-1
First Samhain Publishing, Ltd. electronic publication: November 2008
First Samhain Publishing, Ltd. print publication: September 2009

Contents

Mistress to the Beast

Eve Vaughn

Dedication

To Gwen for being such a sweetie!

Chapter One

"He can't do this to you! We'll fight him and his damn company—if that's what needs to be done, but Saunders will remain in business!" Lila slammed her fist on the dinner table, making the plates and utensils clatter against it.

James Saunders wagged his finger from side to side with a shake of his head. "Watch your language, young lady."

Even at twenty-seven, Lila had to censor her words around her father, who thought it unladylike for women to swear. Lately, she'd been doing a lot of it.

"I'm sorry, Dad, but we can't sit back and watch everything you've worked so hard to build be destroyed by some reclusive property developer. This is your livelihood and home." Tears stung the backs of her eyes as she blinked them away. It didn't seem fair they should lose everything on some rich man's whim.

"Dad, there has to be something we can do to stop them. They can't just take our home like this! Saunders is your life." She wiped away an angry tear that had escaped the corner of her eye. Lila didn't want to break down in front of her father, especially when he was probably trying to stay strong for her. But emotion threatened to overwhelm her.

James pushed his half-eaten dinner away and placed his head in his hands. "You're right. It's my life, not yours, and I've depended on you for far too long."

Lila's breath caught in her throat. Surely he wasn't thinking of giving up. "What are you trying to say, Dad?"

Her father lifted his head with the suspicious sheen of tears glistening in his eyes. "Baby, this is my battle to fight. Not yours. I'm guilty of leaning on you a lot more than I should have. I ought to be the one taking care of you, not the other way around."

She waved her hand dismissively. "Don't be ridiculous. If you can't count on family, who else can you depend on? I'm not doing anything I don't want to do."

"Lila, your heart is in the right place, but maybe it's time to wave the white flag. I'm an old man, and although there's nothing I'd like more than to keep the shop running until the day I die, I don't think I can do it on my own *and* fight Ramsey's."

Lila reached across the table and grasped her father's hand in earnest. "Daddy, you have me."

"And that's the problem," he sighed.

She wasn't sure whether to be hurt or angry at his comment. "Why is my being here a problem?"

He held up his hand. "That came out wrong."

"How else am I supposed to take it when you imply you don't need me, that you don't want me around?"

Her father took her hands in his. "Baby girl, I'll always need you, but like I said, I can't keep leaning on you so much. You're a young, beautiful woman—exceptionally so."

Lila snorted, rolling her eyes. "Don't start that again."

"It's true."

"Fathers are supposed to say things like that to their daughters."

"I don't say anything I don't mean. I see the way men look at you. You're the image of your mother, God rest her soul. I used to wonder how a mug like me was lucky enough to end up with an angel like my Eloise. She could have had anyone she wanted, you know, but for some reason she chose me."

A smile touched Lila's lips at the mention of her mother.

She didn't remember her, but listening to her father reminisce made Lila feel closer to the woman who'd given her life. "Who are you trying to kid? You know you're a good-looking man. Mrs. Reyes comes by the shop everyday and it's *not* to purchase milk. She has a crush on you." Lila giggled. There were quite a few women who gave him more than a second glance.

It was her father's turn to brush her comments aside. "Gloria is a nice lady. She's just looking for a little conversation."

"And a lot of you."

His lips firmed to one thin line as he shook his head. "You won't distract me from the topic. As I was saying, you're young and you should have a life of your own. You need to go back to your job, and find a nice young man to settle down with and give me some grandbabies."

Not this subject again. She should have known he would somehow steer the conversation in this direction. "Dad, I'm not interested in a relationship right now."

"Is that what you told that doctor you were seeing before I had my stroke?"

"That was nothing." The words came out a bit quicker than she intended.

James lifted a brow, a knowing expression on his face. "You used to talk about him nonstop. I thought the two of you would get married."

"It wasn't serious, Dad." Lila couldn't quite meet his eyes. She didn't like lying to her dad. The truth was, Jason had asked her to marry him, but he couldn't understand why she had devoted so much of her time toward seeing her father get better.

"For God's sake, hire a private nurse! I'll pay for it. I don't think it's too much of me to expect my woman to spend some time with me," he'd said one day after another heated argument. Jason Webster wasn't used to being neglected by anyone and had no problem letting her know it.

"I'm a nurse. How could I put him in someone else's care

13

when I'm quite capable of handling the job myself? I can't just ignore that fact. He needs me."

"I need you. You're going to have to make a decision: It's either me or him."

That ultimatum had been the final straw in a string of problems between the two of them. She did love Jason, or at least Lila thought she did, but how could she stay with someone who would force her to make such a choice? Lila realized then she couldn't. Jason hadn't taken it well, and not even a week later he was dating someone else, another nurse at the hospital. His actions had reaffirmed to Lila she'd made the right decision.

James gave his daughter a long hard look. "You haven't lied to me since you were five years old and didn't want me to find out you'd broken your mother's favorite vase. You're not very good at lying, baby. I believe I'm doing the right thing."

Lila's heart beat a tattoo against her breast. "What? You've made a decision?"

"I'm going to sell. I won't let you waste your life taking care of me and fighting a war we can't win." Pain oozed from his voice, and his dark face looked gray all of a sudden.

Alarm shot through her. "Daddy, are you all right?" She rushed to his side.

"Don't you worry, child. It's just this old heart. Get me my pills and I'll be okay."

Lila wasted no time retrieving the prescription bottle from the medicine cabinet and a glass of water. On top of recovering from a stroke, he often suffered heart palpitations due to stress and unhealthy eating habits even though she tried her best to regulate the latter. The entire situation had taken its toll on him physically and mentally.

How could she let him give up something that meant so much to him? If only he didn't have the worry of what would happen to the shop, Lila was sure he'd get better. Selling the place would kill him, slowly but surely.

There had to be something she could do. Thus far, none of her efforts from writing Ramsey's, the local newspapers, and attending town council meetings, were getting her anywhere. Her one last resort would be to go to Ramsey's headquarters in Manhattan and demand a meeting with the CEO. Failure was not an option.

Later that night, after she'd done the cleaning up and her father was in bed, Lila flopped on the couch from exhaustion. Was it already three years since they'd received that damned letter, an offer to purchase the building they lived in? The problem being, it wasn't only their home, but where her father's business was housed. Shortly afterwards, her father suffered his stroke. Lila had taken leave from her position as a geriatric nurse to assist during her father's recovery and rehabilitation, as well as manage the store while dealing with a property developer.

After refusing to sell out for months, Lila learned the city was interested in purchasing their property under eminent domain. Apparently the powers that be at Ramsey's had friends in high places. If the city bought their home, they could sell it for as much—or as little—to Ramsey's as they wanted to. From that point on, her father seemed to age before her very eyes.

She picked up one of the newspapers she'd saved. It was months old, but it had an article within in it that talked of the plans for the shopping center and all the stores that would be included—in her neighborhood. Who were they kidding? Didn't they realize people had lost their homes and businesses in order for this waste of mortar to be built? She scanned the rest of the article which discussed the developers of the project and the head man himself, Hunter Jamison.

Dubbed "the Beast" for his aggressive business tactics, he'd taken over the nearly bankrupt Ramsey's over ten years ago and turned it into one of the largest companies of its kind in the country. The paper contained an earlier picture of him and he looked every bit the Viking he was said to be descended from. Larger than life in the photograph, with his broad shoulders

Eve Vaughn

and barrel-sized chest, he seemed more suited for a football field than an office.

Wavy blond hair framed an extremely attractive face with its square jaw, long straight nose, and surprisingly full lips. Lila thought he looked a little too perfect. Too bad for all his looks, he harbored a black heart.

Though she'd read this article a dozen times, she continued on, looking for some kind of clue that might help her. Lila placed the newspaper on the coffee table and picked up a more recent issue. This particular article focused solely on the man and the accident which had nearly cost him his life. Obviously the accident didn't prevent him from ruining her father's life. Lila was tired of this waiting game. She had to act now.

It was time to confront the Beast.

Chapter Two

"I'm sorry, Hunter, but I can't do this anymore." Jessica delivered the statement with a voice full of contrition, but it still sounded artificial to Hunter's ears. Who did she think she was kidding?

"Do what?" he spoke with quiet menace. If she thought he'd let her off so easy then she had another think coming. He'd been down this road before and didn't want to be lied to. If Jessica wanted to end their affair, she'd have to be woman enough to be honest about her reasons.

She licked her glossy lips, a move that had once turned him on, but now simply annoyed him. "You know perfectly well what I mean. It's over between us. This relationship."

He lifted a brow. "What relationship? There hasn't been much of one in weeks. The only reason you've contacted me lately is to ensure your bills get paid on time. You knew exactly what you were getting into when you got involved with me. Did you think you could just spend my money without delivering the goods? Even you aren't that beautiful."

Her mouth gaped open. "It wasn't like that," she protested, although she couldn't look him in the eyes when she said it.

"Then tell me what it was like. Tell me why you've reneged on this deal when you seemed so eager in the beginning." Hunter tried to keep the bitterness from seeping into his voice, but as he thought of how she'd double-crossed him, he found the task more difficult with each passing moment. He knew exactly why she wanted out, but he wanted to hear the words from her mouth.

"I—I can't say."

"Say it, Goddamn you!" Hunter slammed his fist on the big oak desk separating them. If it wasn't in the way, he was sure his fingers would be wrapped around her lovely white throat.

She jumped, fear entering her eyes for the first time since she'd entered his office. Good. It was better than pity or revulsion. He should have known this would happen when Jessica decided to visit him at his office instead of coming to his home as she normally did. More witnesses. He'd known it was a matter of time before she left him like the others, but it didn't ease the pain searing within his chest. Did he have the right to be this angry or should he be grateful for the time she had given him? After all, who would want to stay with a disfigured freak like him? Still, a deal was a deal.

"Hunter, please don't make this more difficult for me than it already is."

"Why should I make this easy for you? Do you think things have been a piece of cake for me? Look at my face!"

She shook her head, dark red hair swirling around her face. "Don't make me. I can't...I can't handle it. I thought I could but the money isn't worth it. I—" She broke off with a sob. There were a number of hurtful things she could have said, but this by far was the worst.

"Just go," he whispered, not bothering to hide his disgust in himself or with her. He should have been used to this by now, but it hurt as bad as it did the first time. Lowering his head, Hunter waited for her to leave. When he didn't hear the sound of retreating feet, he roared, "What the hell are you still standing there for?"

A squeak escaped her lips. "But you said you'd take care of my bills this month."

The greedy little bitch. It would have served her right if he told her where to go, but the faster she was out of his life, the better.

"Forward them to my personal assistant and they'll be taken care of."

"Thank you." Jessica smiled, moving closer to his desk as if to shake his hand, but Hunter narrowed his eyes, not bothering to hide the rage building within him. She stopped in her tracks and nodded. "Uh, thank you. I'm sorry things didn't work out for us."

"Save your lies for the next sap."

Wisely she didn't respond.

When the door clicked shut, Hunter released a frustrated growl. With a sweep of his arm, he knocked everything off his desk, computer monitor and all. The items went crashing to the ground with a loud clatter.

Seconds later, the executive vice president, his second in command, opened his door and stuck his head in the office. "What the hell happened here?" Thomas inquired as he surveyed the mess Hunter had made.

No one in the Ramsey's organization dared talk to Hunter this way or question him, except Thomas. His years of service and friendship had given him that right. Thomas was also the only one who still looked Hunter directly in the face without flinching.

"What does it look like happened?" Hunter sneered, not wanting to discuss the loss of yet another lover.

"It looks like an adult has thrown a childish temper tantrum. I passed by your latest paramour in the hallway. I take it by the clutter you've made, you two are finished?"

"Nice guess work, Sherlock. What are you going to tell me next? That it's Tuesday?"

"If you ask me, you're better off without her. And you should have known better before getting involved with her in the first place. The only thing she was interested in was your wallet."

Sometimes Hunter wished Thomas wasn't so open with his thoughts. His situation was humiliating enough as it was with the reminder. "But I didn't ask you, so keep your damn opinions to yourself."

"Someone needs to open your eyes to a few home truths."

Hunter exhaled slowly, wishing his friend would just go away. "And I suppose you've appointed yourself to the task?"

"I'm only saying this because I care."

Hunter wasn't in the mood to listen. He turned his swivel chair around to face the window. "Don't you think I know what Jessica was after? Maybe that's why I chose her in the first place. At least that way there'd be no pretense of an emotion that doesn't exist."

Thomas released a sigh. "Why do you even bother with these women in the first place? You may get a temporary bedmate, but is it really satisfying if you have to pay for them? Jessica was little better than a prostitute."

"I believe the term is called mistress."

"Whatever you want to call it, you basically had to pay for her time. You can do better than that, Hunter."

Hunter turned around then to face Thomas. "And what would you have me do? Stroll into a party and chat up some random woman as if I don't look like a monster?"

Thomas rolled his eyes heavenward. "You're not a monster, and if you allowed someone to take the time to get to know you, then maybe these situations could be avoided."

"Considering you have no clue what I'm going through, it's easy for you to say."

Thomas raked his fingers through his dark hair. "Look, if you're going to have another pity party then you're going to be the only guest."

"Then fucking leave! I didn't ask you to come in here to begin with!"

Thomas advanced, stopping when he stood directly in front

of the desk. "I should, but someone has to deal with your disgruntled ass. Hunter, I can't pretend to know what it's like to go through what you have, but it can't be healthy to cut yourself off from the rest of the world. You stay holed up in that damned house of yours for days at a time, only coming to the office occasionally. And when you do show up here, you make such a big production of slipping in like a damn thief in the night because, heaven forbid, someone might catch a glimpse of the face you keep covered with hair. Did you ever think people are only reacting to what you project?"

"I don't—"

Thomas held up his hand. "Let me finish. You've had your say so I'm going to have mine. You refuse to meet with our business associates and it makes people wonder about your competency to run Ramsey's."

"Do you have any complaints about how I conduct business?"

"That wasn't my point and you know it. Do you know what your problem is?"

Hunter's fingers curled into fists as he struggled to hold on to his threadbare temper. "No, but I'm sure you'll enlighten me."

"You're being an ass. Don't you realize how lucky you are to be alive? You might have a few scars, but at least you still have your life."

This had to be the hundredth time Thomas had delivered this speech and it was just as annoying this time around. "Saying it's a few scars is an understatement. And maybe I would have been better off dead, at least then I wouldn't have to go through life looking like a circus sideshow attraction."

Thomas shook his head. "You sound incredibly ridiculous right now. Get over yourself. It's time to come out of hiding."

Hunter pulled back his hair and stared defiantly at his friend. "Care to take another look and revise your expert opinion?" His scars were the very reason he refused to look in any mirrors and why he avoided them like the plague. God's little joke on him had been to leave one side of his face intact while the other side was a hideous roadmap of imperfections. The doctors had offered skin grafting, but had informed him that while some of the damage could be corrected, he would still never be the same as he was before.

There was a time when Hunter had been considered handsome. He'd even been featured in a local paper as one of New York's sexiest bachelors. He'd taken his looks for granted, but the accident changed everything. Now, he couldn't walk down the street without making small children cry. The humiliation of dealing with people's reactions made him isolate himself and withdraw from the social whirl he'd once enjoyed.

The most humbling aspect of life after the accident was the loneliness. Were it not for Thomas forcing him to handle his responsibility to Ramsey's, Hunter would probably never bother leaving his home. Even the women he'd set up as mistresses couldn't stomach him for long, as demonstrated by Jessica.

He shouldn't bother, but goddammit, he was still a man with needs. Masturbation would only satisfy him to a point, but what choice did he have other than choosing some random woman off the street. The very thought disgusted him. At least when he had a steady lover, they were exclusive with him and he'd always verified their clean bills of health before entering into an agreement. Perhaps it was a part of his life he'd have to let go. He wasn't sure if he could deal with the constant rejection, because it was slowly killing him on the inside.

Some would probably say he was getting exactly what he deserved. Remembering what an ex-lover had told him a few years back, he closed his eyes.

He'd just ended their affair with his customary parting gift of diamond earrings and a matching tennis bracelet. "You're a bastard, Hunter Jamison, and one day you're going to get your comeuppance. You're going to fall for a woman who won't love you back, and by God, I wish I could be there to see it!" his ex had cried.

Hunter, in his cocky insolence, had laughed in her face before dismissing her from his thoughts. He'd found her words amusing though. What did he need with love? He had wealth, power, and access to unlimited pussy. Love was for losers. Hadn't he learned that particular lesson well enough from his mother who went through husbands like most people did underwear and his father who spent years pining for a woman who didn't care for anyone but herself?

Hunter had yet to find a woman worthy of the emotion *if* it even existed. Still, it didn't mean he wanted to go without companionship. Who would?

Thomas finally threw his arms up in the air in his exasperation. "I wish you'd get over yourself, Hunter. Yes, you're scarred, but you still have your health and your life. You have a successful business and several possessions most people would kill for. How about being thankful for the things you do have?"

"Because those things don't mean a thing as long as I look like this." Hunter pointed to his face.

Thomas shook his head, annoyance etched on every line of his round face. "I give up. Have it your way. You're a disfigured monstrosity who no one will ever love. There. Is that what you'd rather hear?"

Hunter shrugged. "It's the truth."

"I hope you really don't believe that."

"I do."

"Then I feel sorry for you."

"I didn't ask for your pity, nor do I want it."

"Fine. I'll leave you to your misery."

Hunter knew Thomas meant well. Regardless of the fact they didn't see eye to eye on this particular subject, he didn't want his friend to leave on this note. "Wait. Don't leave. You obviously had a reason for coming to my office in the first place. What's up?"

Thomas looked like he was heavily debating staying or going, but finally took a seat across from Hunter's desk.

"We're still having problems with the last owner on Hudson Street. He still refuses to sell. According to the attorneys, he's had some health problems of late and his daughter is making most of the decisions for him."

This was the one project that Hunter still had interest in. It had been his baby from the beginning. "She's crazy if she thinks we'll offer more money. It doesn't have much worth now that everyone else has sold."

"Exactly. We've already initiated plan B. We have a couple council members who owe us some favors. I believe the property will be ours before the year is out, but we can at least start building around it."

"Good, I think—" Loud shouting on the other side of the door greeted Hunter's ears, making him wonder what the hell was going on out there.

"You can't go in there! Oww! I'm calling the police!" That sounded like his usually unflappable personal assistant.

"Fine. Do what you have to do, and so will I," answered someone whose voice Hunter didn't recognize. A woman's voice.

Seconds later the door flew open, and standing in the doorway was one of the most beautiful women he'd ever seen.

And she looked pissed.

Chapter Three

The moment Lila stepped into her adversary's office, all the courage she'd summoned for this confrontation flew out the window. Staring at her with the greenest eyes she'd ever seen was the legend himself. Hunter Jamison.

Her feet wouldn't carry her forward, and she couldn't tear her eyes away from the man sitting behind the large oak desk in the corner of the office.

"Mr. Jamison, I tried to keep her out, but she assaulted me. I've called the police and security is on their way upstairs." The woman who'd tried to restrain her entered the office. She sounded out of breath. Probably from chasing Lila, who'd run past her.

Lila didn't set out to give the woman a hard time, but she was determined to have this meeting come hell or high water. Turning around to face her accuser, Lila pasted a smile on her face, and delivered her next line in a saccharine sweet tone. "I didn't assault you. If my heel connected with your foot, it was because you were standing in my way. I can't help if you don't understand the meaning of the words 'excuse me'."

The woman gasped, her mouth opening and then shutting as if she couldn't believe what she was hearing. Lila twirled back around and noticed a stocky dark-haired man with glasses standing by the boss man. Had he been there already? He must have, but Lila only had eyes for Mr. Jamison.

Refocusing her attention on the still figure, she noticed a

thick mane of wavy blond hair resting in a cascade around his shoulders and obscuring most of his face. The only features she could really make out were those arresting eyes, a long blade of a nose, and thick lips, which were now pulled down into a frown.

"Miss, whoever the hell you are, you're going to have to leave," the dark-haired man spoke.

Lila spared him a brief glance, daring him to touch her. "I'm not going anywhere until *he* agrees to cease and desist!" She jerked her thumb in Jamison's direction and advanced toward the desk. "Don't you understand what you're doing? Do you get your kicks from destroying people's lives?"

The unknown man walked toward her, but she backed away when it looked as if he'd touch her. "Ma'am, I'm not sure what the problem is, but perhaps if you come to my office, we can work something out to your satisfaction. My name is Thomas Ruby and I'm just as capable to see to your problem as anyone in this organization."

It was a tactic to get her to leave if she'd ever heard one. Lila wasn't stupid. He'd have her ass hauled out the door the minute she stepped out of this room.

"No! The only person I want to talk to is Hunter Jamison, and if that's not your name, I don't want to hear you."

Why wasn't the big blond saying anything? His head was bowed now, but she sensed his anger simmering just below the surface. Good. That made two of them.

"Look, Miss..." Mr. Ruby trailed off in an attempt to get her name.

"Saunders. Lila Saunders," she bit out through gritted teeth.

Mr. Ruby stepped away from her, mouth agape. "Miss Saunders, I—" His words were cut off when two uniformed security guards burst into the office and ran over to her.

Each of them grabbed one of her arms. Lila refused to let this crusade end at the hands of a couple of rent-a-cops. "Let go of me!" She wiggled and struggled against their grasps, trying to pull free even though the more she moved, the tighter their hold became. They were too strong for her. *Please don't let it end this way,* she silently prayed.

"The police are on their way, sir," a pimple-faced guard said as his nails dug into her skin. "We'll keep her downstairs until they arrive. We're not sure how she got up here, but it won't happen again."

Lila continued to fight, trying to yank free. "Let go!"

"Let her go." The deep booming voice that resonated throughout the entire office came from the man himself, shocking her so much she froze.

"But, Mr. Jamison, we—"

"Let her go. I'll deal with this matter myself." Hunter Jamison pushed away from his desk and stood up to reveal his magnificent height. He had to be at least six feet six and he was very broad.

"But the police are on the way!" the woman whined.

"Then tell them you've wasted their time. I'll talk to Miss Saunders."

"But—" The woman didn't seem ready to give in so easily.

"This discussion isn't up for debate, Ann," Mr. Jamison said the words softly enough, but the underlying message was there: do as I say or else.

The security guards released Lila's arms with obvious reluctance. She rubbed her aching limbs to increase the blood flow to the areas they'd squeezed, shooting each guard a glare.

"Thomas, please leave us," Jamison ordered.

Mr. Ruby remained where he stood for a moment, but one look from the boss had his shoulders sagging in defeat. "Fine, but if you need me, I'll be in my office." He gave Lila a shaky smile before following the other three out. He closed the door behind him with a decisive click.

Once she and Mr. Jamison were alone, Lila squared her

shoulders and took a deep breath. His large frame would have intimidated anyone, but she refused to be cowed by him. She raised her chin in a gesture of defiance and met his gaze.

"Miss Saunders, please have a seat," he offered. The way he stared at her made Lila feel self-conscious. She couldn't quite read his expression, especially with all that hair in his face, but she felt like a very juicy mouse beneath the hungry gaze of a cat.

Placing her hands on her hips, she shook her head. "No, thank you. I'd prefer to stand. What I have to say won't take long."

He shrugged one massive shoulder. "Suit yourself. I'll sit, if you don't mind."

The office was huge, but he seemed to dominate every square inch of it, though she did wonder why there was a huge mess in front of his desk, including a computer monitor. Lila didn't like the way she was so aware of his larger than life presence. She licked her suddenly dry lips. "N-no I don't mind."

"Good, Miss... May I call you Lila?"

"Yes."

"Lila," he said her name slowly, as though testing it on his tongue. "Did you know your name means dark-haired beauty? I took a little Arabic in college."

She did, actually. Her father had mentioned it to her once, and how it was the only name he and her mother had agreed on. "I didn't come here to talk about the meaning of my name."

He inclined his head slightly forward, making his hair cover up even more of his face. Was he really as badly scarred as the newspapers suggested? "Fair enough. Then tell me why you've come to see 'the Beast'"

Lila knew he was toying with her, but she was in no mood for games. She'd be damned if she let him frighten her. "I'm sure you already know."

"You're the one who burst into my office. If you have the guts to do that, surely you can follow through by sharing your grievance."

Bastard. Did he want her to beg? On the verge of telling him to go to hell, she remembered how sick and weak her father had seemed this morning. If Hunter Jamison wanted his pound of flesh, she'd give it to him. She would do whatever it took to save Saunders.

"I'm asking you to reconsider your offer on my father's property."

"Our plans have been finalized. The shopping center will go up as planned."

"But you can build around Saunders, can't you? I've seen the blueprints. My father's building will be just on the outskirts of it."

"The shopping complex could use the space for parking," he countered. "Anyway, it's in your best interest to sell out, don't you think? Wouldn't your father's little business suffer from the competition?"

Lila gritted her teeth at his condescending tone. Her fingers itched to slap him. "We'll make it work somehow."

His lips tilted into a small brief smile. "You sound like you actually believe that, but I'm afraid you're wasting your time. I'm sure you're already aware the city council has taken an interest in your father's property. Once they're involved, there's little I can do about it."

Lila bit back the expletive hovering on her tongue, silently counting to ten before speaking. "If you wanted to, you could."

He grinned. "You're right. I could, but I don't feel so inclined.

"What you're doing is illegal."

Again, he shrugged. "Tell that to someone who's interested, sweetheart."

Lila wasn't prepared to let things end like this. There had to be something she could do. As much as she loathed to do so, she was willing to beg. "Please, Mr. Jamison, there must be some other way. I'm pleading with you. Don't do this. If my father loses his business, it would kill him."

"Don't you think you're being a tad dramatic, Lila?"

Her hands balled into fists at her sides as she willed herself to remain where she stood. "I'm telling the truth."

Jamison stifled a yawn, not looking the least bit impressed. "If keeping his business is so important, why isn't your father here pleading his own case? What kind of man would allow his daughter to fight his battles for him? This doesn't sound like the kind of person I'd do a favor for."

Lila knew he was trying to bait her, but she wouldn't let him. No matter how much she wanted to tell the smug son of a bitch where to go, she'd have to keep her cool.

"My father doesn't know I'm here. He's...he hasn't been well lately, but the only thing that makes him better is working at the store. He lives for that place. If you take it away from him, he'd have nothing to live for."

"Do you mean you're not reason enough for him to live?"

"You're twisting my words around. That isn't what I meant at all. To be honest, he plans on giving up and just taking the money."

Jamison's brows knitted, his bewilderment evident. "Then why are you here?"

"Because I know he doesn't want to. He's doing it for me. He thinks if he sells, I can move on with my life. My father believes he's a burden to me."

"Perhaps there's some wisdom in his decision. You're young, beautiful...and desirable. Why would you want to throw your life away taking care of an old man?"

Lila tightened her fists. *I will stay calm. I will stay calm,* she chanted in her mind. "My father could never be a burden to me because I love him very much, but then again, I wouldn't expect a cold bastard like you to understand."

Jamison leaned back in his chair, raising a dark blond

brow. "Strong words for someone who wants my help."

Lila turned her head unable to meet his taunting green gaze. "I'm sorry, I shouldn't have said it."

"Don't be. It's what you meant. I can respect that."

She forced herself to look at him again. "Look, Mr. Jamison, I know if you'll just let us be, he'll get better and won't worry so much. Due to pressure your company is placing on him, I fear this stress is taking a toll on his health."

His lips twitched into a mockery of a smile. "Beautiful and compassionate. A rare combination. You're to be commended on your concern for your father, but you've made a miscalculation."

"What do you mean?" she whispered, almost afraid to hear the answer.

"You bet all your hopes on the fact I'd give a damn. Unfortunately for you, I don't."

Lila's breath caught in her throat as she blinked hard. She vowed not to cry in front of this jerk. It took several moments before she could compose herself enough to reply. "I'll do anything if you would reconsider."

He stiffened and his eyes narrowed. "Anything?"

Lila closed her eyes tightly to block the sight of his hateful presence. Did those words actually leave her mouth? "Anything."

"I'm not sure you know what you're saying. When you make a provocative statement like that, you're asking for trouble." His gaze blatantly roamed her body, leaving no doubt in her mind what he was thinking. "Now tell me, Lila, are you willing to back up that statement? Because I have no time for little girls playing adult games."

Was she really propositioning him? Her father had taught her to have respect for herself and her body, yet here she was offering to act the whore for someone she despised more than anything. Could she go through with this? She moistened her lips with the tip of her tongue nervously. Not trusting herself to speak, she nodded.

"Would you sleep with me?" he asked softly.

Even though she'd known this was the direction the conversation was headed when she'd made her bold declaration, his words still came as a shock. To actually hear them said aloud made her feel sleazy, but now that it was all on the table, there was no turning back.

Lila felt like a character in a bad B movie. Did things like this really happen? Her stomach twisted in knots and her hands shook. If she pinched herself, would she wake up from the horrible nightmare? "Yes," she finally answered after nearly losing her nerve.

"What I want is a mistress. I find myself without one at the moment, and I think you'll do quite nicely. Would you be willing to stay with me for three months at my house, at my beck and call—seeing to me every need?"

"But my father—"

"Would be taken care of."

"I don't want to be away from him for that long."

"Then you obviously don't care as much about saving his business as you've let on. Good day, Miss Saunders."

The tears that had threatened to spill earlier sprang to her eyes once again. "Wait! The answer is yes, but only if you arrange for a nurse to occasionally stop by to see my dad takes his medication and for someone to help him around the store."

"While it's pretty bold of you to make demands considering you're the one who wants a favor of me, that can easily be arranged."

She let her head fall, as shame washed over her. What had she done? "Okay, then it's a deal."

"And would you be ready for me to fuck you whenever and however I want?"

She flinched. "You don't have to be so crude about it."

"Sweetheart, I don't have time to tiptoe around your

ladylike sensibilities. Besides, I won't insult either of us by calling it making love."

"It could never be that," she hissed.

"I like your spirit, Lila." He stood up and then stalked over to her.

She took a step back. "Hold on. How do I know you'll honor your end of the bargain and leave my father's business alone?"

"I'll have my attorney draft a contract and make it legal and binding. At the end of our agreement, you'll receive a generous settlement in addition to services rendered."

Lila shook her head. "I don't want your money, just your promise to leave my father be."

Jamison raised a brow. "Persistent, aren't you? But before we reach a formal agreement, I think there's something you should see...in case you want to change your mind."

"I won't."

"We'll see." Slowly he raised his hands to his face and pulled his hair back, revealing what it had been hiding. On one side of his face was an angry jumble of deep, red scars running from his temple to his neck. They created such a contrast to the other side of his face which was virtually untouched, she gasped in horror.

Maybe it was nerves, but the room began to spin, and everything suddenly went black. Her last conscious memory was the sensation of falling.

What the hell had he been thinking to throw that impulsive offer at Lila Saunders? Had he become that desperate? One thing he knew for certain, she was one of, if not *the* most stunning woman he'd laid eyes on.

Tall and voluptuous with curves that cried out to be caressed, she had the face of an angel. Hunter had memorized

Eve Vaughn

her every feature, from her rich mocha skin, full bow-shaped lips and tilt-tipped nose. Her hair had been pulled back in a tight ponytail, emphasizing high cheek bones. He wondered how her dark tresses would look flowing around her shoulders, or arranged around her head against a pillow—in his bed.

His cock grew hard at the mere thought. Lila's most arresting feature he'd determined, were a pair of large dark gold eyes framed by long thick lashes. She was a real beauty.

Hunter took another swig of his scotch as he remembered the look of horror on her face when he'd revealed his scars. As he'd suspected, Lila was just like the others. She'd talked a good game, but she didn't have the nerve to back it up. Despite this being a business transaction, he should have known a woman who looked like her couldn't possibly be attracted to him. In most cases, he would have brushed off her reaction and written her off, but for some reason, he couldn't.

He should have sent Lila on her way the second she'd come to, but in the moment he'd caught her from falling, holding her in his arms, Hunter had realized it was something he wanted to experience over and over again. But still, his pride wouldn't allow him to demand she follow through with her offer. Instead, he'd handed her his card and informed her she had twenty-four hours to contact him before the offer was taken off the table.

He wouldn't hear from her, he was sure.

She may have been able to give her delectable body to him if he kept the scars hidden, but as long as they were out in the open, she couldn't handle it. It figured.

Hunter couldn't remember the last time he'd wanted someone with the intensity that he felt for Lila, but he knew he'd have to get over it fast and get used to living a life of solitude. Maybe when the shopping center project was over, he'd resign from the company and sell his stocks. Going out in public was becoming more difficult each time.

"Mr. Jamison, you have a phone call," his housekeeper, Mrs. Coates interrupted his thoughts.

He hadn't heard it ring, not that it mattered. It was probably Thomas. "Tell Thomas I'll call him later."

"It's not Mr. Ruby. It's a Miss Saunders. Would you like to speak to her or should I tell her you're unavailable?"

Lila? Was this a courtesy call to tell him she had changed her mind? He set the decanter and his glass aside. "I'll take it in here. Thank you."

Mrs. Coates nodded and left the room. Hunter picked up the receiver and waited for his housekeeper to hang up the other line before speaking. "Lila. To what do I owe the pleasure of your call?" He silently congratulated himself for sounding calm.

"You know." She spoke in a hushed whisper as if someone was there with her.

"So what's your answer?"

She took so long to reply, he thought the line had disconnected.

"Hello?"

A sigh greeted his ears. "Yes. My answer is yes—that is, if you still want me."

She had no idea how much.

Chapter Four

It looked like Hunter had thought of everything, from hiring a private nurse for her father to ensuring the store would be taken care of properly in her absence. Lila had even taken a physical and STD tests at his insistence, verifying her clean bill of health. Lila had been on the pill since she was a teenager to regulate her cycle, but it had been humiliating to be asked whether she was on some type of birth control. As a show of good faith, he'd presented her his medical records to prove his vitality and disease-free status.

Hunter had told Lila he wanted her without any barriers between them.

She had to be crazy to go through with this. To actually be this man's kept woman for the next few months was something that had kept her awake at night since she'd said yes. He'd wanted her to come as she was, with the clothes on her back he'd said, and nothing more other than what was necessary as everything else would be provided for her.

He'd even sent a car to pick her up and take her to his home. The hardest part in preparing to spend this time with him was coming up with an excuse to give her father for being away. Lila hated lying to him. He'd been so trusting when she told him she'd been offered a private nursing assignment.

In fact, her story seemed to make him happy, to see her venture out "and not be closed in with the old man" as he'd put it. Lila hadn't been able to look him in the eye. How could one tell their dad they were going to whore themselves out—after all, what she was doing was little better than prostitution.

Shivering as a pair of brilliant green eyes flashed through her mind, she was tempted to tell the driver to turn the car around and take her home. The words hovered on the tip of her tongue, but they wouldn't come out. For the past few weeks, the amount of time Hunter had given her to change her mind, she'd fought desperately to come to terms with what she'd agreed to.

She'd have to let him touch and screw her in ways she'd let no other man do to her before. The odd thing was, the thought didn't make her cringe as she felt it should have. What was wrong with her? Did she look forward to being debased by him?

"Ma'am, we're here."

The cool burst of air hitting her skin signaled to Lila the rear passenger door was open. She'd been so lost in her musings, she hadn't realized the car had stopped. The sudden urge to get out and run and keep running grabbed her momentarily. Once she entered Hunter Jamison's home, there would be no turning back. Could she go through with this?

Clenching her fists at her sides, she closed her eyes and squeezed them tight, attempting to work up enough nerve to get out of the car.

"Ma'am, we're here," the driver repeated.

Lila nodded, opening her eyes. It wasn't just a nightmare. Damn. "Okay. Thank you." Taking a deep breath, she took the hand offered her. For the first time since the car had stopped she looked at surroundings. So this was where she'd be staying? To say the house—no the mansion—was large would have been an understatement. Lila had only seen something of its kind on those television shows which gave peeks into the opulent lives of celebrities. The large beige Georgian style manor with its imposing columns could have been considered a work of art in its beauty.

The estate gave her another reason to hate Hunter Jamison. Here he lived high on the hog while harassing working class people like her father and forcing them out of their livelihoods.

Squaring her shoulders, she allowed the driver to lead her up the pathway to a side entrance. When they entered, Lila couldn't help but be awed by the grandness. She made a mental note not to touch anything while she was here because any of the treasures decorating this place would be far too dear for her to replace.

A tall, slender woman with warm, sherry-colored eyes and iron gray hair approached, a half smile on her lips. "Welcome, Miss Saunders. I'm Maddie Coates. I take care of this house for Mr. Jamison and during your stay here, I'll see to your needs. My husband, Ernest, drove you here. He'll also be on hand if I'm not available. There's an intercom in every room so you'll be able to contact us at anytime."

Lila shook her head, nervous laughter trilling from her throat. "I won't bother you at all hours of the night. And please, call me Lila. Must we be so formal?"

"If that's your wish...Miss Lila. Please follow me." The woman seemed nice enough, but Lila could tell she was a stickler for propriety. Sheesh, Lila hadn't realized people like Mrs. Coates existed outside of television and books. She and her husband were faithful retainers to the core. But then again, none of what was happening to her seemed real.

Already, Lila felt grossly out of place in a pair of slacks and a blouse she'd always believed she looked nice in. But her surroundings were a jarring reminder that her clothes had come off the rack and not in one of those fancy boutiques where someone who was used to this set up shopped. Her jaw dropped when she saw the room she'd be staying in. It was larger than all the rooms combined in the apartment she shared with her father.

"I hope this room is to your satisfaction, Miss Lila."

She could only nod in response. The room would have been adequate for the Queen of England. "Yes...it's very nice."

"Your private bathroom is through that door." Mrs. Coates pointed to a door at the far corner of the room. Then she walked to another section and opened a set of double doors. "This is your closet. You'll find all your clothing in here and the dresser drawers. I'll leave you to freshen up and change into something for dinner, which will be served in a half hour. Mr. Jamison will be waiting for you in the dining room. Is there anything you require in the meantime?"

Lila was still trying to acclimate herself to the sheer luxury around her. "No, thank you."

Mrs. Coates hesitated at the door. "Mr. Jamison would like for you to choose something suitable to wear. He said you'd you know what he meant." The distaste in the other woman's tone brought heat to Lila's cheeks.

It was one thing to deal with her shame privately, but to have someone judging her put things in a whole different ball court. "Umm, yes," she murmured, not meeting the other woman's eyes.

Once the door clicked shut behind the housekeeper, Lila was able to let her guard down. What was she getting herself into to by agreeing to this crazy deal? Living in his home, and being fed and clothed by him? Would he be a selfish lover, demanding all she had, taking while giving nothing back? Yes, that's how it would be. A man who would steamroll over an entire neighborhood was probably not good in bed.

Not that it mattered. He could be Don Juan for all she cared. Lila was determined to not enjoy it. She tried to stave off the tremble that moved up her spine. She'd made this bargain with the devil. Now, she'd have to figure out how not to get burned.

Hunter gripped the stem of his wine goblet, swirling the burgundy contents inside. What the hell was taking her so long? He knew the exact time she'd arrived—an hour ago. He'd left instructions with Mrs. Coates to escort Lila to the dining room a half hour after her arrival. He'd seen her get out of the car from his office window—saw how she'd looked at her surroundings with an air of uncertainty, touching something deep within him. Then he'd witnessed her lift that determined little chin of hers and stride into his house as proud as a queen.

Lila didn't strike him as the type to back down from a challenge, which made him wonder why she hadn't come downstairs to the dining room as he'd ordered. Had she lost her nerve? Hunter gritted his teeth, slamming the glass on the table, uncaring of the droplets of merlot splashing on the white lace tablecloth. He'd spent every single night since making this arrangement with her, lying awake, imagining his hands caressing her creamy chocolate body, her lush lips crushed beneath his. Then, he'd think about turning her over and riding that voluptuous rump and asking himself how she'd respond to toys. He tortured himself with questions of how things would be between them.

He supposed time would tell if only she would get her ass downstairs so he could lay down some ground rules. Glancing impatiently at the platinum Rolex adorning his wrist, Hunter decided he'd give her five more minutes before he stormed upstairs and dragged her down—by her hair, if he needed to.

The soft clicking of heels against the marble floor in the foyer alerted him to someone's approach. Lila.

Folding his hands in front of him, he tried to project an air of nonchalance he didn't feel. His pulse raced, and breath caught in his throat when she appeared.

Wearing a little black dress, which dipped in the front to reveal the top of her tempting cleavage and accentuated her curves to a tee, she stood proud and graceful. He could probably span her tiny waist with his hands. Lila wore her hair piled on top of her head and her face was bare of makeup save for a touch of gloss.

She was absolutely gorgeous. And late.

"You were supposed to be down here a half hour ago!" The words rushed from his mouth like an angry roar. It was a bit harsher than he'd intended. Hunter hadn't meant to let on how eager he'd been for her to join him.

Lila jumped at his brutal rejoinder before standing even straighter and taking a seat at the foot of the formal dining room table. "I'm here now." She replied so calmly, it raised his ire.

"You're too far away. Come down here."

Golden brown eyes narrowed as she raised her chin in defiance. "I prefer where I'm sitting, thank you."

There could only be one reason why she wouldn't want to be so close to him. Well, that was too damned bad. She'd have to accept him, scars and all. She'd already seen them and knew exactly what she was getting into. "Perhaps you've forgotten, but I call the shots around here. Not you. But seeing as how you'd like to test me, I'll give you two options, you can either take the seat here," he pointed to the table setting next to his, "or I'll come get you. I don't think you'd appreciate the experience."

Lila went completely still, her gaze locking with his. For a moment he believed she'd stand her ground, but in an abrupt movement, she pushed her chair back, and stood, her lips tightened to a thin, angry line.

Disappointment at her reluctance to be close nagged at him. One of the first things that had struck him during their initial meeting was the way she'd seemed unaffected by his appearance. Oh, he'd seen that look of horror flash in her eyes upon his reveal, and of course she'd fainted, but after she'd come to it was as if she'd forgotten about them. Could he have just imagined it? Was it simply wishful thinking on his part? Probably. He was a fool.

She was no different than anyone else. Too bad for her she'd have to deal with him for the next three months. Hunter had given up a great deal to give in to her demands, including hours with board members, executives, contractors and on top of that coming up with a feasible alternative to his previous plans. He'd be damned if he allowed her to treat him like a fucking nuisance.

When she plopped down in the seat cattycorner to him, Lila lifted her shoulders in a shrug. "Okay. I'm here."

A floral scent wafted to his nostrils making Hunter want to bury his face against neck. Her proximity was doing things to his equilibrium he didn't think possible. His cock stirred and stiffened, straining against his pants. Goddamn. This woman had to be part witch because she'd cast a spell on him. There was only one way to grab control of the situation and that was to let her know right away who was in charge.

"Rule number one, when I say jump, you'll say how high. Two, when I tell you to be somewhere at a designated time, I expect you to make every effort to obey. Three, you will always be courteous to my staff. And last but not least, failure to obey my rules will result in punishment."

Her lips twisted into a smirk. "Punishment? What do you plan on doing? Give me a time out?"

"You'll find out when you fail to do as I ask."

Mrs. Coates chose that moment to enter the dining room. "Mr. Jamison, are you ready for me to serve the meal?"

"Yes, thank you."

The housekeeper turned to Lila. "Would you like a glass of wine, Miss Lila?"

"Yes, she would."

With a nod Mrs. Coates left them alone once again.

Fire flashed from the depths of her golden eyes and if looks could kill, Hunter was sure he'd be dead on the spot. A smile tugged at the corners of her lips. He couldn't help admiring her spirit.

"I can speak for myself and I don't particularly care for wine at the moment."

"Do you have some objection to drinking alcohol?"

"I don't, but I'd rather not have any now."

"But I want you to have some. It would please me."

Her lips quirked. "And what you say goes right?"

"You're learning fast." He allowed his gaze to drift to the tops of her breasts. Unable to go another second without touching her, Hunter reached over and ran his finger across her tantalizing décolletage.

Lila gasped, eyes widening. She jerked away from his hand. "Don't."

"It's my prerogative to touch you. Remember our bargain... How is your father by the way?"

"You're a beast," she mumbled under her breath.

A chuckle escaped his lips. "So they say. And you, my dear, are a beauty and you're mine—that is unless you've changed your mind?"

Through the narrowed slits of her eyes, Hunter thought he saw a suspicious gleam of moisture. He should have been ashamed for what he was in essence making her do, but he pushed that feeling away quickly. Lila was here of her own free will. It wasn't as if he were holding a gun to her head to make her stay. So she could save her tears for someone who gave a shit. "Has anyone ever told you how beautiful you are when you're angry? I'm happy to see the clothes the personal shopper selected for you fit so well."

Lila shrugged. "I don't see why I couldn't bring my own things."

"Because it suits me to see you dressed in satins and silks. My women wouldn't be caught in anything but the best. When our agreement is over, you may take them with you."

The chin was raised once again. "I'll walk away with what I came into this house with, if it's all the same to you."

He lifted his wine goblet and took a healthy sip before

returning it to the table. "Suit yourself. They're yours to do with as you wish."

Mrs. Coates returned, wheeling a cart with their dinner on it.

Hunter leaned against the back of his chair, realizing Lila had barely looked at his face since she'd entered the dining room. Even those few times when she'd dared to catch his gaze, Lila had quickly looked away. The old insecurities hit him like a sledgehammer. *It doesn't matter what she thinks. She's yours for the taking.*

With slow deliberation, he pushed his hair away from his face. A perverse need for her to look at him as he was took over. "Look at me, Lila." He kept his voice low and soft, but left no room for doubt that he'd issued a command.

She raised her head with obvious reluctance and looked him square in eyes, gold fire sparking within the depths of her gaze. "Do you get off by telling me what to do?" She bit the words out, tight-lipped.

Hunter laughed. "Not from giving orders, but I plan on getting off in quite another way very soon."

Mrs. Coates placed his plate in front of him, her movements stiff. She was too much of a professional to give away her true thoughts, but Hunter had a feeling his housekeeper didn't approve of his arrangement. He'd brought women to the house before, but he'd never had one stay longer than a weekend. Not that it mattered what his employee thought anyway. This was his house, and he'd do what he saw fit in it.

Once he and Lila were alone again, he took another sip of his wine, watching as she pushed the food around her plate with her fork, not attempting to eat any of it.

"Do you have anything against your dinner?"

Her head came up again, bewilderment crinkling her forehead.

"You've been stabbing that steak with your fork as if it's

done something to you. Is it too rare for your liking or do you not eat meat?"

She pushed her plate away. "I have no problem with eating meat. I'm not hungry."

"Try to eat something. You'll need your strength for later on."

Her eyes widened, her mouth forming a perfect, "o". "Look, Mr. Jamison—"

"Hunter. I hope you don't intend to go all formal on me every time I annoy you. Seeing as how we'll be getting to know each other." He paused to allow his gaze to rake over the length of her beckoning curves, quite intimately. "There's no need for formalities."

Closing her eyes briefly, she took a deep breath. "Hunter. This is my first night here. Can't we just get to know each other a little better before we do *that*?"

Raising a brow, he met her angry gaze. "Fuck you mean?"

Lila lowered her head but not before she shot him a glare. "You don't have to be so graphic."

"Should I pretty it up and give you some flowery speech?"

"All I want from you is to keep your promise." Her voice was low with an undertone of fury.

Yes, she'd be a hellcat in bed. The very thought of it had his cock jumping to life, straining against his pants to break free. Shifting in his chair to alleviate the ache within his throbbing balls, Hunter knew he wouldn't last much longer before taking her and burying himself inside her tight cunt.

He ran his tongue across his lips in anticipation. Would she taste as sweet as she looked? Examining her tightened lips and hands gripping the arms of her chair until her dark knuckles turned several shades lighter, Hunter realized he'd have to work at getting her hot.

It was a challenge he looked forward to tackling.

Chapter Five

"As long as you keep yours," Hunter finally answered. "Look, I've had plenty of lady friends before, but I've never been in an arrangement quite like this either, but it doesn't mean I'm willing to permit you to set the pace."

"But surely you can understand my dilemma. I'm not used to jumping into bed with men I hardly know. I'm only asking for a little time for us to be better acquainted before we sleep together." Lila hoped her plea would appeal to his good nature, that was, if he had one.

Part of her wanted to run out of there and never look back, but what kept her planted in her seat, sitting across from this loathsome man, was thought of her father. After she'd told him Ramsey's wouldn't pursue buying his property, he'd seemed to lose all the worry clouding his eyes. He walked around with a spring in his step that had been missing for months and whistled, looking happier than he had in a long time. She wouldn't have his decline on her conscience, but still, how would she get through this ordeal without losing every ounce of self-respect she possessed?

"I gave you three weeks to back out of our agreement. But the very fact that you're here tells me you're fully prepared to honor your end of the deal. No. I won't allow you to fob me off now because you'll keep coming up with excuses as to why we should wait. In light of rearranging plans for the megaplex and in essence putting my business reputation on the line, you had better get used to the idea of sharing my bed, and fast. And as for my sleeping with you, I have more productive things in mind than that."

Lila willed herself to remain still, otherwise she knew she'd slap the bastard into next week. If that was the way he wanted things to go down, she'd make sure she conveyed in every look, motion and sound that she didn't want to be here. She had agreed to allow him the use her of body, but he never said she had to like it. "Fine," she delivered between clenched teeth.

The sound of his chuckles were tormenting to her ears. He was getting off on her misery!

"I like your spirit, Lila Saunders, but if this is to be a battle of wills, I'll have you know, I don't intend to lose. And no worries, my dear, there's no better way of getting to know each other than in bed. I look forward to the experience."

She kept her head bowed, refusing to rise to the bait.

"Eat."

"I'm not hungry."

"Eat!"

She jumped as his roar reverberated through the dining room. Did she dare defy him? As appetizing as her meal appeared to be, her stomach was too tied in knots to ingest a single bite. But still, if she didn't he'd press the issue. Lila didn't think she had the strength to continue the argument. She picked up her fork and stabbed a string bean with its prongs before popping it into her mouth. The vegetable could have been cardboard as far as she was concerned. She tasted nothing. "There. I ate."

Hunter watched her with those devastating green eyes, his expression giving nothing away. Would he take this as an act of disobedience? He lifted his wine glass and downed the remainder of its contents and stood up. "If you're through, then by all means, let's retire."

When he held out his hand to her, panic set in. There had to be a way to buy some more time. Lila shook her head. "Just give me tonight. I promise, I'll be ready for you tomorrow."

Nostrils flared as he narrowed his eyes. "Lila, I don't make a habit of repeating myself. Get up now or by God, I'll drag you upstairs."

"Sir, is there anything else you'll need?" Mrs. Coates poked her head into the dining room.

"Go away!" Hunter growled.

The older woman disappeared as quickly as she appeared.

Lila gasped. "Do you make a habit of talking to your staff that way? You are a hypocrite. How can you expect other people to be courteous to those who work for you, when you don't know the meaning of the word?"

For his answer he grabbed her by the arm, practically yanking it out of its socket as he hauled her out of her seat and pulled her roughly against his body.

Her fighting instinct emerged. She didn't care what kind of bargain they had, there was no way she'd let him get away with manhandling her. Lashing out, she smacked his broad chest. "Don't ever do that to me again! You have no right—"

"That's where you're wrong, Lila. My house, my rules. You didn't have to agree to the terms set before you, but you did so now you'll have to deal with the consequences. So far my words have had no effect on you so I think the time calls for action."

Before she could utter another word of protest, Hunter bent over to lift and toss her over his shoulder like a sack of potatoes. The wind whooshed out of her lungs, making it difficult for her to speak. Stunned, she hung helplessly as he strode out of the dining room, took the stairs two at a time and carried her to a bedroom she assumed was his. Once her feet touched the floor again, her ability to talk had returned and she was pissed!

"Who the hell do you think you are? I'm not a rag doll you can lug around as you please."

Hunter's response was to loosen his tie and shrug out of his black dining jacket. His outward calm only served to enrage her further.

"Did you hear me?" she yelled.

He unbuttoned his shirt, revealing a chest Mr. Olympus would have been proud of. Her gaze slid along the crested hills of his torso, sprinkled liberally with dark blond hair that trailed down the center of hard rippled abs. He'd seemed huge with his clothes on, but topless, he was a hulk.

Lila gulped, taking a step back. Shaking her head as though to deny what was happening, she held her hands out in front of her. "Don't."

He unbuckled his belt and pulled it out of the loops of his pants. "As we've already established, there's no backing out."

"No. You established it. I didn't. I don't think it was asking too much of you to give me a little time to adjust to this situation."

"But I believe it was. Just as it was a lot for you to ask me to rearrange my plans for a multi-million dollar project, which took weeks of finagling to get the board to agree to. I complied with your plea because I thought you to be a woman of your word. Was I wrong about you, Lila? Are you the type of woman who'll make pretty promises until she gets what she wants and then doesn't fulfill them?"

"No. When I say I'll do something I will..." With a groan, she covered her mouth. She'd basically backed herself in a corner. If she didn't go through with this, she would look like she was reneging and, judging from the smug smirk tilting those sensually curved lips, Hunter knew it too.

Damn him.

"That's what I thought." Kicking out of his pants, he placed his hand on the elastic band of his black boxers.

Lila shook her head, closing her eyes at the sight of his cock tenting his silk underwear. She wrapped her arms around her body, letting her mind wander to any place other than here. Once he touched her, there would be no going back. She'd be no better than a whore.

A cry escaped her lips when he reached out and grazed the side of her cheek with the back of his hand.

"Open your eyes, Lila. I won't allow you to pretend I'm someone else." Once again there was steel in his soft words, daring her to disobey his order.

Slowly she raised her lids, her insides churning with nerves. Why couldn't she stop shaking and dear Lord, why was he so—naked? Though she attempted to keep her gaze above waist level something drove her to look down.

Her mouth fell open. His dick was huge! It jutted forward, not a few inches away from her, long, proud and obscenely thick; she couldn't tear her eyes away from it.

"Do you like what you see?"

"No." The word had come out a little too quickly, even to her own ears.

"The mouth says one thing, but the eyes don't lie. This is what you did to me. Have you any idea how many nights I've lain awake thinking about this moment? When you came downstairs for dinner, I could barely sit still. I'm so fucking horny, I can't promise our first time together will be as nice and slow as I'd like it to be."

Hunter pulled her against him, grinding his hardness against the juncture of her thighs before burying his face against her neck.

She stiffened. *I will not like this. He can do what he'd like to my body, but he'll never have all of me,* she silently vowed. Unfortunately, her body wasn't in tune with her mind. To Lila's utter shame, warmth worked its way from her core and spread throughout her being at the gentle press of his lips on her flesh.

What had she expected? That he'd fling her on the bed, hump her a few times and be done? That's exactly what she'd believed.

Calloused hands slid across her shoulders and pushed the spaghetti straps of her dress down. "Beautiful chocolate skin," he murmured, caressing her with what almost seemed like awe.

A tremble made its way up her spine. No! This couldn't be happening to her. She didn't want to like this, didn't want it to feel good. Keeping her arms firmly at her sides, her fists clenched tight, she tried to maintain a steady breathing pattern.

Hunter pushed her dress to her waist with practiced ease. Her nipples stiffened as the cool air hit them. He lifted his head and cupped her breasts. His thumbs grazed over the turgid peaks, bringing her to painful awareness of the stirring between her legs.

"Sexy. Like dark Hershey Kisses."

"Please" She whispered one last protest, not wanting to give in to the burning ache searing through her system.

"Oh, I definitely intend to." Hunter laughed softly and dipped his head to flick his tongue over one stiff tip, circling and teasing it until Lila began to shake uncontrollably.

Heat flooded her pussy, forming moisture in her panties. She bit her bottom lip to hold back the moan that nearly escaped.

Hunter pulled the burgeoning point into his hot mouth, sucking with fervent tugs.

Almost involuntarily, her hands found their way to his silky blond tresses, digging into them and holding his head against her chest. It had been so long since she'd been held and touched like this, and she couldn't believe how easily her body reacted to him. Lila pressed her thighs together to temper the heat pulsing between them. Hunter seemed to relish his task, taking his time and working her body into a frenzy.

He turned his attention to her other nipple, giving it homage, teasing and tormenting it until she whimpered from pleasure overload. He surprised her by dropping to his knees, taking her dress down with him until her garment formed a little black puddle at her feet.

Hunter jerked her panties down and nudged her thighs further apart, before burying his face between her legs, inhaling deeply. "Mmm. I love the scent of your arousal. You're so responsive. I like that."

Lila looked down to see he was eye level with her pussy. Why did he have to torture her this way? And why was she so turned on by the simple act of him staring at her?

"I'm glad you're not completely shaved down here. I like my women to look like women and not little girls and you're all woman, aren't you, Lila?" He brushed the nest of tight curls with the heel of his palm.

The warring emotions raging through her were making this ordeal more difficult to bear. Despite his skillful ministrations and her body's responses to them, she had to somehow get herself under control or she wouldn't be able to think straight. "Please, c-can't you just get this over with? I-I don't want this."

He lifted his head to look her in the face with knowing eyes. "I won't dignify that comment with a response, especially when you're so hot a trail of cream is running down the inside of your delectable thigh." And to prove his point, he ran his tongue along the very line he'd pointed out.

Lila had to grip his shoulders to remain on her feet, otherwise her wobbly knees would have given out on her. Besides, she was still wearing the black heels she'd donned earlier, and it grew increasingly difficult to hold steady on them.

Parting the slick folds of her pussy, Hunter leaned forward and placed a kiss against her swollen clit and followed it with a long broad lick.

Her nails dug into his skin as she attempted to hold on to the last bit of her sanity. Lila could no longer kid herself. She wanted him. She was probably damned for feeling this way, but by God, the fire flowing through her veins could no longer be denied, especially when he sucked her hot nubbin into his mouth, his teeth grazing against it until she could no longer hold her excited moans back.

"Please." This time her impassioned plea was not for him to stop, but for him not to.

"Throw your leg over my shoulder."

He gave her no choice but to obey because he grasped her ankle and lifted it for her, his impatience evident. This time when he lowered his head, he attacked her pussy like a man hell bent on staking his claim, conquering—devouring. With his lips sealed tightly around her clit, Hunter eased his middle finger into her sopping-wet sheath, pushing knuckle deep. In that moment, she was lost. There was no turning back.

Thoughts of why she was here, her father, her vow to not enjoy this had fled completely. All that mattered was the irresolute desire rolling through her core and sliding along her central nervous system. "Hunter, that feels so good."

Lila ground her hips against the thrust of his finger burrowing inside of her. It was soon joined by another, stretching her walls as though she was being prepared for the intrusion of his cock. He used his mouth and fingers to lick, suck and fuck her wet box until the slow build up of passion exploded within her.

Her climax came hard and fast. Cream gushed from her pussy and Lila held on to him so tight, her nails furrowed into his skin, breaking it and drawing blood. Hunter seemed unfazed, continuing his onslaught.

Dizzy from what he was doing to her, Lila's could barely breathe as stars danced before her eyes. The man was after his pound of flesh and there was absolutely nothing she could do to stop him. "I can't take any more," she groaned, close to her second orgasm.

Hunter looked at her, green eyes blazing. "Oh, you will, my dear, and so much more." Pushing her leg off his shoulder, he stood up. Then he scooped her into his arms and carried Lila the short distance to his massive king sized bed.

"My shoes," she murmured, remembering she was still wearing them.

"Call it a little quirk of mine, but I find it highly arousing to make love to a woman in heels." Pushing her legs apart, he settled between her thighs and shoved his tongue between her slick opening.

"There's nothing more satisfying than feasting on a beautiful woman's cunt. I may not have had dinner, but this dessert more than makes up for it." He moved his palms over her belly, never lifting his head, until his hands reached her breasts, squeezing and shaping them.

Lila wiggled and writhed, mashing her pussy against his mouth. Never in her wildest imaginings would she have thought Hunter Jamison could make her feel this way, yet she was too caught up in a whirlwind of pleasure to care. There'd be plenty of time to deal with the fallout later. It wasn't long before she reached yet another peak.

Hunter lapped at her juices, slurping, grunting and savoring every drop. She was too weak to think coherently when she saw him rise to his knees. Grasping her thighs, he yanked her closer.

Closing her eyes, Lila refused to watch his final act of possession. Bracing herself, she clutched the down comforter beneath her as he pressed the bulbous head of his cock against her entrance, moving it up and down her slit, wetting it.

"Open your eyes, Lila. I've already told you, I won't allow you to pretend I'm anyone else. I want you fully aware of who it is inside of you."

Reluctantly, she complied, not quite looking at him but at some point beyond his shoulder.

He had been so gentle up until this point that it took her by surprise when he slammed into her balls-deep, filling her passage so thoroughly for an instant she believed he'd split her open.

"Goddamn you're tight. And so wet and ready for me." He uttered his words through clenched teeth as though he was having difficulty getting them out.

His fingers inside of her had been nothing compared to the feeling of being so completely stuffed by a thick hard cock. Not giving her much time to adjust to the sheer size of him, Hunter began to move, straining and pushing into her until it almost hurt, but it was the kind of sensation that hovered the line between pleasure and pain.

Her mind screamed this wasn't supposed to happen, but her body was in complete control. Lila gave over to the torrential heat consuming her. Grinding her hips, she met his cock as it plunged in and out of her. She gripped his dick with her pussy, tightening her muscles around him, causing Hunter to grunt incoherently.

They moved liked two dancers in a choreographed piece, so in sync with one another. She held on to him as they bumped, thrust and meshed their bodies together until Lila wasn't sure where Hunter began and she ended. This time when she reached her climax, it was more intense, raw and powerful. "Hunter!" The cry fled her lips before she could stop it.

"That's it, baby. Scream my name. Say it again."

"Hunter."

"Again."

"Hunter."

"Louder!"

"Hunter!" She yelled his name at the top of her lungs, making her throat burn.

"Oh God, I'm coming." Slamming into her one last time, he tensed before collapsing on top of her. He rested his sweat dampened forehead against her own as he gasped for breath.

As she slowly regained control of her hormones, reality smacked her in the face. She'd just allowed this man to use her body. What was worse—she'd liked it, couldn't get enough of what he'd done. Her shame was now complete.

Placing her hands against the hard wall of her chest, she gave him a shove with what strength she still possessed. Once she'd dislodged him, she rolled to her side, scooting to the edge of the bed as far away from him as she could get. Blinking hard, she tried to fight off the tears, but when Hunter touched her back, she lost it.

Stuffing her knuckles into her mouth, she muffled her sobs. Once she began crying, she couldn't stop. How could she have behaved like this? And how in the world would she be able to stop him from taking her again? Especially when she wanted him to?

Hunter removed his hand.

In her misery, she barely registered him rolling off the bed. It was only when a door slammed that she realized he'd left her alone.

Chapter Six

Pressing his hands against the shower wall, his arms holding him braced, Hunter stood under the scalding sting of the water's spray. He must have been in here for at least a half an hour. At this rate, he'd be a shriveled prune. But no matter the length of time he remained in the stall, the rage, sadness, and guilt would not be abated. Never had an experience with a woman touched on so many different emotions.

Holding and touching her had far surpassed the fantasy, but having her turn away from him at the end and cry as though her heart were breaking had been like a punch in the gut. Did he disgust her so much? Were his scars so hideous to her she couldn't believe she'd stooped to letting him have his way with her?

Hunter had been so sure Lila wanted him, too. Hell, he knew she did. The gasping moans, the way her body shook with just a stroke of his finger and the way her pussy had gotten so wonderfully wet couldn't be faked by even the most skilled actress.

Now that he knew what it could be like between them, one taste wasn't enough. He had to have her again. The very sight of how his pale hands had splayed across her dark body sent blood racing to his cock, stiffening it to near pain. He'd been with black women before, but out of the couple he'd dated, one had lovely cafe au lait skin while the other was not much darker than him. They didn't have Lila's rich cocoa hue. Not that they hadn't been lovely. They were. But they weren't Lila. Because there was such a huge contrast in their skin tones, Hunter never realized how something so simple could be an erotic turn on.

She was the epitome of perfection from the blue-black nipples cresting the well-formed mounds of her breasts to that pretty pink pussy, wrapped so tightly around his cock. He'd almost come the second he'd entered her.

For as long as he lived, Hunter would never forget how she'd made him feel. Being one with Lila had been like a dream, but then it had turned into a nightmare. His. At least the other women he'd taken to his bed since the accident pretended to enjoy the aftermath. Not Lila. She'd broken down completely. It had angered him at first. She had no right to pretend she was some vestal virgin who'd been taken by force. She'd been far from it. Hadn't he given her the opportunity to change her mind? Up until the very last minute, Hunter left her with the option to back out, but she hadn't.

Then, the shame had come. He wasn't the one who'd put her up to this. She was here for her father and he knew it. That's when the depression kicked in. While he'd fucked her, he could almost imagine she was there for him, not because he'd forced her hand.

With a sigh of resignation, he turned the nozzles of the shower off. Standing under rapidly chilling water wasn't going to change things. If he had any decency within him, he'd let her go home. But he couldn't, at least not until he'd had his fill of her and Hunter had a feeling that wouldn't be for a very long time.

Once he was dried off, he threw on the terry cloth robe hanging on the back of the bathroom door. He put his hand on the knob, but caught his reflection through the steam in the mirror. Walking over to it, he wiped the mist away. Hunter flinched at the sight of his scars.

Raising his hand, he touched them. It was no wonder Lila

could barely look at him. He'd noticed it. There wasn't much about her that had escaped his attention. His fingers grazed the patchwork of imperfections criss-crossing the side of his face. When would the pain and desolation end? When would it cease to hurt so much? Was this to be his eternal punishment for the way he once used and discarded the women in his life? He wasn't crazy enough to believe any of them had cared about him beyond his wallet, so why him?

The right side of his face in its untouched state mocked him, reminding Hunter of the man he used to be. With a frustrated grunt, he turned away, his anger renewed. Lila wouldn't get out of their bargain by shedding a few tears. He wouldn't allow them to sway his decision in keeping her here.

Storming out of the bathroom with every intention of telling her so, the wind was knocked out of his sails when Hunter saw Lila lying in the same position she'd been in when he'd left her. She was curled up into a tight ball, her even, steady breathing indicating she was sleeping.

His gaze trailed down the curve of her back to her rear. He wanted to snuggle next to her, mold his body to hers, but didn't dare. Walking to the other side of the bed, he knelt in front of her.

Lila looked so vulnerable in this state, much younger than her twenty-seven years. Tear tracks stained her cheeks and again guilt briefly assailed him.

Hunter brushed aside a stray lock of hair that had fallen across her forehead. He used his knuckles to graze the softness of her cheek. In her sleep, she murmured something he couldn't quite make out before a small smile touched her full lips. Unable to help himself, he brushed their tempting fullness with his mouth.

When she stirred, he pulled back. It was probably best if he took her back to her own room. Besides, if she stayed in here with him, there was no way he could trust himself not to take her again. Nor did he have the stomach to wake up to her screams.

Hunter shuddered, remembering the last time he'd allowed a woman to fall asleep in his bed. After a night of sexual aerobics, he'd made the mistake of letting his guard down. When he woke up the following morning, Tina was still sleeping. Sliding on top of her still resting form, he'd planted kisses on her face and neck in hopes they would wake her.

The pure terror in her eyes was like a dagger through his heart. He'd never repeated that error again and he certainly wasn't going to do it with Lila. For some reason, screams coming from her would be far worse.

Careful not to wake her, he lifted her in his arms and took her to the room he'd designated as hers. Gently, Hunter eased her between the covers and dragged them up to her chin. For several moments, he stood, watching her sleep.

God, she was beautiful and for the next three months she'd be his for the taking. The sudden urge to wake her and slide his cock deep into her hot cunt again warred through him, but he pushed that feeling back.

He'd allow her a respite for the remainder of the night, because come tomorrow, there would be none.

Lila snuggled within the warmth surrounding her. Something cold and wet touched her face and then licked her lips. A pair of green eyes flashed in her mind and a delicious sensation heated her to the very core, sending little bursts of flames up her spine.

The damp stroke of what felt like a tongue grew more insistent. Why was he licking her face? She frowned not wanting to open her eyes, but then something spongy and moist nuzzled the side of her neck and sniffed. The sound of panting greeted her ears, followed by the scent of stale breath.

What the hell?

She turned her head to evade the questing tongue and rank morning breath, but it didn't stop. In fact, it grew more persistent. Her lids popped open and Lila found herself staring into a pair of round, pale blue eyes.

Shooting up into a sitting position, she wiped her mouth with the back of her hand, her stomach suddenly feeling nauseous. Standing next to her bed was the biggest dog she'd ever seen. No, that wasn't a dog, it was a horse. Scooting away from the animal, she gagged. Yuck! While she liked dogs, it wasn't her cup of tea to be French kissed by one.

"Shoo." She gave it a gentle shove, but the huge black monstrosity wouldn't budge. As a matter of fact, it seemed to think she was playing a game.

Placing his huge paws on the bed, it climbed up beside her. Its mouth was turned into what looked like a smile.

"No. Bad dog."

But, it wasn't listening. Jumping up and down, he nudged her with his head.

Despite herself, Lila began to giggle. "You're just a big kid aren't you? A big hairy kid." She patted his shiny black coat and the dog preened at the attention.

"Miss Lila! I'm so sorry." Mrs. Coates rushed into the room. The housekeeper tugged the dog's collar. "Shadow, get down this instant. I guarantee this won't happen again. Usually, the dogs stay in the kennel when there is company or they're at Mr. Jamison's side. I think he caught the scent of a new person. Shadow is a people dog, I'm afraid."

Giving the dog one last rub, Lila smiled. "It's okay. He's a sweetie." She yawned. "What time is it anyway?"

"It's about ten past one."

"In the afternoon?"

"Yes."

Lila groaned. "I've never slept this late before in my life. I need to get up. It's no wonder I feel so lethargic."

"Take your time, Miss Lila. Whenever you're ready for something to eat, you can either come downstairs or I'll bring you up a tray if you buzz me on the intercom."

"I'll be down. I'm really not the type to laze around in bed all day."

The older woman shrugged. "I imagine you had a late night. Mr. Jamison said you were not to be disturbed."

Heat rushed to Lila's cheeks at the insinuation. Studying the housekeeper's face, she saw nothing malicious in Mrs. Coates's face. The statement was probably innocent, but it again reminded her of why she was here. No longer could she look Mrs. Coates in the eyes. Lila bowed her head, folding her hands in her lap. "That was thoughtful of him."

"Let me know if you need anything."

"Wait!"

The other woman halted mid-step. "Yes, Miss Lila."

"Umm, is Mr. Jamison expecting me for lunch?"

The housekeeper frowned. "I don't think so. He usually stays in his office most of the day to work. He should be done by dinnertime."

"Oh." Then what the hell was she supposed to do all day? She wasn't used to sitting around idly. Would she be forced to stay in her room all day, bored out of her skull, waiting for him to be ready for her again? She trembled at the thought, but not from revulsion or cold. More from how she'd reacted to him the night before. Lila shook her head to rid herself of the carnal images of the night before from her mind.

"Is that all for now, Miss Lila?" Mrs. Coates broke into her thoughts.

"Umm, what am I supposed to do for the remainder of the day? Maybe I can help you around the house?"

Mrs. Coates's chin rose and her lips tightened briefly. "That won't be necessary. There's a library in the west wing if you like to read and the basement has been converted to a game room. The in-house theater is on the first floor and the weather is nice enough to take a swim if you're so inclined. I didn't get a chance to show you the place properly yesterday, but I'll be happy to do so today."

"Actually if you don't mind, I'd like to explore the place on my own…that is if you don't mind?"

"That should be fine, but please stay away from Mr. Jamison's office. He doesn't like to be disturbed while he's working."

"Which one is his office?"

"It's two doors down from the kitchen."

"Okay. Thank you."

The housekeeper gave her attention to the Great Dane who looked as though he was contemplating jumping on the bed again.

Lila shot him a look. *Not a chance buddy.*

"Come on Shadow." When Mrs. Coates closed the door behind her, Lila slid out of bed pulling a sheet off with her and wrapping it around her body. She wasn't used to sleeping in the nude. It suddenly dawned on her that she was back in her room. Hunter must have brought her here sometime during the night. As much as she tried to block last night from her mind, she couldn't.

All her intentions to not respond to his ardent caresses had been futile. He'd possessed her with the skills of a man who knew exactly how to please a woman. Images of his hands running along her body, tongue circling her skin, and cock stuffing her so fully, infiltrated her mind. Her pussy throbbed and nipples pebbled against the silk sheets.

No! She mustn't let that man get the better of her. It was only physical. Once the three months were over, she would walk away without a backward glance. Or could she? Strangely enough, she was experiencing something more than physical pleasure. If she wasn't, Lila might have been able to deal with these feelings, but no, it was something more—something she couldn't quite put her finger on.

He puzzled her. She had expected him to be rough with no regard for her pleasure, but he'd taken his time to make sure she was thoroughly sated, giving her not one, but three orgasms. No one had set her insides on fire like he had, yet there was no one she had more reason to hate than him. This ordeal was going to be much harder to get through than she'd originally thought.

Chapter Seven

It was difficult to get any work done while sporting a serious hard-on. Just knowing Lila was in the same house with him made his pulse race. Eager for the night to come when he could have her again, Hunter spent most of the day staring into space and rubbing his painfully engorged cock to ease the tension rather than focusing on his project.

He'd barely touched the food Mrs. Coates had brought in for lunch. What was Lila doing right now? Was she thinking of him? He snorted. Probably not. She was most likely counting the days until she could leave him. Why did that thought cause him pain?

Glancing at his watch, he noted it was going on five. Normally, he would get so engrossed in what he was doing that a lot of times he didn't rise from his desk until well into the night. With a frustrated grunt, he shut down his computer. There was no point in sitting here getting eye strain for nothing. Hell, who said he had to wait until dinner to have her again?

He was horny now!

If only he knew where the hell she was. Lila wasn't in her room, nor was she in the game room. Had she managed to leave without notifying him? Pain swelled within his chest. He knew she didn't care about him, but he could have sworn after last night she wasn't completely adverse to his touch. He walked into the closest bedroom and was about to press the call button on the intercom, but he saw Mrs. Coates coming down the hallway.

She inclined her head toward him. "Good afternoon, Mr. Jamison."

"Have you seen Miss Saunders?"

"No. I haven't see her since she came down for lunch and that was a few hours ago. She did mention something about visiting the kennel to see the dogs. I'm sure she's around here somewhere. If I see her, I'll let her know you're looking for her."

He held up his hand. "No. That won't be necessary. I'll look for her myself." The last thing he wanted was to appear too anxious.

She nodded and looked like she was about to move on but hesitated.

Hunter raised a brow. "Is there something you wanted to say?"

"No, Mr. Jamison."

Frowning, he wondered what could be on the woman's mind. In all the time she and her husband had been in his employ, she never gave her feelings away, but in the past couple days, he had the feeling she didn't quite approve of what was going on. "Are you sure?"

"Of course."

He couldn't force her to spill whatever was on her mind if she didn't want to share. Continuing on his quest, his anxiety was fast becoming anger. Was she hiding from him? He was about to pass the library when movement caught the corner of his eye. Sitting curled up in the far corner of the room with Shadow resting his head on her lap, was Lila. She seemed to be engrossed in her book while her hand absently stroked the dog's sleek coat.

Deja, his golden bull mastiff, lay at her feet. Usually, he let the dogs roam the house freely as they were both housetrained and caused very little mischief for dogs of their size. But when there were guests in his home, especially of the female persuasion, Hunter kept them locked in their kennel. In his experience, people were squeamish around large animals. Shadow was nearly two hundred pounds and Deja was one twenty-five. They were gentle creatures who wouldn't hurt a fly, but still intimidating in looks. Hunter had an affinity with them because people often judged them by the way they looked—kind of like him. So it amazed him to see Lila so comfortable with them. She was full of surprises.

Dear Lord, she was lovely. He'd found himself entranced by her beauty on several occasions, but each time he looked at her Hunter was fascinated how each emotion she experienced seemed to enhance her looks. When she was angry with fire blazing in the dark gold pools of her eyes, she was like an avenging fury. In her highest state of arousal, she was a sex goddess beckoning him to enter her Garden of Eden and sample her forbidden fruit. Now as she sat in calm repose, there was a calm about her, making Hunter want to cocoon himself within her warmth.

Unable to help himself, he took a step closer to the door. The movement brought both dogs' heads up. Deja and Shadow jumped to their feet and ran to him, their tails wagging. Hunter gave the panting animals each an affectionate rub behind the ears, but his gaze never left Lila.

She closed the book on her lap and wobbled to her feet, her expression wary. "I hope you don't mind my making use of your library, or letting the dogs out of the kennel. They didn't look too happy being cooped up behind that fence."

"I'd like your stay to be as comfortable as possible. Feel free to roam as you will. As for these two big babies, as long as you don't mind, I don't. Mrs. Coates keeps them in the kennel during dinnertime however, or they'll steal food off the table."

A smile turned the corners of her full lips. "Really? These two seem like angels."

He grimaced. "Trust me, you'd only get a few bites of your meal with these two around. Between them trying to swipe the food from your plate, they'll whine until you give in."

"Hmm, I guess that would get old pretty fast. They're gorgeous creatures. How long have you had them?"

"Three years. I got them when they were puppies. They were a great comfort to me after my—they're good dogs," he finished lamely. In a self-conscious movement he smoothed the hair covering his check. Never had he come so close to talking about his accident as he had just now—not that Lila would be interested anyway.

The simple fact he'd basically blackmailed her to be here with him told Hunter she would probably be repulsed by his ordeal. Even now she didn't quite look him in the face, instead keeping her attention focused on his dogs. Recalling how she'd turned her head when he'd tried to kiss her last night was all the rejection he could take in such a short period. There was no way in hell he'd open himself up to it again. He had to steel himself to not expect more from her than the limits of their bargain.

He ran his gaze over her jeans-clad figure. They were the same clothes she'd arrived in. "Is there a problem with the outfits I've provided you?"

Lila shifted on her feet, wrapping her arms around her body. "The wardrobe is lovely, but I...I don't feel comfortable wearing them."

Hunter furrowed his brows. He'd had the personal shopper pick out clothing from the top designers, nothing even the most discriminating of fashion plates could object to. "Not comfortable? Do they not fit?"

"They fit fine."

"Then what's the problem?"

She rolled her eyes heavenward. "If you insist I wear them, I will, but I'm a jeans and T-shirt kind of girl. Those clothes are far too beautiful for hanging around the house. Besides, when I was wearing that dress last night, which probably cost more than I earn in a month, I was so scared of spilling something on it."

"So what? Spills happen. You could have easily changed into a different outfit."

"That's the thing. I don't think I should have to. I don't like feeling this way."

"I see. If you're not happy with the items, I could have Ernest take you out tomorrow so you can buy whatever you like."

She shook her head. "That's okay."

"Don't worry about money. You can charge the clothes on my credit cards. After all, I did insist you not bring anything here but yourself."

"Because for some perverse reason you wanted to dress me up like a paper doll." The bitterness was clear in her voice. "If that's what you want then okay. I'll play along, but let's not pretend it was an act of generosity on your part. If anything, it's an attempt to control me. You always have to have the upper hand don't you?"

The mercurial mood swing took Hunter aback. The dogs must have sensed the tension in the room because they began to whimper. Her words were like daggers cutting into him. He hadn't sought her out to have an argument. But he wasn't going to let her to see how her obvious hatred affected him.

Narrowing his eyes, he gave her a long hard stare. "Seeing as how you think I'm trying to control you, I may as well live up to my reputation. I don't want to see you in that outfit for the remainder of your stay. Dinner will be served in an hour. Wear something appropriate and don't keep me waiting like you did last night."

Lila folded her arms beneath her breasts. "Or what?"

"Or I'll paddle your ass raw."

Her mouth opened, eyes widening. "You wouldn't dare."

"I don't issue idle threats, Lila. Six o' clock...and choose something sexy."

"I hate you"

"Hate me all you like, but for the next several weeks you'll follow my rules or would you rather call the whole deal off?"

For a moment, she looked like she wanted to do just that. With her fists balled at her sides, Hunter believed if he were standing closer to her, she'd probably belt him one.

"It's easy for you to challenge me when you know I have no recourse. Fine. You win, but so we're absolutely clear with each other, you make me sick to my stomach. Whenever you touch me, my skin crawls."

Hunter laughed out loud to show her barb hadn't been like an arrow to the chest—even though it was. "How easily you forget the way you screamed my name last night and clung to me like you couldn't get enough of what I was giving to you. I believe I need to jog your memory." He advanced further into the room, stalking toward her like a panther with an eye on his prey.

Though she took a step back, Lila wasn't quick enough to evade his grasp. "Let me go!" She struggled against his hold.

Hunter slammed her against him, crushing her breasts between their bodies. He moved to capture her lips, but she turned her head. "Don't!"

He grasped her ponytail and gave it a healthy tug, exposing the silken column of her neck. "You're in no position to dictate my actions." He circled her beating pulse with the tip of his tongue. At the small contact, her stiff body relented and she began to tremble.

The hands that had been pressed against his chest, poised to push him away, fisted in the folds of his shirt. Releasing her hair, Hunter allowed his hands to slide down her back to cup her ass and gave it a squeeze.

Lila moaned, her eyes widened, but the expression he read within them wasn't one of outrage, but arousal.

His cock grew to painful stiffness. More than anything he wanted to toss her to the floor and bury himself deep inside her tight sheath, but knowing Lila wanted it too was enough to get him through dinner. He released her with an abruptness that had her stumbling backwards.

Righting herself, Lila glared at him, her eyes narrowing. "I hate you so much."

"You keep saying that, sweetheart, but your body doesn't." He chuckled to drive his point home. Hunter didn't really want to taunt her. Hold, kiss, caress and worship her body was what he wanted to do. Not this bickering. Hell, this was only her second day here and they were already at each other's throats. He didn't want things to be this way between them, but what else could he have expected?

A little more amiability? Perhaps he'd envisioned—no. Hunter knew how it would be between the two of them when they made their bargain. There was no point in dwelling on the should've, could've, would'ves. But, why did he feel so empty inside?

Lila's glare became venomous. "Maybe my body does want you, but it's only that, my body. My mind, heart and soul don't."

"Fortunately for me, then, your body is all I require. I'll see you at dinner." Turning on his heels before she could make another retort, he strode out of the room with the dogs following him.

That man! One day she'd bring him to his knees and he wouldn't know what hit him. It was extremely inconvenient to respond sexually to him even when she knew what kind of man he was, the type to plow over those with less money and power than him. A man who felt he could do or say what he wanted because of his position in life. Strangely though, in her brief stay in his home, she caught glimpses of another side of him.

Lila couldn't quite place her finger on what it was, but then again, did she care? Should she? Probably not. She couldn't remember being this confused about anything in a long time. When she was younger, she used to run to her father and he

Eve Vaughn

always seemed to know the right things to say.

If only she could hear his voice now, she'd feel so much better. Remembering there was a phone in her room, she decided to give him a call, hoping he'd be in the apartment and not in the store. She cursed herself for not replacing her lost cell phone before she came, but her mind had been on other things.

Hunter hadn't said she couldn't make calls. Once she was in the safety of her room, Lila's hand trembled as she punched the numbers, her heart pounding when the other line began to ring. Even if her father wasn't there, hearing him on the answering machine would have to do. At this point, she would take any crumbs she was offered.

"Saunders' residence."

Just to hear him brought tears to her eyes. More than anything she wanted to be there with him while he held her and told her everything would be alright. Too choked up to get the words out, her lips moved soundlessly.

"Hello? Who is this?" he prompted. "If this is a prank caller or a telemarketer, I'm hanging up."

"Daddy, it's me."

"Baby?" His pleasure in hearing her was evident and it made her feel better.

"Yes, it's me. H-how are you?"

"I'm doing fine. I just woke up from my afternoon nap."

"Since when have you started napping?"

"Doctor's orders. Your old man is getting up there in years, baby girl."

"So I take it all is going well."

"Yes. Those teenagers working in the store have been very helpful. They hardly let me do anything. It's given me a chance to work on the books. And that nurse you got for me came by today. How is your patient doing?"

Patient? Then Lila remembered how she'd lied to him about

72

her reason for being here. "Fine. He's f-fine. I—" A sob tore from her throat and she broke out into noisy tears.

"Baby? What's the matter?"

It took several moments before she could regain her composure. She felt like a fool for worrying him like this.

"It's okay, Lila. Get it out, you have to. Daddy's here."

"It's just—I miss you so much and wanted to talk to you."

"Are you sure? You've been away from me before. Tell me what's really going on. You haven't cried like this since you were a child."

"It's..." Did she dare tell him the truth? Knowing how much pride her father had, he'd probably make her come home. Then what? He'd lose the store for sure. She should have waited to get herself together before calling him. "I know, but I had a bad dream last night that something happened and I just wanted to make sure you were okay." The lie didn't come easily, but she hoped it sounded convincing to him.

"Child, I'm fine. That nurse makes a bigger fuss over me than you and like I said, Reg and Carla are good kids if not a little talkative. Gloria is coming over tonight with one of her casseroles."

"Mrs. Perez?"

"That's the only Gloria I know. She's a nice lady."

Lila grinned. Her absence might not be such a terrible thing for him after all. James Saunders was still a good looking man. It came as no surprise to her that he still got his fair share of attention from the ladies. Lila liked Mrs. Perez so she was glad her father would have some companionship in her absence.

"Tell her I said hello."

"Will do. Is everything going well with your job? Do I have to kick someone's ass?"

She giggled, wiping the tear streaks from her face. "Now that I know you're alright, I am too."

"Is your employer treating you well?"

Lila paused for a moment before crossing her fingers. "As well as could be expected. This isn't the typical patient. He's...very moody." It wasn't exactly an untruth.

James chortled. "I'm sure you'll have him eating out the palm of your hand by the time your assignment is over. You can charm the bees from honey."

She snorted. "Hardly. You have much more faith in my abilities than I do."

"Since you were small, you had something in you people flocked to. Some people have it and others don't. You have it, baby girl. And if your boss can't see it, then there's something wrong with him."

Lila wondered what her father would say if he ever came face to face with Hunter. "It's not really a matter of me being charming. I'm here to do a job and that's it."

"Hmm, then why do I get the sense there's something going on you're not telling me?"

She closed her eyes against the lie she knew she'd have to tell. "I guess I'm a little stressed is all. My, uh patient is more than a little moody at times. He can be an absolute beast and there's only so far my charm will go with him. When he wants something, he expects me to do it immediately, or else."

"Used to getting his own way."

"Definitely."

"Does he have any family or friends who visit?"

"Not that I'm aware of."

"Maybe he's simply a lonely man who isn't used to social interaction."

It was so like her father to try to see the good in other people. Lila doubted he'd find many redeeming qualities in Hunter Jamison. She toyed with the idea of telling him the reason why she was really here and being done with it. As much as she hated lying to him, Lila dreaded disappointing him even more and this would definitely qualify as that. "You could be on to something. He's had a really bad time recovering from his injuries."

"It could be one of the reasons he's so moody as you put it."

She snorted. "I think he was probably a jerk long before the accident."

"If that's the case, then this can't be easy for him. And haven't I taught you better about judging people? You never know what someone else is going through unless you walk a mile in their shoes. Maybe what this guy really needs is a little understanding. I know he's a client, but maybe what he really needs is a friend. Maybe you should try a little harder to see things from his perspective."

Could her father be right? Was she being too hard on Hunter? Maybe what Hunter really needed was a little understanding, but would he accept an olive branch from her? Lila had made damn sure Hunter knew her only reason for agreeing to their arrangement was for the sake of her father. Should she have been so blunt? Perhaps he was just as ashamed of their deal as she was. After all, it must have been quite an ego crusher for him, a former playboy, to resort to blackmail in order to get what he wanted from a woman. That he even had to was kind of sad. Confusion assailed her. She wasn't supposed to feel sorry for someone she'd vowed to hate. Lila shook her head to rid it of her guilty thoughts.

She and her father chatted idly for another few minutes before he had to get back to the store. The conversation had made her feel much better, but it didn't change matters. She still had three months to put up with "the Beast" himself. It would be a miracle if she could walk away from this mess unscathed.

Chapter Eight

Tonight she chose a cream off the shoulder dress which dipped to the small of her back. The skirt rested mid-thigh. The fine material crested over her curves like a second skin and Lila had to admit she looked good in it. But she couldn't shake the feeling of being some kind of mannequin dressed for Hunter's pleasure.

Glancing at herself in the full length mirror, Lila ran her fingers through the hair that fell to her shoulders to assure her appearance was in order. She'd stalled as long as she could. It was time for dinner.

"Miss Lila?" Mrs. Coates's voice chimed in over the intercom.

Lila rolled her eyes, realizing she was being summoned. She walked over to the offending box on the wall and pressed the talk button. "Yes, Mrs. Coates?"

"Dinner will be served in five minutes."

"I'm on my way down."

"I'll let Mr. Jamison know."

"I'm sure you will." Lila spoke softly, but she heard every word.

"Did you say something, Miss Lila?"

Damn. Her finger was still on the button. Still, the woman had bat ears. "Umm, no."

"Very well. I'll see you shortly."

Lila felt like she was in grade school all over again and teacher had caught her passing notes. There was no point in delaying the inevitable. She had to face Hunter sometime. With an impending sense of doom, she trudged down the stairs and walked to the dining room.

Hunter was waiting for her. He stood when she drew close, his bright eyes gleaming with naked appreciation. She didn't want to be pleased by his blatant desire for her, but a tingling sensation spread through her body.

"You look lovely tonight."

Keeping her lids lowered as she took her seat, she gave him a brief smile. She didn't see why they couldn't at least be cordial to one another. "Thank you."

If it was his intention to play nice, she was willing to go along with it. Frankly, all the bickering was starting to wear on her nerves and she hadn't even been here that long. Lila didn't like the hostile feelings she harbored toward this man, even if he did deserve them. Perhaps for her own peace of mind it was better to try and get along with him rather than look for an argument. Her father's words came back to her and Lila steeled herself to get through the rest of this night with as little conflict as possible.

Hunter sat once again, taking the bottle of white wine and pouring some into her glass. "Try this. I think you'll like it."

"I'm not—" It was on the tip of her tongue to tell him she didn't want any, but she stopped herself. If she was going to get through the next several weeks with her nerves intact, arguing with Hunter wouldn't be the way to go.

She brought the glass to her lips and took a sip. She wasn't much of a drinker but this wasn't bad. In fact, the mixture of fruity flavor with just a hint of sweetness was pleasing to her taste buds. "It's very good."

"I'm glad you like it. It's from my vineyard."

Lila raised a brow in surprise. This was news to her. "I thought you were strictly into property development."

"That's my main interest, but my fingers are in several pies. For instance, I'm part owner of a car dealership, several restaurants and various businesses."

"You must stay pretty busy if you're running all of those things."

"I don't do it all on my own. There are people who work under me who see to my business holdings."

"Figures," she muttered before taking another sip of wine.

He stared at her from over the rim of his wineglass. "What's that supposed to mean?"

"Nothing." Lila silently cursed herself for letting her mouth get ahead of her thoughts. If she didn't want to start any arguments with him she'd have to guard her tongue more carefully.

"Are you by any chance surmising that I sit on some kind of throne while the worker bees do everything for me?"

She shook her head vehemently. "Not at all. Forget I said anything."

"I assure you, Lila, I don't demand anything of my employees that I'm not willing to put out myself," he continued as if she hadn't spoken. "A company can't run properly if it has a weak link in the chain and as the leader, it's my job to keep that chain strong. Most days, I'm working from dawn until well after midnight."

"That can't be healthy."

He gave her a lopsided grin. "You actually sound like you care."

"I guess it's the nurse in me. I'd feel this way about anyone."

He raised his glass and brought it to his lips and took a sip before saluting her with it. "Honest to a fault. If I had any ego before you arrived, I certainly won't have one for very much longer."

Lila nibbled on her bottom lip. There she went again,

putting her foot in her mouth. She would get this conversation on better footing if it killed her. "I didn't mean it that way. And of course I'm genuinely concerned. You're not doing your body any favor by working such a grueling schedule."

"Probably not, but work is all I've had since..." His eyes narrowed slightly before he took another sip from his wine glass.

"The accident?" For the first time since she'd joined him, Lila looked at his face. His hair which he still wore parted in the middle and hanging down on either side of his head obscured most of his scars. She could still see angry red lines peeking through, however.

They weren't so bad, compared to some of the things she'd seen throughout her career. Probably having one side of his face still untouched was a constant reminder to him of how he used to look. If the society papers were correct about his former playboy lifestyle, having half of his face disfigured would be harder to deal with for him than it would have been for other people.

She could tell how self-conscious he was about it by the way Hunter was constantly patting his hair down over the marks, which is what he was doing at this very moment. Didn't he know it only drew more attention to him? Lila would have pointed this out, but the last thing she wanted was to make him feel more insecure than he already was.

"It's all right if you don't want to talk about it. I'm sorry I brought it up."

"You didn't. I did. And yes, I've worked more hours since my accident, but I worked a lot before it so I'm used to it."

Mrs. Coates appeared, wheeling in a cart with their dinners and then proceeded to serve them.

The Chicken Francese lined with roasted potatoes and asparagus had Lila's mouth watering. She didn't plan on making the same mistake twice by not eating dinner. "It looks delicious."

The older woman nodded. "Thank you, Miss Lila." She turned her attention to Hunter. "Will that be all?"

He nodded his head in approval. "Yes. Thank you."

Only after the housekeeper was gone did Hunter reply to her last statement. "To answer your question, my work has pretty much been my life since the accident."

"Why do you hold yourself away from the rest of the world? Maybe people make such a big deal about your face because you do." She cut into her chicken, attempting to add a casualness to her voice she didn't quite feel.

Hunter stiffened his fork halfway to his mouth. "You seem to have it all figured out don't you?"

Lila took a sip of her wine before answering. "It's pretty obvious. For instance, you keep your hair in your face. That probably draws attention rather than detracts from it."

Hunter didn't reply. Lila could have kicked herself. She'd resolved not to mention what was on her mind and did exactly that. This wasn't a good time to suffer from run-of-the-mouth-itis. But for a moment Lila had caught a sad look in his green gaze which had touched something deep within her. In that moment there was much more to him than just the business tyrant or the scarred recluse. Surely there must be something charming about him. How else would he have earned the reputation of ladies' man before his car wreck? *What was he like then*? she wondered.

Lila cleared her throat and began her next attempt at conversation. "What do you like to do besides work? Do you have any hobbies?"

"No." The answer was curt and Hunter offered no further elaboration.

The remainder of dinner was eaten in silence, only broken when Mrs. Coates would come in to check on them. By the time dessert had come around, the tension was so thick it could be cut with a knife. Lila couldn't take it any longer.

"Hunter," she began tentatively, "I won't bring it up again if it bothers you. I didn't mean any offense. I was only..."

"Making small talk?"

"No. Well, yes. But seeing as how we're stuck together for the next three months, we may as well get to know each other better."

He placed his fork down and leaned back in his chair. "Say what you really mean, Lila."

She frowned. "What are you talking about?"

"You said we're stuck together. What you meant was *you're* stuck here with me. Isn't it?"

Lila shook her head. "I said what I meant. You're twisting my words."

"Am I? So in other words, if I weren't holding something over your head you'd be here on your own volition?"

"Probably not." The words spilled out before she thought about how they may have sounded.

Hunter's lips twisted into a grimace. "That's what I thought."

"I didn't mean it as it sounded. No, I probably wouldn't be here because our paths probably wouldn't have crossed otherwise. I'm hot dogs and beer. You're caviar and champagne."

"Very nicely put, but let's not pretend you meant anything other than what was said. I appreciate your honesty far more than your lies."

"But you don't understand. I really didn't mean it the way you think. And anyway, even if we did move in the same social circles, I wouldn't want to be here because of your actions, not the way you look. You have to admit, your reputation wasn't particularly stellar before your injury. And the fact you were trying to destroy something my father and me held dear didn't make you a recipient of the good guy award, in my book. I wouldn't care if you looked like a movie star, I'd still not want to be here, but since I am we may as well make the best of it."

Eve Vaughn

Green eyes narrowed. "So looks don't matter to you?"

"Not particularly."

He rolled his eyes, disbelief etched in every line on his face. "Go ahead and pull the other one. You may have fooled yourself into believing that bullshit, but you sure as hell haven't convinced me."

"That's because you care so much about them, it puzzles you when someone else doesn't."

He leaned back in his seat and studied her with his intense stare as he absently swirled his wine around his glass. "There's no need to pretend with me if they do. It won't make any difference one way or another."

"It's the truth. I'm not that shallow."

"Then you're one in a billion. I've found more women of my acquaintance would rather cross the street when they see me coming than look at my face. I can't see how you're any different."

"You must be exaggerating." He had to be. Or was he? Perhaps that's why he was so bitter. No one deserved to be shunned the way he had, even if karma had finally caught up to him. Lila squirmed in her seat, suddenly uncomfortable with this sympathy she was beginning to feel for him. The last thing she wanted was to care, to see him as a human being who hurt like everyone else. Getting along was one thing, but understanding was quite another.

"Am I? I can't have imagined the look of horror in my lover's face when the bandages came off. You see, the irony of the whole situation was, she was in the vehicle during the accident. We argued because I wanted to end the affair. She'd grown a little too clingy for my taste. Dawn, on the other hand, thought we should take the relationship to the next level. She made such a scene in the restaurant, I had to take her home." He paused for a moment and gulped the remainder of his wine down.

Lila could see the pain radiating out of every pore in his

body and it touched a part of her she didn't expect. She sat silently, waiting for him to continue.

"When I was taking her home, she cried, yelled and begged for another chance, but it grew tedious very quickly. I was so agitated with her tears and protests of love that I didn't notice that drunk fool driving down the wrong side of the road. Fortunately for her, she survived with a few minor abrasions, while I lay in a hospital bed for weeks in pain, bandaged like a mummy, not knowing how extensive the damage would be. Dawn came by to visit diligently and I was grateful for her company. I even began to think maybe she did love me as she'd claimed to. I'd certainly never given credence to that word before, but I started to depend on those visits. I even fantasized about a possible future with me and Dawn." He closed his eyes briefly as if having difficulty getting the words out.

Lila's heart ached for him. She wanted to wring this superficial woman's neck for callously discarding Hunter at his most vulnerable. Lila most certainly could never have treated anyone so cruelly. "You don't have to finish."

He shook his head. "I want to. Besides, if you're so eager to learn about my life, you might as well hear the bad. Where was I? Oh yes...then came the unraveling and I don't think I need to go into detail, but, she couldn't get out of the hospital fast enough. She, of course, said she'd be back, but it was the last time I saw her. I should have guessed right away, but I found out later she'd moved on to the next shlub—an heir to a toilet bowl company."

"Then obviously she didn't love you. She wouldn't have been able to walk away so easily otherwise."

"No shit."

"You can't lump all women in the same category just because one woman did you wrong."

"She wasn't the only one, just the first in a line of many. When word spread I was single again, my exes appeared in droves thinking they would be my Florence Nightingale, until

83

they got a look at my face. I may have been able to handle the rejection a little better if it wasn't for how other people would treat me. It got to a point where I couldn't go to my office or out in public without looks of fear and disgust. I might have gotten past that, but I couldn't take the pity. I made a small child cry once."

"That's horrible." Lila wanted to offer words of comfort, but she knew he'd probably take them as pity.

He laughed humorlessly. "For the child, I'm sure."

"No. For you. I can't imagine how you must have felt."

"Of course, you can't. Because a person like you has probably had it easy. Most beautiful people do. I took my looks for granted until I lost them."

"I don't spend time obsessing on how I look, Hunter. I have too much going on in my life to do that. Besides, with so much hatred in the world, doesn't it stand to reason that I've been judged by the color of my skin? It doesn't feel good, but the people who do that to me aren't worth my time."

"I concede there are small minded people in the world, but it's not exactly the same. I'm sure there are more people who admire the way you look than not."

"Again, it's way too trivial to dwell on."

"Then you're a rare human being if you don't think looks matter."

Lila shrugged. "I'm not so naive to think they don't with most people and I acknowledge there has to be some degree of attraction between two people if they want some kind of relationship, but in the grand scheme of things, the surface doesn't matter much. What counts is how a person is on the inside. One of my favorite quotes is 'beauty fades, but dumb is forever'."

Hunter's lips turned up in a half smile. "Is that something your father taught you?"

She grinned. "No. Judge Judy. But she had a point. If I had to choose between the two, I'd much rather be smart than pretty."

"Says the beautiful woman." His voice dripped with scorn.

"You're the one who's got a hang up about my looks, not me. Anyway when it comes right down to it, once you get used to a person you want more than just a pretty face. You want a little substance. When I finally settle down, I'd rather be with a man who makes me laugh and is a good person rather than a Denzel Washington or Hugh Jackman look alike who's a jerk."

"You actually sound as though you believe that drivel you're speaking."

"It's not drivel. And I do believe it." She was beginning to get a little annoyed. Lila wasn't used to anyone questioning her integrity or trying to find double meaning in her statements. "Anyway, you're not completely innocent either."

"Oh?"

"Yeah, I've seen some old articles about you in the society pages. I've never seen you with anyone who didn't look like a supermodel. So don't sit there and pretend like you've never judged anyone based on their looks. I bet there are plenty of genuine women who wouldn't care about your wealth or position, but you didn't give them the time of day because they didn't have perfect bodies, or they weren't up to your standards of beauty. You reap what you sow and if you chose to date nothing but gold diggers, you can't expect them to be around in your time of need."

Blood rushed to Hunter's face, turning it a deep shade of red. His nostrils flared and he flexed his fingers as if he was contemplating strangling her. But finally after a moment of tense silence, he relaxed. "Perhaps." Hunter leaned forward. "Tell me, Lila of the noble heart, why did you cry last night? You sit there with your Pollyanna attitude of the world while you can't stand to look directly at me. You're no better than the other women I've come across. In fact you're worse. You're a hypocrite. The worst kind of woman."

Lila slammed her hand on her the table. "Don't compare

me to the trash you used to date. They may wear expensive clothes and mingle in the highest of social circles, but they lack the one thing you can't buy and that's class. And I don't appreciate you calling me a hypocrite."

"I'm just calling it like I see it. They at least were more upfront. Everyone has a price, Lila. Some women are just more expensive than others. If you were honest with yourself you'd realize you have one as well."

She took the napkin off her lap and threw it on the table, her appetite gone. All resolve to make it through this dinner with little conflict flew out the window. This man had to be one of the most obstinate people she'd ever met. It was no wonder he'd been dubbed the Beast, although she could think of a few more titles that would suit him even more. "I don't have to sit here and take this."

"Oh, but that's where you're wrong. And I see you've neatly skirted around my original question."

Lila stiffened. "What question?" She knew exactly what he was referring to, but admitting her reasons why would be her final humiliation. She should have known she couldn't get away with that fib. Hunter was much too shrewd not to guess.

His lips twisted and eyes flashed his disbelief. "You're trying my patience, Lila. I don't make a habit of repeating myself, but I'll ask one more time: why did you cry last night? Were you so disgusted by me you couldn't take it or is it a habit of yours to weep after sex? If it is, it's not much of a turn on."

"It's not something I ordinarily do."

"Then answer my question." He spoke with such dead calm, it sent a chill down her spine.

"I-I can't." As much as he'd just angered her, telling him the truth would probably hurt him and it wasn't in her to do that to him.

"That's what I thought. You make pretty speeches, but they don't mean jack squat. You're starting to sound tedious and I'm getting tired of it. When you speak to me, you're looking everywhere but my face." He pushed his hair behind his ears, revealing the full extent of his disfigurement.

Lila flinched, but not because she feared him, but because it saddened her as she imagined how horrible it must have been for him to suffer as he had.

"You say my scars don't matter, so prove it. Come here and kiss me."

Why did he have to ask of her the one thing she couldn't do.

"Look at me, Lila." His voice was soft but the underlying steel in his tone left no doubt in her mind that his statement wasn't a mere request.

Tears stung the backs of her eyes at the raw pain she heard in his words. She didn't want to look at him the way he ordered her to because then she'd start to care as she feared she was very close to doing so anyway. She couldn't afford to care.

"Look at me!" he roared, making her jump.

A tear escaped the corner of her eye which she hastily wiped away. Lila shook her head. "Don't make me."

"You'll fucking do as you're told. I've had enough of your defiance and if you don't do as I say, by God, I'm going to make you!"

Chapter Nine

Hunter leaped out of his chair, rage guiding his movements. He'd had enough of her lies. She wouldn't meet his gaze yet she chose to stand behind her lie. Lila was like the rest of the women in his acquaintance. No. She was far worse because she'd nearly had him believing that bullshit she'd been spouting.

He yanked Lila out of her seat and led her out of the dining room, moving so fast she had no choice but to follow him, otherwise she would have fallen.

She tried to pull away, slapping at his arm. "Stop this right now, Hunter! It doesn't have to be this way."

He turned to shoot her a glare before continuing on. "Yes it does. I promised you punishment and now it's time to pay the piper."

"No! You misinterpreted my words. If you would have given me a chance to explain why I couldn't do as you asked then maybe you'd calm down."

"Don't bother. My bullshit tolerance is extremely low, and I'm not in the mood to hear any more of it."

Digging her heels in, Lila halted. "What do you plan on doing to me? A-a-are you going to spank me?" she croaked.

Hunter smirked. "As tempting as that sounds, I've thought of something much more fitting. For every action, there's a consequence and you're about to find out what yours is."

"Hunter if you go through with this—"

"What? You'll hate me? I've heard that before, remember. It's time you came up with some new material." For a brief moment, he caught a glimpse of what looked like fear swimming in her eyes. Guilt surfaced inside of him. She had to know he wouldn't hurt her physically. But he wouldn't relent on what he planned on doing. He would make her eat her words. "I would rather you hadn't tested me on this, but you've made your choice so now you'll have to deal with it."

Lila's struggles renewed. Hunter wrapped his arms around her waist and carried her the rest of the way to his bedroom. He dumped her unceremoniously on the bed and then walked over to his closet and pulled out a box he hadn't used in ages.

He looked over his shoulder to see her watching him, her expression wary. "What is that?" Her eyes darted from side to side as if she were staking out an escape route.

"You'll find out soon enough."

She tried to scramble off the bed, but he intercepted her, using his body as a blockade.

"You're not going anywhere." Hunter opened the box and removed a length of nylon rope and then tossed the container aside.

Lila took a step back. "I won't let you tie me up."

Instead of answering her, he laughed menacingly. "Take off your dress."

"No." She moved further away from him until her back hit the wall.

Hunter placed the rope on the bed and slowly made his way toward her not stopping until he was only a few inches away.

She held up her hands. "Okay. I'll do it." Her anger was palpable.

"I'm glad you're beginning to see things my way," he taunted.

"Do I have a choice? If I refused, you'd find a way to bully me into it anyway."

"Don't try to worm your way out of this."

"I'm only voicing the truth. You're a bully and I despise you for it."

"You're starting to sound like a broken record. Do you keep saying it to convince me or yourself? Perhaps you do hate me, but you love what I do to your body, don't you?"

She placed her hands over her ears. "Shut up!"

He grabbed her arms and pulled them down roughly. "Hit a nerve, didn't I?"

Lila lashed out at him, her palm connecting with his cheek.

Hunter closed his eyes against the sting of her blow, almost welcoming the physical pain to replace the internal torment.

She gasped, her hands flying to her mouth. "I'm sorry."

"I'm sure you've been itching to do that for a long time, haven't you?"

"I still shouldn't have done that. I abhor violence." She trembled and he wondered if it was because she was truly sorry for what she'd done or because she was scared of what he might do to her because of it.

"I don't want your apology, I want you to undress. Do it now!"

Her lips quivered for a moment and she raised that stubborn chin of hers again before reaching behind her and unzipping her dress. She pushed it down until it fell at her feet. Looking straight ahead, she balled her fists at her side not attempting to cover her naked flesh.

Hunter's dick sprang to attention at the sight of her delectable naked body. It was insane how he could want a woman as much as he did her. "The panties, too."

Lila hesitated for the briefest of seconds, but then complied.

He couldn't tear his eyes away from the magnificence of her feminine curves, but he wouldn't allow them to sway him from his course of action. He had to show her who was boss, teach her a lesson. For all the people who'd shunned him, the women who'd hurt him, Lila was the embodiment of them all. So beautiful on the outside, but inside she harbored the heart of the biggest hypocrite.

"You're no different from anyone else. When these three months are over, you'll go back to your life and feel better about yourself because you did a noble thing. I know your kind, Lila Saunders. You're a do-gooder out tilting at windmills and preaching your 'We are the World' bullshit. And in the meantime, you sit around patting yourself on the back, wondering how these ignorant people could have possibly gotten along without you. I think it suits your martyr complex to be here right now, doesn't it? Going toe to toe with the Beast? Do you see yourself as some kind of savior? You're no better than me."

Her mouth opened slightly then closed before she spoke. "That isn't true."

"Of course it is. Even now you can't stand the sight of me, but that's okay, because I intend to break you out of the habit." He retrieved the rope from the bed. "Give me your wrists."

Hunter expected her to argue, but instead her shoulders slumped and she slowly presented them. Still, she wouldn't look at him. That only served to piss him off.

Taking her wrists, he wrapped the rope around them. It had been a long time since he'd included this in his sex play, but with her tied to the bed, she couldn't turn away from him so easily. Once he was sure the knots were secure, he led Lila to the bed. Where had her fight gone? Why didn't she protest?

"On the bed," he ordered.

Again, she complied without another word. Hunter took the end of the rope and looped it around the post, raising her arms above her head.

She lay completely motionless, her lids lowered. He realized the game she was playing. He wouldn't stand for her passive-aggressive defiance and he knew just how to deal with it.

Eve Vaughn

Once the rope anchoring her arms to the bed was tied to his satisfaction, he undressed with hurried motions, anxious to possess her. He vowed by the time he got through with her, Lila would know who the master of her body truly was. Standing naked, Hunter perused every inch of her frame, contemplating where he'd start first.

He sat down beside her, the bed depressing under his weight, and stroked her cheek. "Look at me," he whispered softly.

"You have me where you want me and the power to do anything you'd like. Why do you have to keep pushing the issue?"

Hunter clenched his jaw muscle. The gauntlet had been tossed and this was a battle he intended to win. He grazed her flat stomach and then cupped one well-shaped breast. Lowering his head, he flicked her nipple with the tip of his tongue. The little bud came to life, puckering to a taut peak. He took it fully into his mouth and then fondled her breast in his palm.

"Oh," Lila sighed, her body writhing beneath his ministrations.

His body tightened at her responsiveness. He loved her naturally passionate nature. Tugging the hard tip between his teeth, Hunter applied enough pressure to make her cry out, but not enough to cause serious injury.

Lila's skin was so soft and tasted so good. Hunter gave her other breast the same treatment until Lila was moaning incoherently, her body wildly wiggling.

Hunter lifted his head then. "Look at me."

She squeezed her eyes shut, but he wasn't about to give up. He'd have her surrender by the end of the night if it killed him. Slipping his arms underneath her body, he flipped Lila onto her stomach.

He then pulled her to her knees, forcing her to use her restraint as leverage. She began to tremble. Her apparent fear wasn't something he wanted, but at least it was an honest

92

emotion. Deep down, he wished it could be different between them, but he was the one who'd made the rules and he'd have to abide by them.

Running his hand down the curve of her back, he didn't stop until it rested on the seat of her ass. "You have beautiful skin. When I first saw you, this is what I wanted to do." He placed a light kiss on her shoulder then pushed her hair aside and pressed his lips against the nape of her neck.

As he moved his mouth over her satiny skin, Hunter slid his hand between her legs, pushing them further apart. The inside of her thighs were wet. A small smile touched his lips when he saw this evidence of her arousal. Even if she wanted to fight him, her body would always be her Judas.

He dipped his finger between the cleft of her pussy and rubbed her dewy clit.

"Hunter," she moaned, squirming against his touch.

"That's it, sweetheart. Say my name. Know that I'm the one who's doing this to you," he whispered against her skin. He rolled the hot button between his thumb and forefinger.

Lila bucked her hips. "Oh God!" She tugged at her restraints as though trying to break free, but Hunter knew it was her fiery nature making her writhe so wildly. It was one of the reasons he'd tied her up in the first place, because a woman as passionate as she would barely be able to stand being bound, unable to use her hands as she willed.

Hunter knew his touch was driving her wild and he loved seeing her so turned on and ready to be fucked. The very scent of her arousal was driving him to the brink of insanity. He'd set out to conquer, but feared he might be the one to succumb to her charms.

He removed his fingers and grasped her ass, spreading her cheeks apart as he studied the beauty of her tight hole resting above her pussy. One of these days, he'd take her in that forbidden place, but tonight he had other plans. Eager to sample her fragrant cunt, he moved behind her. Parting her slick folds, he shoved his tongue into her tight passage.

"That feels so good," she sobbed, pushing back against his mouth.

Hunter slid his tongue in and out of her channel as he reveled in Lila's tangy, musky and tantalizing flavor. He could easily get drunk from the very taste of her.

Her body started to shake and he realized her climax was near. Though he wanted to continue, Hunter pulled back.

"Please don't stop."

He ran his tongue over her pussy lips to capture the last bit of her cream and sat back, watching her suffer with wanting him.

"Hunter?" Uncertainty making her voice wobble.

"Yes?"

"Why...why did you stop?"

"It's part of your punishment. You don't come until I say you do."

"And when will you say?"

"When you beg for it."

She gasped her outrage. "I won't."

"But I think you will."

"If you believe that, then you'll have a very long wait."

Hunter smirked. "Somehow, I doubt it." Sliding his fingers into her pussy, he pushed them deep. He could tell she was fighting the urge to respond but soon gave in just as he knew she would.

Lila relaxed her stiffened stance and moved against his thrusts.

Hunter fingered her slowly and then leaned forward and whispered in her ear. "All you have to do is say the words and this can be my dick. Admit you want it, or I swear I'll stop."

She bit her bottom lip. It was obvious she was trying to decide what to do. "Yes," she finally spoke so softly he could barely hear her.

Hunter hadn't realized he was holding his breath until the tension from waiting on her answer eased out of his body. "I didn't hear you."

"Yes!" she yelled, her resentment clear. "Just stop torturing me. I want you. There. Are you happy?"

He was certainly getting to that point, but he was much too horny to gloat. With a swift movement, he flipped Lila on her back again and pushed her knees apart. Without hesitation, he positioned his cock at her entrance. "Look at me."

When she turned her head, he wanted to pull back, but knew he would be hurting himself as much as her. Hunter pushed into her tight channel with a loud grunt.

Her walls tightened around and gripped his shaft, sucking him so deep, he felt like he would shoot his load right away. His eyes squeezed shut, he moved within her, relishing the feel of her.

"Hunter."

Hearing his name on her lips was like music to his ears. He opened his eyes and noticed hers were still shut. Something within his snapped. A primal urge to demonstrate his supremacy took over.

He slammed into her so hard, Lila cried out. Hunter continued to plow relentlessly into her, fucking her with a combination of lust, anger and a perverse need to make her pay for making him feel inadequate—like a hideous monster she couldn't bear to look at.

Despite his rough savagery, she moved with him, taking all he dished out until her body tensed and shook. Lila cried her climax. Her pussy gushed around his cock, but Hunter wasn't finished with her, not by a long shot.

Gripping her face to ensure she couldn't turn her head away from him, he rode her even harder. "Open your eyes."

When they remained closed, he forced her hand. "Open them!" he bellowed, clenching her face in a vise. "Now!"

Slowly her eyelids rose.

"Do you see me? I'm the one who's fucking and giving you pleasure. Take a good look at me Lila. Can you honestly say that looks don't matter now?"

She didn't answer, but the unshed tears in her eyes said it all.

Releasing her face, Hunter screwed her until his orgasm hit him like a series of fireworks going off in his body. He shot his seed deep inside her hot hole. As he gasped for breath, he rolled off her, horrified at what he'd just done.

Why had he let his temper get the best of him? Despite what he thought of her, she didn't deserve his rough treatment and shame kept the apology lodged in his throat.

Lila lay so still beside him, Hunter wondered what was roaming through her mind. She was probably wishing she was anywhere but here with him at the moment.

He moved to a sitting position and untied the rope from the bedpost. She offered her wrists without being asked and he undid the knots. Hunter then rolled off the bed and grabbed his boxers off the floor, quickly donning them.

It took him a moment to speak as he searched for the appropriate words to say. What could he say after what he'd done? With a frustrated sigh, he raked his fingers through his hair wishing he could go back in time to before he'd ever met her, and then at least he'd have most of his sanity still intact.

"I assure you, this won't happen again," he began gruffly.

If he was any kind of gentleman, he'd let Lila out of their agreement, but he couldn't bring himself to say the words. The very idea of her walking out of his life and never seeing her again caused him pain. It was ridiculous feeling this way about someone in so short an acquaintance, but Hunter knew if she left, it wouldn't be something he could get over easily.

"My behavior was inexcusable and for that, I apologize. If you would like to stay in this room tonight, I'll go to one of the other bedrooms, or you can return to your room whenever you're ready."

Lila sat up, massaging her rope-burned flesh. For the first time since she'd arrived, she was looking at him without his directive. "I think I'd like to stay here for the night—with you."

Chapter Ten

Hunter took a step back, shaking his head as if he couldn't believe what he'd heard. "What?"

Lila climbed off the bed and stood in front of him, tilting her head back to stare at him directly in the face. One of the main reasons she'd avoided looking at him for so long was because she knew she'd be forced to throw out her preconceived notions about this man. In her mind, Lila had wanted him to remain a tyrant—not a man who hurt and experienced emotions like anyone else. Now that she'd seen this side of him, she could no longer treat him with the indifference she'd set out to do.

Hunter flinched at her boldness. Inwardly, she chided herself for having behaved so cowardly. In a way, she was glad he'd forced her to take a good look at his face in full, scars and all, because it gave her a glimpse into his tortured soul. She could no longer ignore his anguish, the pain lurking deep within him. There was something inside of him which touched her in a way she didn't think possible. A connection was made she couldn't quite put her finger on, but it was there nonetheless.

It had probably been there all along, but she'd been so hell bent on fighting it. Now there was nothing left but to deal with these feelings brewing inside of her. Did he feel the bond between them or was it only one-sided on her end? Perhaps the question she should have asked herself is, was she insane? This man was supposed to be her enemy. There should be no tender emotions toward him. Yet there were. By no means did she think it was love, but it was something nonetheless.

Lila would be with him for the next three months and she might as well stop fighting Hunter every step of the way. From now on, if there was to be any conflict between them, it wouldn't originate from her. She placed her hand against his chest. "I said I would rather stay here with you."

His gaze roamed her face. He was probably trying to figure out whether she was serious. Abruptly, Hunter turned his back on her. "I don't want your fucking pity."

She pushed away the urge to match his anger. Breaking the barrier he'd erected between them wouldn't be easy. Besides, Lila realized he'd be suspicious of her motives. Since she'd come to his home she'd told him in not so many words of the contempt she felt toward him. Of course he'd question the sincerity of her change of heart. There had to be some way she could reach him. "That's good because you won't be getting any from me."

He snorted. "Then why the sudden about face?"

"Could you please turn around and look at me while I'm speaking to you?" The irony of her words wasn't lost on Lila.

"Why? Haven't you had your fill of me already? Do you want to stare at the freak some more?"

The man had more barriers than Fort Knox. She circled him until they were facing each other again. "You probably don't want to hear it, but I'm sorry for how I acted. I mean, yes I was resentful about being here, but it has nothing to do with how you look."

He rolled his eyes in his apparent disbelief. "Go ahead and pull the other one." Hunter turned his head to show off his scars.

Lila suspected he did that to deliberately put her off, but she wouldn't let him. Not anymore. For some reason it had become important to her convince him he wasn't the monster he believed himself to be.

She could tell Hunter was still determined to call her bluff. There was only one thing she could do. Capturing his face between her palms, Lila stood on her tip toes and kissed his lips.

Hunter stiffened, remaining immobile as she moved her mouth over his. She ran her tongue along the seam of his lips before pushing it past his teeth to fully explore the cavern of his mouth. His taste was so wonderfully male, she deepened the kiss. She'd never been so forward with any man before and she found the experience of taking the lead titillating.

With a groan, Hunter wrapped his arms around Lila, giving in to her insistent kiss. His tongue met hers in an erotic dance. He ground his lips over hers as if he was afraid to let her go.

Lila pressed her body against his, twining her fingers through his loose blond locks. Heat surged through her and she wanted him all over again, but this time it would be different. She'd let her defenses down.

He was no longer the man she'd grown to dislike. Hunter Jamison was simply a man and she was a woman; two people who were in desperate need of a little compassion and loving. She was the one who finally broke the tight seal of their lips, but only to catch her breath.

Then, she kissed his jaw line on his scarred side.

"Lila," he growled softly.

"Shut up, Hunter. I'm in charge now," she shot back before touching her tongue to where her lips had been. Lila refused to let him deter her from what she intended to do. Running her hands over his hair-roughened chest, she slid her fingers down until they encountered his cock.

He was rock hard.

"Lila, I don't know what kind of game you're playing..."

"This is no game." She moved down the length of his toned torso to his ripped abs and then went to her knees. Wrapping her fingers around his thick rod, she touched the velvety smooth hood with her lips. With her free hand, she cupped his throbbing balls and fondled them lightly. "Do you like this, Hunter?"

He inhaled sharply. "You know I do," he groaned.

She glided her lips along his cock and sucked him into her mouth, one delicious inch at a time, not stopping until its tip touched the back of her throat. As she bobbed her head back and forth, Lila continued to squeeze and play with his tense sack.

Hunter moaned out loud, placing his hands on either side of his head. "What are you doing to me, woman?"

She pulled back, releasing his cock with a decisive, wet pop and looked up at him. "Making you feel good, I hope."

The hunger in his gaze told her that was exactly what she was doing. His heavy breathing was all the confirmation she needed. Lila licked his rod along the side before taking it back into her mouth.

Giving him pleasure filled her with a blistering heat that surprised her. She hadn't expected to feel this way. Her pussy was on fire. Needing to ease some of the ache burning between her legs, she released his balls, and speared her pussy with two fingers, working them inside her channel in cadence with her mouth moving over his cock. Her movements grew frenzied as the intensity of her arousal increased. She sucked him harder, fingering herself deeper.

Hunter's grip on her head grew firmer as he guided it along his dick. "Lila, I'm going to come." He tried to pull away, but she wouldn't let him. "Lila!" he yelled hoarsely.

His seed filled her mouth and she attempted to swallow as much of his essence as she could. She was so close to her own orgasm, she shoved another finger into her passage, stretching it until an explosion ripped through her body.

He reached down and hauled her against his body, then crushed her mouth beneath his. His kiss was hard and hungry. She didn't notice they'd moved until she realized Hunter was laying her on the bed.

She eyed his erect cock in amazement. "You're ready for me again?"

Covering her body with his, he slid easily into her wet hole. "Did you think after that I could leave you alone?" His gaze roamed her face with tenderness lurking within its depths.

Something twisted inside her heart as he began to move inside of her. "Come here," she whispered.

He pressed his body into hers and she wrapped her arms around his neck and her legs around his waist. This time their coming together transcended fucking and mere sex. It was something different entirely, as though their souls were coming together. He was so gentle, Lila felt like crying all over again, but not from anger, pain or shame, but because of the deep connection she felt with him in this beautiful moment.

Lifting her hips to meet him thrust for thrust, she moved and strained against his body. Her nails grazed the back of his neck. When Lila came yet again her climax gave her peace. A wave of contentment flowed over her.

Hunter pushed in and out of her for several more strokes before reaching his climax. Resting his forehead on hers, his breath mingled with hers. "That was amazing. You were amazing," he whispered.

A smile tugged the corners of her mouth, exhaustion making it difficult for her to reply verbally. Hunter was heavy, but she welcomed the pressure of his weight, pressing her into the bed. It felt right for some reason.

He was the one to break the silence, lifting his head with wonder in his eyes. "Why?"

She brushed the side of his face with the back of her hand. "Why not?"

He captured her hand and gave it a squeeze. "Don't."

"I thought you enjoyed my touch."

His expression grew stormy, his bright green eyes turning a

deep jade. Hunter rolled off her and sat up, shaking his head which made his hair fall into the style he usually wore it. "I told you I didn't want your pity."

Lila joined him in a sitting position, wrapping the comforter around her body. She'd need to be patient with him if she wanted to break through the wall he'd erected around himself. "Hunter, after what just happened, do you honestly think what I did was out of pity?"

He raised his shoulders in a shrug. "I don't know what to make of what you did. One minute you can't look at me, and then the next you can't stop. What am I supposed to believe?"

If she was to gain his trust, Lila knew she'd have to be honest with him. "You'll probably think I'm silly, but the reason why I never looked at you was because I didn't want to think of you as a real person. As nutty as this sounds, in my mind, I had you built up as some monster who was trying to destroy everything I held dear. And before you get defensive, I'm not referring to your face. I hated you, or at least I thought so before I learned of your accident."

"Because of your father's store?"

"Exactly. Deep down, I always knew what your company was doing isn't something new, or anything another property developer in your position wouldn't have done, but Ramsey's was going after something I loved and the stress was damaging my father's health. If it weren't you, my anger would have been directed to whoever was in charge, but I had to fight. Maybe you're right about one thing. I probably do have a do-gooder complex. In my wild imaginings, my father and I were the victims and you were the villain."

"I see, but that still doesn't quite explain everything."

She placed a hand on his arm. "Please let me finish."

"Okay, but I still don't understand."

"'I guess I'm not explaining myself very well. Basically, when we received that last letter from your company, I thought you were a completely reprehensible man to do something so underhanded. It gave me this preconceived notion of what you were like. Coupled with all the stories of your playboy lifestyle, I even began to believe you deserved what happened to you."

Hunter flinched at her statement. "Perhaps I did. A lot of my business associates and women I've dated would probably agree with you."

"But I was wrong. Don't misunderstand me. I'm still willing to fight tooth and nail for my father's business. I just believe my way of thinking was a bit overboard. When I stormed into your office that day, I wasn't really prepared to see your scars, but when I did, they made me angry, they humanized you, gave you a vulnerability I didn't want to associate with you. I saw your pain and then I knew if I kept looking at you I wouldn't be able to hate you as I had before. I couldn't compartmentalize you into a neat little body. Knowing this, I tried not to look at you because I was afraid of caring about you. And before you ask, I fainted because I hadn't eaten all day."

Hunter furrowed his brows. "Are you saying you care about me?"

"No. I'm saying I could, and that's what I was fighting so hard against."

She brushed the hair on his face aside and touched his scars, wanting him to know she wasn't frightened of him. "I don't want to fight with you anymore, Hunter. I'd like us to be friends."

His mouth slanted into a half smile. "Are you by any chance trying to wiggle your way out of sleeping with me?"

She laughed. "I don't think that would happen even if I tried."

"Damn right it wouldn't."

"I don't want to stop." Heat rushed to her cheeks and Lila felt shy all of a sudden.

"Lila if you're messing with me..."

"I'm not. I'd like us to be friends. Since I'm going to be here, we might as well try getting along outside of bed as well. Is this something you'd be agreeable to?"

Hunter stroked his chin. "I've never had any female friends before."

"Maybe that's why your relationships didn't work in the past. Women are more than playthings and so am I. Look, I know our arrangement isn't conventional, but we might as well make the most of the situation."

"Ok. Why not? Do you really not care about the way I look?"

"Your scars take some getting used to, but they don't define the person you are. I'm a nurse and trust me, I've seen a lot worse. I once had a patient who'd been a victim of a gunshot wound to the face. I won't bother getting graphic about it, but I'll always remember that kid. He was only sixteen when it had happened, but he was always upbeat and positive. It makes one appreciate their own life. When you think you have it bad, remember, someone always has it much worse."

"When put like that, you probably think I'm a shallow son of a bitch."

"A little."

He scowled. "Your honesty is going to take some getting used to."

"Friends are honest with each other."

Hunter's gaze roamed her face for several moments before he replied. "You're really trying to push this friendship thing aren't you? I'm surprised you'd want to tangle with the Beast?"

"I wouldn't call you that, although I'm still annoyed about the city council getting involved."

Hunter exhaled deeply. "Honestly, that was the work of an over-enthusiastic executive who thought he could score some points that way. It's not normally how I do business."

"But you taunted me about it when I confronted you."

"And I'm sorry for it. My day wasn't going well, and I'd only just learned what that executive had done."

"Would you have really gone through with it?"

"To be truthful, Lila, I don't know how I would have dealt with the situation and now neither of us ever will because you chose that very day to storm into my office. But I will say it's not a tactic I've ever used before. In most cases, Ramsey's usually builds in abandoned areas or on vacant land."

"But not this time."

"No. But as we were planning, we tried to find an area which would displace the least amount of people. I can't apologize for that."

Lila appreciated his honesty, but it was still a sore topic for her so she decided to change the subject. "How did you get such an awful nickname anyway?"

"When I took over Ramsey's, I felt I had a lot to prove because most of the employees felt I didn't deserve my position."

"Why not?"

"One of my stepfathers took me under his wing. At times, I was probably more aggressive than I should have been, but my business decisions often got positive results for the company, hence the nickname."

"Ah, your stepfather used to run this business." She at least understood how he'd come to work for the company he now ran.

"Yes. Ben had no children of his own and he was pleased when I wanted to learn the business."

"You said stepfathers in the plural."

"Yes, I've had a few growing up, but I'm sure you don't want to hear my life story."

"I wouldn't mind. It would give me some insight into the man himself, and maybe I'll understand this chip on your shoulder in regard to women."

"I don't have a—"

"Yes you do, and it's the size of a boulder. Spill it."

"Are you sure I won't bore you to death?"

She winked at him. "As long as you resuscitate me if I show any signs of dying, I think I'll be okay."

"If nothing else can be said about you, you're definitely a persistent lady, Lila."

"So they tell me. Now stop stalling."

"Truthfully, there's really not much to tell. I had a pretty average childhood until my father died when I was ten."

"I'm sorry. I only had my dad growing up, so I know what it's like to only have one parent."

"You, at least, had the advantage of being close to your father. I'm sure Mom cared about me as best she could, but she wasn't the most maternal of women. She wasn't the kind of woman who liked to be alone. She remarried within three months of my dad's heart attack. She was—is—an attractive woman and has never been short on male attention. I guess I grew a bit resentful at how quickly she was able to move on while I was still grieving."

"Do you think that's where your mistrust of women began?"

"I won't say I mistrust women entirely. In my experience, unfortunately the ones I've had dealings with were more interested in what a man could give them rather than the other way around."

"We're not all like that. I'm not."

"So you keep saying."

"Because it's the truth."

"Hmm." He neither agreed or disagreed.

Lila silently counted to five before she spoke again. She had to remember it would take time for him to get over his hang-ups. "What happened when your mother remarried?"

"My first stepfather wasn't a bad guy. Ben was as good to me as any man who'd had a ten year old stepson suddenly thrust upon him. He'd even offered me the Ramsey name. I refused out of respect for my father though. I was just starting to get used to the arrangement when Mom decided she couldn't handle what she called his workaholic attitude. I was fourteen then."

"That's a shame."

"It was upsetting, but Ben and I kept in contact in the following years. Stepfather number two was a widower with a daughter. He resented the hell out of my presence and made no secret of it. Being a self-made man who'd come from nothing he liked to throw his money around, making sure everyone knew how much he shelled out for everything. Ted made sure I realized I was in his house because of his largesse. I hated him for constantly putting me down but I started to despise my mother even more for letting him. In retrospect, I didn't exactly demonstrate model behavior."

"But you were a teenager, he was a grown man."

Hunter's lip quirked briefly. "You're very generous."

"I'm just calling it like I see it. Did you get along with your stepsister at least?"

"Karen didn't make matters easier for me."

"She teased you?"

"In the worst way a girl could do to any hot-blooded teenage boy. She loved to show off her body, flashing me when no one was looking, and touching my knee and rubbing my crotch under the dinner table."

Lila gasped. "How old was this girl?"

"Seventeen and very developed. I didn't stand a chance. I don't think I have to tell you what happened next. She came on to me and I took what she offered. Unlucky for us, or me rather, we were caught. Ted gave me an ass kicking I'll never forget for taking advantage of his innocent angel." He snorted. "She wasn't a virgin when I had her, but she was always so well behaved around him."

"But she was older than you—knew better. Surely he could see she was just as responsible.

"Karen could do no wrong in Ted's eyes. Hell, she even

turned on the waterworks and said I'd forced her. That earned me another pummeling, although I did get some nice shots in myself. Anyway, I was sent to boarding school after that incident because he refused to have me under his roof anymore. Mom stood back and said nothing as usual."

"You can't hold women responsible for what your mother and some *girl* did to you."

"Maybe I shouldn't but I haven't seen any shining examples of female virtue. After I took over Ramsey's for Ben and made it what it is today, all the attention from the women went to my head. In my mind, I was getting a little of my own back for past hurts. I didn't give a lot of them a proper chance to find out who was using me and who genuinely liked me. They were all the same to me. My earlier experiences hardened me against the fairer sex. I suppose my accident didn't help matters. Until tonight, I didn't realize how bitter and angry I'd become at people, the world and myself." He took her hand in his. "I don't want to be this way anymore. I want to heal. Teach me how, Lila."

Her heart went out to him. Hunter's impassioned plea touched a part of her she didn't believe he was capable of. Her response was to lean over and offer her lips him.

With a groan, Hunter lowered his head to accept. For the first time since her arrival, Lila didn't feel homesick.

Chapter Eleven

Lila touched his sleeve, compassion etched in every line on her lovely face. "If you're not comfortable coming out, I don't mind if we get takeout and go back to the house."

Though she kept her voice light and casual, Hunter could hear the anxious undertone of her words. Ever since he'd decided to take her out for dinner, he couldn't fight the nerves coursing through his body. Going to work and dealing with his colleagues was a trial in itself, but it was a necessity. This on the other hand was different, voluntarily putting himself out there to be scrutinized by the public, inviting the stares, trying to ignore the whispers behind cupped hands. Perspiration beaded his forehead when he thought about it.

Clenching his fists to prevent his hands from shaking, he pasted a smile on his lips. Lila had turned out to be everything he could possibly want in a companion, and more. Because he hated seeing that look of abject longing he saw in her eyes when she didn't think he was watching, Hunter had suggested they go out for a night on the town. To say Lila was thrilled at the suggestion was an understatement. Throwing her arms around him, she'd thanked him profusely and Hunter knew there was no turning back.

How could he tell her he'd changed his mind, when he hadn't seen her face light up like that before? Hunter hadn't realized how much making Lila happy meant to him until that moment. As much as he wanted to tell Ernest to turn the car around, he didn't have the heart to do it.

Pasting a smile on his lips, he hoped it looked natural. Hunter patted her hand, letting his fingers graze her soft skin. God, he loved touching her. "No, I don't want to go home, besides, I can't think of a better way to spend my evening than with a beautiful woman enjoying a fine dining experience."

Lila's grin widened, making her dark eyes sparkle. She leaned over and planted her glossy lips against his cheek. "Thank you. This means a lot to me."

A warmth spread throughout his body from the touch of her lips. "It's my pleasure. You look fantastic, by the way." And she did. Though he would have preferred her hair to be worn loose, it was pinned in a stylish topknot with loose strands framing her heart-shaped face. She didn't wear as much gunk on her face as the other women who'd flitted in and out of his life, yet none of them could hold a candle to her natural beauty.

Her dress was one of the items he'd purchased for her. A strapless jade gown which hugged her curves like a second skin. His cock stiffened with the mere thought of his plan to undress her when they got home. How he'd undo her hair to let it cascade around his shoulders. How he'd kiss every inch of her soft chocolate skin, until she cried out his name, begging him for more.

Hunter wasn't thrilled at the prospect of being in an uncontrolled environment. But he didn't want to disappoint Lila when he knew it meant so much to her to have a night out. That she didn't seem to mind she was spending it with him gave him the courage to see this thing through.

Her full lips curved to a smile. "And you don't look so bad yourself. You clean up rather nicely."

Hunter shook his head. "Just because I pay you a compliment, don't feel obligated to give me one back. We both know what I look like."

One finely arched brow shot up. "Oh? And since when did you become a mind reader? I happen to think you look very handsome right now. If you didn't have so many damn hang-ups, maybe you'd be able to accept what I say at face value rather than scrutinizing everything."

"What I accept is you're the kind of person who doesn't like to hurt people's feelings, but let's not try to sugarcoat this joke I call a face."

Folding her arms across her chest, she turned away from him. "I wish you wouldn't start this again, Hunter. I'm not interested in joining your pity party tonight."

"I'm not having a goddamn—" Realizing he'd raised his voice when he saw her flinch, Hunter paused. Taking a deep breath, he placed his hand on her thigh and gave it a light squeeze. "You're right. Learning how to accept myself as I am now is going to take some time, but I'll keep trying. For you."

Lila turned and faced him again, her dark brown gaze roaming his face. Hunter tried not to fidget under her penetrating scrutiny. Placing her hand on the scarred side of his face, she shook her head. "No. Do it for you."

There was no mistaking the sincerity in her voice. Lila Saunders was as genuine as they came, and he should have seen it right away. But he'd let his prejudices about women get in the way. Maybe he should let her go now instead of forcing her to spend time with him. But the moment the thought entered his mind, he immediately buried it again.

He'd have to let her go soon enough, but for now, he wanted to spend as much time with her as possible. Needed it. He enjoyed her company far more than he believed he would at the beginning of this arrangement. No, he wouldn't let her go just yet. Hunter intended to keep her with him for as long as he possibly could, even though deep down he knew it was wrong.

Dinner was every bit the ordeal Hunter pictured it would be. Besides the stares he drew in his direction, the minute they'd stepped into the restaurant, Hunter was aware of the hushed whispers and stunned gasps. He'd known this was what to expect, knew people would pause in the middle of eating and stare, some pretending not to, while others watched him openly.

What made matters worse was knowing what they were thinking. He could tell by the sympathetic stares some shot Lila's way. *What is that beautiful woman doing with that monster? He must be incredibly rich because she couldn't possibly be with someone like him.* And they wouldn't have been so far from the truth. What would they say if they knew he'd blackmailed her to be with him? They'd condemn him for being every bit the monster they believed him to be.

There was only so much of this he could take.

"Hunter." Lila stretched her arm over the table as she waved her hand in his face. "Earth to Hunter."

He shook his head to rid himself of the disconcerting thoughts swimming in his mind. "I'm sorry, were you saying something?"

"Can I go too?"

"What?"

"Wherever you were just now. I've been trying to get your attention for the last five minutes."

He was doing exactly what he promised her he wouldn't, feeling sorry for himself. *Come on, Hunter, you're being an ass. Pull yourself together.* Pasting a smile on his face, he gave her his undivided attention, determined to block out the curious glances thrown his way. "I apologize. I was thinking about how long it's been since I've been out like this."

"Are you enjoying yourself?"

"Of course. How could I not when I have the company of such a lovely companion?"

"You don't have to lay it on so thick, Hunter."

"It's true. You're gorgeous, and I think you know it."

She raised her shoulder in a nonchalant shrug.

"You don't give a damn about your looks do you?"

Lila shook her head. "Not really. I'd be lying if I said I didn't know I was attractive, but there are far more important things in life than being pretty. Eventually, my looks will fade and I'm okay with that because I have so much more going on in my life than my face. And I suspect you were the same way before your accident. You didn't give a damn about your looks before it happened, did you?"

It was on the tip of his tongue to deny it, but she was correct. Sure he knew what a good looking man he used to be, but he'd taken his face for granted. It was only now when he was deformed that it mattered to him so much. He twisted his lips into a half smile. "You never appreciate what you have until it's gone. What you say makes sense, but it's hard to not to be uncomfortable when people are staring at me like I'm a circus freak."

Lila sat back in her chair, crossing her arms over her chest, looking at him with a suspicious gleam of amusement in her eyes. Her glossy painted lips were slightly curved. Hunter didn't quite trust that look. He was beginning to learn what her expressions meant, and when the cogs were spinning. She was up to something.

"What's that look for?"

Her grin widened to reveal her even white teeth. "What look?"

"The one that tells me you're plotting."

She tossed her head back showing off the graceful column of her neck as she laughed. "I'm sure I don't know what you're talking about, Hunter. Has anyone ever told you you're paranoid?"

Hunter raised a brow. "When I'm given a good reason to be, I am." He stiffened at the feel of her stockinged foot easing its way up his leg. "What are you doing?"

Instead of answering, she picked up her fork and knife, cut a piece of asparagus and popped it into her mouth as if her foot wasn't sliding along his thigh.

Hunter's cock jumped to attention and her toes were mere

inches from his crotch. Yet she sat across from as if nothing out of the ordinary was happening. "What are you doing?"

"You've already asked me that. I'm eating." She pressed the ball of her foot against his erection making him jump.

He inhaled sharply as heat rushed through his body. "Good God, woman, what are you doing to me?"

"Giving you something else to think about. Is it working?" She moved her foot against his cock in circular motions."

Hunter clenched the tablecloth between his fists as sweat broke out along his forehead. Not only was he no longer concerned about what people around them thought about his face, he doubted he'd make it ten minutes without fucking her senseless.

"You're asking for it," he said through clenched teeth, trying to hold on to his last bit of self control.

Lila continued to stroke him with her foot, all while eating her meal as if nothing out of the ordinary was going on. When she put her fork down and winked at him, Hunter could take no more.

He yanked his cell phone from his breast pocket and punched in Ernest's number.

"Yes, Mr. Jamison?"

"Meet us out front in five minutes."

"Sure thing, boss."

Hunter clicked off and replaced his phone.

Lila pulled her foot away, a frown marring her forehead. "Why are we leaving?"

"You know why," he growled. Hunter pulled out his credit card to pay for their meal before signaling the waiter. "I think you know."

"But I'm not finished with my meal."

"You should have thought about that before you pulled your little stunt. Now, I'm going to finish what you started."

With their coats collected, and the bill paid, Hunter hustled her out of the restaurant in record time. He couldn't get her home fast enough to ease his aching hard-on.

Ernest had the car parked in front of the building as instructed. Wisely, the driver didn't ask questions about their dinner ending so abruptly.

Hunter held Lila against him, nuzzling her neck and inhaling the sweet scent of her fragrant skin. He gripped her thigh, pushing the hem of her skirt higher as he caressed her soft skin.

"Hunter, not here," she whispered, her eyes darting to Ernest, though she made no move to pull away from his caresses. In fact, she leaned into his touch, her body seeming to beg for more even though her mouth said otherwise.

"Payback is a bitch isn't it? All you have to say is stop and I will."

A whimper escaped her lips and Hunter knew he couldn't go another minute without tasting her. Lowering his head, he smothered her succulent mouth with his, plunging his tongue forward to sample her sweet essence.

With a sigh, she returned his kiss wholeheartedly, tangling her fingers through his hair and holding his head to hers. Not being able to touch her had been pure torture. He cupped her face to deepen the kiss, taking charge and showing how much he needed her. His body was on fire for her and his dick was so hard and sensitive it was almost painful to endure.

The ride home wasn't long, but Hunter didn't know how much longer he could hold out without being inside her hot, tight pussy. Kissing wasn't enough. He needed her. By the time they pulled up to the house however, Hunter didn't have the patience to make it to the bedroom.

He broke the tight seal of their lips only for a moment to leave instructions for his driver. "You can leave the keys in the ignition, Ernest. I'll pull the car into the garage when Miss Saunders and I have finished talking." Talking was the last thing Hunter had in mind, but he knew his employee was too professional to say otherwise.

"Of course, Mr. Jamison. Have a good night."

Ernest slid out of the car and closed the door behind him with a decisive click. Once they were alone, Hunter pulled Lila across his lap with every intention of finishing what they'd started, but she placed her hands against his chest, halting the descent of his mouth on hers.

"Wait, Hunter. Shouldn't we go in?"

He ran his tongue over his lips to lick up the taste of her still clinging to them. "No. Remember, you started this."

"But in the car?"

He ran a finger along the top of her breasts peeking out of her dress. "Yes, in the car."

A gasp parted her lips and her shoulders shook with a shiver. "Ernest probably thinks we're depraved."

"He's not paid to think about what I do within the confines of my property. We're both consenting adults. What's the matter, sweetheart? Don't tell me you didn't mean it." Hunter buried his face against her neck. She trembled within the circle of his arms, but he could still feel her resistance. By the time he was finished with Lila, he would have her absolute surrender.

"Mean what?"

"You were obviously trying to get a rise out of me back at the restaurant and you got one. I'd hate to think you don't plan on following through."

"I do." She arched her neck, granting him the access he desired.

A smile curved his lips. Lila was weakening just as he knew she would. One thing he loved about her was how wonderfully responsive she was to his touch. The ways she'd shake at his every caress, moan and writhe against his passionate ministrations was enough to drive him to the brink of insanity. Nibbling on the soft flesh where her neck and shoulder met, he took his time exploring her creamy flesh before raising his head to meet her passion-glazed brown eyes. "Then what's the problem?"

"I was—oh! I can't think when you do that."

Hunter's hand slowly eased up her thigh, pushing her dress up as he made his way up. "Don't mind me. Finish your thought."

"You're infuriating, do you know that?"

"Mmm, so I've been told." He was more interested in getting her panties off so he could be inside of her, but he would humor her a couple minutes more. There was only so long she could hold him off. His concentration was on his task as he traced the fastening of her garter belt. "You were saying?"

"I was only trying to relax you when we were at the restaurant. I didn't mean for things to go this far."

"I see," he said solemnly, moving his hand higher until the tip of his fingers touched the edge of her panties. "Well, it certainly worked. I'm so relaxed, I can't think of anything other than fucking you, and you know what? I think I will.

She clamped her thighs together, trapping his hand between them. "Don't."

He raised a brow. "You don't want me to stop, Lila, not when I feel your heat. It's practically scorching my hand. I bet you're wet for me aren't you, darling?"

She averted her gaze as if she had something to hide. Hunter smiled, enjoying this game of cat and mouse, a game he fully intended to win.

"Hunter..."

"Open up for me, baby. Don't deny what we both want."

Her nibbled her bottom lip before slowly parting her thighs.

With her silent encouragement, Hunter grazed the crotch of her panties with his fingertips. "Hmm, just as I suspected, you're soaking wet. I think we're going to have to do something about that. Don't you think?"

She met his gaze once more with narrowed eyes. "Does it

really matter what I think?"

"Of course it does. All you have to do is tell me to stop, but I don't think you want me to, do you?"

Clutching his shoulders, she hung her head in defeat. "You know I won't, although I didn't realize my actions would lead to vehicular sex."

"This is only the beginning, dear." He dipped his finger inside her panties and searched for her hot little treasure. When he grasped her clit between his thumb and forefinger, she bucked her hips forward.

"Hunter!"

"That's it, baby. Let it happen. Don't hold back. Admit it, Lila, this was exactly what you wanted when you did what you did."

"Mmm." She wiggled her hips against his hands. Lila didn't need to admit anything, because he already knew. Hunter had learned in the few short weeks they'd been together how Lila, though a very passionate and giving lover, was still basically shy when it came to vocalizing her sexual needs. She probably fooled herself into believing her attempt at seduction was to relax him, but Hunter was certain she'd done it as much for her benefit as for his. Lila wanted this as much as he did. The more time they were spending together though, she was opening up more and more.

Hunter released her clit and slid two fingers into her damp sheath, pushing them deep. "Your pussy is tightening around my fingers. You want it bad don't you, Lila?"

She ran her tongue across her lips, and nodded, her eyes tightly shut.

Chuckling, Hunter brushed his lips against the column of her throat. "You don't get off that easily. You're going to have to tell me how much you want this."

"You know…"

He slipped his fingers in and out of her, making her shake and moan. Hunter couldn't remember when he'd enjoyed a

119

moment as much as this one. To have this gorgeous woman squirming on his lap, her cunt so wet and ready to be fucked... She was his for the taking and he couldn't wait to have her. But he'd have her admit it first. It was the least she owed him for the sexual torment she'd dealt out earlier.

"I do, but that doesn't mean I don't want to hear you say it. Tell me."

"I want you. Please. I need it. I need you. Don't tease me anymore."

Hunter had her where he wanted her. Debating on whether he should prolong her sensual torture, he decided against it. His rigid cock strained against his pants, threatening to break through. To continue teasing her as she deserved would have been just as hard on him if not more so. Besides, the evidence of her arousal soaked his hand.

Easing his fingers out of her tight cunt, Hunter brought them to his mouth and licked her juices off, never breaking eye contact with her. She watched him open-mouthed, her body trembling. Hunger lurked within the depths of her gaze as her tongue slid across her now bare lips.

He had to have her right here and right now. "Come here." Grasping her shoulders, he guided her until she straddled him with her knees resting on the leather upholstery. Her dress was hiked around her waist and her breasts hovered dangerously on the brink of popping out of the bodice clinging so tightly to her. Hunter grasped either side of her head with a groan and smashed his lips against hers.

Lila's mouth parted as her tongue darted forward to collide with his in a duel for sexual supremacy, but it was a battle Hunter fully intended to win. He held her head steady until he was satisfied in his exploration of the sweet recesses of her delectable mouth. Damn she tasted good, but once again, the ache of his groin reminded him of his other pressing need.

Tearing his mouth from hers, Hunter took a few gasps of air before softly commanding, "Undo may pants and take out my cock."

Lila opened her mouth as if she wanted to say something, but instead she merely nodded. Lifting her hips up just enough to maneuver her hands between their bodies, she fumbled with his belt buckle, unsuccessfully at first, but her second attempt was met with triumph. In hurried movements, she yanked down his zipper and slid her hand through the slit in his boxers.

When her fingers wrapped around his cock, Hunter felt as if he'd explode right then and there, silently praying not to come too soon. No, he wanted to save that for when he was inside of her. "Hurry!" So close to getting what he wanted, yet not quite, was driving him insane with a manic need.

Lila gently pulled his cock out of his pants and Hunter hooked his finger inside the crotch of her panties and pushed it aside. "Lower yourself onto me. Take every inch of me inside of you."

She positioned his dick against her wet opening before dropping her hips just enough for the head of his cock to enter her. "Hunter." The soft sigh of her voice was just enough to drive him over the edge.

With impatience, Hunter grasped her hips and surged up, sending his cock deep into her tight sheath. Wonder filled his being as he inhaled sharply. This wasn't the first time they'd fucked, but he still couldn't get over how right it felt being inside of her. How tight she was and how her muscles clenched so tightly around him. Most other times, he would have remained still for a moment to savor how absolutely perfect this feeling of being one with Lila was, but he was far too horny. There'd be time for that later.

Lila gripped his shoulders as she bounced her hips up and down, moving until his cock was nearly out of her and then going back down until he was so deep inside of her, Hunter wasn't sure where he ended and she began. His fingers dug into the tender flesh of her hips while he bucked his hips to meet her thrust for thrust. It took a few strokes to catch his rhythm, but soon their movements were so synchronized, it was almost like they'd practiced it many times before.

Having Lila here like this excited him like nothing else. The thrill of taking her, fucking her in a new location and her absolute surrender was a potent aphrodisiac he knew he'd succumb to any minute now. Gritting his teeth and willing himself not to climax just yet made his pulse race.

One of her breasts spilled out of her dress. Its dark nipple hardened as though beckoning him to taste, presenting a temptation he couldn't resist. This was how Adam must have felt when Eve presented him the apple, though Lila's offering was far more inviting. Leaning forward, Hunter captured the taut tip between his lips and sucked with desperate tugs. He couldn't get enough of her.

"Yes. Hunter. That feels so good."

Her moans egged him on as he explored the contours of her breast with his tongue, their bodies never missing a beat. She tasted so good, smelled so wonderful, felt so right. Releasing her nipple with a wet pop, Hunter raised his head with the intention of finding her lips. But something happened in that moment. Their gazes clashed and he saw something in her eyes, an emotion he couldn't quite make out, one he wasn't really familiar with, but it was a look that changed everything—shifted this joining of their bodies beyond mere fucking, to something much more profound.

Hunter couldn't put his finger on what it was, didn't have the courage to further examine it, but it happened nonetheless. The urgency suddenly left him, but the need increased. The longer they maintained contact, Hunter could tell, the same thing was running through Lila's mind. Slowly their mouths fitted together, and her arms went around his neck and her hands clasped the back of her head. Hunter held her against him knowing he must for no other reason than it was something he had to do.

They moved together, his cock still deeply imbedded in her

pussy, their lips melded together as if it were their last kiss. He wasn't sure how long they stayed like that, but finally Lila was the one to turn her head away as she gasped, "I'm coming." Crying out, her head flopped back and forth and her shudders racked her body.

Hunter was close to his own orgasm, but the inner workings in his brain wouldn't allow him to speak. He shoved deeper into her, getting closer and closer to his climax until the buildup that had started in his toes moved along every inch of his body, throughout every limb, every fingertip and every nerve ending, resulting in something so powerful he shouted his release. "Lila! Lila! Lila!"

Shooting his load into her pussy, he held on to her so tight, never wanting to let her go, frightened that he'd never experience this almost spiritual feeling coursing through his soul again. Hunter buried her face against her neck. "Oh, God, Lila. I lo—loved it. That was..."

She nodded. "I know," she said with a whisper, holding on to him just as tightly as he was to her.

Hunter knew they should go inside. It was chilly out, but he wanted to stay like this just a little while longer. Lila didn't seem to be in any particular hurry to move either. What had happened here? Even if he was forced to put it into words, he couldn't. There was one thing he knew for certain: after tonight, things would never be the same between them again.

Chapter Twelve

Finally, the damn meeting was over and Hunter couldn't wait to get the hell out there. If he left now, he could make it home in under an hour.

Home to Lila.

The very thought of her brought a smile to his lips. Closing his laptop and shoving it into its case, he was ready to leave when Thomas walked over to him.

"Hunter, are you okay?" Confusion crinkled his friend's forehead.

The question took him aback. For the first time in a while, Hunter felt great. "What do you mean?"

"You've been walking around with this shit-eating grin all day. It's kind of creepy, man."

Usually a comment like this would have made him scowl, but nothing could rob him of his good mood today. Plans for the megaplex were going accordingly: in fact the new arrangements he'd proposed a couple months ago were working out better than he anticipated they would. His passion for his job had returned, but it was different. Hunter realized it was only just that. A job. And he wouldn't allow it to consume him as it had before. "Is there a reason why I'm not allowed to smile? It's a beautiful day."

Thomas narrowed his eyes. "Okay. Who are you and what have you done to Hunter Jamison?"

"Can't a man be happy for once?"

"But you're never happy."

Hunter should have been offended but he knew Thomas had a point. It made him feel guilty at how he must have come across to others in his depression. "Sheesh. You make me sound like a miserable bastard."

"I wouldn't be a good friend if I lied to you. I haven't seen you like this since..."

"Before my accident? Don't worry. You can say it."

"Now I know something's up. What's going on? First you come into the office whistling. Then, during our meeting not once did you halt Peter in the middle of one of his pompous tirades. Your tolerance is usually pretty low for his crap. To top it off, you're referring to your accident so casually. What's the deal with you?"

Hunter sighed. There was no point in keeping quiet. Thomas would get it out of him eventually anyway. He was also the only person who knew of Hunter's agreement with Lila because Thomas had wanted to know why he had pushed so hard to change the plans for the megaplex.

"Walk with me to my car." Hunter pulled his cell phone from his pocket and punched in Ernest's number.

The driver answered. "Are you ready, Mr. Jamison?"

"Yes. I'll be out in ten minutes."

"I'll have the car out front."

"Thank you." He flipped the phone shut.

"Okay, shoot," Thomas prompted.

"There's really not much to say other than someone special showed me what an ass I've been. It's never easy to change, but I'm trying."

Thomas adjusted his glasses on the bridge of his nose. "I've been telling you that for years, but you never listened to me."

"You never put it as eloquently as Lila."

Thomas's eyes widened behind his glasses. "Lila? As in Lila Saunders, the woman who could have cost this company hundreds of thousands, possibly millions of dollars? The very one you're practically blackmailing?"

Heat swamped his cheeks and Hunter was sure his face was bright red. He didn't care to be reminded of how he and Lila had come together. Deep down, he knew she wouldn't have looked his way had the circumstances not thrown them together, but the last two months of her stay had meant something to him. He liked to think she actually enjoyed being with him. Not once did she flinch when she looked his way, instead, she had a ready smile that seemed like it was just for him.

She continually sent his body into a tailspin like he'd never experienced with any other woman, and Hunter was glad to face a new day knowing Lila was a part of his life. His cock stirred as he thought of what he intended to do to her later tonight. A more passionate woman, he doubted he'd meet.

When Hunter had first met her, he'd only seen the surface, but as he got to know Lila better, he saw her inner beauty shined as bright as her outer shell. She was a rare jewel.

"Yes. The same one," he finally replied, tight-lipped.

"Don't get all defensive now. I've never seen you so over the moon, especially over a piece of ass."

Hunter halted in mid-stride and turned on the other man, baring his teeth. "If you refer to her as a piece of ass again, I'll knock your teeth in. Her name is Lila. Use it."

Thomas held up his hands. "Whoa. I meant no offense, and it's not more than what you yourself have called your other women."

"But she's not them."

"I guess she's not if you're getting so riled over her. I'm just saying."

"Saying what?"

"If you keep walking around with that dopey grin on your face, I may begin to think you're in love."

"I'm not—" Hunter broke off, wondering if there was any validity to Thomas's words. For so long he'd scorned that emotion, never seeing any proof of its existence. His mother, who seemed to throw that word around so freely, was on her fifth husband. Most of the married couples in his social circle were either bitterly unhappy or trying to put on a front for the rest of the world, while the others didn't bother to pretend.

Was what he felt for Lila more than just lust, friendship and companionship? She made him smile without trying and he missed her when she wasn't around. When she was with him, Hunter didn't want to let her out of his sight. Was that love? He wasn't sure. He didn't have the right to use that word in conjunction with her because in a month she'd leave him. The very thought caused him pain.

"Finish what you were going to say," Thomas interrupted his thoughts.

"I don't know. Look I have to get home, but I'll call into the office tomorrow so you can fill me in on how your meeting went with the Carver group." When he would have moved on, Thomas grasped his arm.

"Wait. I didn't mean to piss you off."

Hunter sighed. "You didn't. I'm just being overly sensitive."

"She must be a remarkable woman. Not only has she managed to tame the Beast, you've been wearing your hair tucked behind your ears. You didn't even turn your head when that jackass in the meeting kept staring at you."

Hunter hadn't noticed. Now that he thought about it, he hadn't dwelled on his scars in weeks. As a force of habit, he touched the imperfect side of his face. Maybe he was healing on the inside so much that the outside didn't matter as much anymore, another thing he had Lila to thank for.

"No. I suppose I haven't and yes, she is pretty special."

"Have you told her how you felt?"

"What do you mean?"

A knowing smile split Thomas's face. "I think you know. I'll

127

talk to you tomorrow."

Hunter didn't bother to dwell on his friend's words. Ernest was outside waiting for him.

His driver hopped out of the car and opened the door for Hunter. "Good afternoon, Mr. Jamison. I trust your meeting went well?"

"Yes, thank you." He was about to get into the car when he remembered something important. "How are the grandkids by the way?"

In all the time the Coates had worked for him, he hadn't bother getting to know them, too wrapped up in his own world to even care. It was through Lila he'd learned more about his two employees in two months than he had in years.

Ernest's grin widened. "They're doing wonderfully. Mary is taking ballet classes, dances like an angel that one. Nathan is into soccer. As you know, his eighth birthday is coming up. I'd like to thank you again for giving Maddie and me the time off to attend."

"Anytime. Please don't hesitate to ask for time off when you need it. I think the two of you are due for a paid vacation pretty soon."

"You'll have a devil of a time convincing Maddie of that. She's not happy unless she's busy." Ernest chuckled. "Now let's get you home. I'm sure Miss Lila is waiting for you."

At the mention of Lila's name, he slid into the car. Usually, Hunter worked on his laptop on the ride home, but he knew he wouldn't be able to concentrate. Thomas's words came back to him. Did he love Lila? He went over it in his mind the entire way home.

When Ernest pulled the car to a halt, Hunter opened the door and got out, not bothering to wait for the engine to shut off. He hurried into the house and called out. "Lila!"

When he didn't get a response, he tore upstairs to the library where she spent a lot of her time. She wasn't there. His next stop was the kitchen. Maybe she and Mrs. Coates were chatting over tea? It amazed him how Lila had even made his normally stiff housekeeper unbend.

Mrs. Coates was there, but Lila wasn't. "Have you seen Lila?" he asked without greeting.

"Good afternoon, Mr. Jamison."

Suddenly remembering his manners, he grinned. "Good afternoon."

His housekeeper smiled. "Miss Lila was out back, the last I saw her."

"Thanks." He didn't stick around for her reply before heading out to the backyard.

Grinning broadly, he paused when he saw Lila running around the yard with the dogs. Her face was animated and she was laughing at Shadow and Deja's antics. She presented a lovely sight. He wondered if he'd ever get used to how lovely she was. Somehow, Hunter doubted it.

He saw she was wearing one of the new outfits she'd bought recently, a hot pink track suit. They had come to a compromise about her clothes. He had Ernest take Lila to her favorite department store to pick out anything she liked, which turned out to be mainly casual clothes. But at night she wore the items he'd selected for her. Hunter was glad he'd relented on that subject. She seemed happier because of it.

He observed her tossing a stick and the dogs running after it. Her face fell and a wistful look suddenly turned into a frown. Something was wrong. Hunter could feel it. His heart skipped a beat as he watched Lila maintain that sorrowful expression. Yes, something was definitely the matter.

"Come on, guys," she spoke to the dogs, "time to go in."

As the three made their way toward Hunter, Shadow and Deja noticed him first. They barked and then ran toward him in their excitement, tails wagging.

Lila's eyes widened in surprise at his appearance and then her smile reappeared, but it couldn't erase from his mind what he'd just seen. As she drew closer, he noticed her eyes were red.

She'd been crying! He'd bet his last dime on it.

"Hi, Hunter. How did things go at the office?"

"They went well. Did you do anything exciting today?"

She shook her head. "Not really. Playing with the dogs has basically been the highlight of my day. You're home earlier than I thought you'd be."

Hunter raised a brow. "Is that a problem?

"Not at all." He studied her face for a moment. She seemed distracted.

Grasping her chin, he dropped a light kiss on her lips. "Are you sure everything is alright?"

She lowered her lids and nodded. "Lila, I thought we were going to be honest with each other. Tell me what's on your mind."

"It's nothing."

"I can't help if you don't tell me."

She nibbled on her bottom lip and looked as though she was debating on whether she could open up.

"Are you unhappy with me?"

Her head came up sharply. "No! You've been great company."

"So what's the problem?"

"I'm so used to keeping busy I'm going out of my skull. Plus I'm getting major cabin fever. I've only been out of this house a couple times since I've been here and it's wearing. I know what our arrangement is and I have no right to complain, but..."

Hunter felt like a jackass. Of course she'd get bored staying cooped up in his house all day. Why hadn't he thought to provide her with something to occupy her time? He'd been so caught up in his own needs, he hadn't dwelled on her. He had a nagging feeling she hadn't told him everything.

"There's more isn't there?"

"I miss my dad. This is the longest I've gone without seeing him. When I talked to him last night, he sounded happy actually. With the construction beginning, he's getting a lot of business from the workers who come in for lunch."

"But?"

"But I miss him and even though he says he's doing fine, I worry."

"Would you like to go home and visit him?" The words were out before he realized what he was saying, but there was no taking them back once he'd said them. When he saw the pure joy flit over her face, he knew what he had to do.

"Do you really mean that? You'd let me go home and see him?" Her eyes lit up and her face became more animated than it had been in days. He hadn't realized how unhappy she was until this moment. So wrapped up in the joy she brought to his life, he hadn't stopped to consider how she must feel. Of course Lila missed her father; he was after all the reason she was here in the first place. And seeing how full of joy she'd become at the mention seeing her father, Hunter knew he couldn't deny her that pleasure.

"Yes."

Just as quickly as it had appeared, the light dimmed from her dark eyes all of a sudden. "I can't."

"Why not? I'll have Ernest drive you there."

"For how long though?"

He shrugged. "For a few hours I suppose."

Lila shook her head. "That's okay. It wouldn't be enough. I appreciate the gesture though."

Hunter's stomach lurched and it felt like it was twisting in knots. He knew the direction this conversation was heading but he found himself saying, "If you'd like I can arrange for you to spend a couple days with him." The thought of her being away from him even for that short period of time caused him pain, but he knew he had to offer because she wouldn't ask.

She caught her bottom lip between her teeth, and looked as though she was contemplating his suggestion before shaking her head again. "Thank you, but no. I have another month in our agreement. It wouldn't be fair to you considering how you've honored your end of the bargain. I need to do the same."

Her statement was like a sledgehammer to his heart. Did she only view the thing between them as mere duty? Just as he was beginning to suspect his feelings for her were so much more than sexual attraction she'd dealt him a painful blow. The sad part was: Lila probably wasn't aware of what she'd just done.

Had he been a fool to think she'd come to care about him a little? Did it even matter? Hunter had known things would eventually come to an end. If it truly made her unhappy to be here with him, how could he even justify keeping her? Sure they had a deal, but could he really live with himself knowing she was counting the days until she was out of here? He should never have thrown this offer at her in the first place. But now that he had, he'd have to deal with it. "It's okay. I don't mind. Besides, we can add two more days on if it makes you feel better."

With a smile she leaned forward and brushed her warm lips against his cheek. "You're a sweetheart, but seriously, I can hold out for a little while longer to see him. I'd much rather make the rest of our time together special."

Hunter wanted that too, more than he could ever put into words, but Pandora's Box had been opened and dammit, there was no closing it. Though it pained him to ask, he had to at least gauge if she felt something deeper for him than just the mere friendship she'd offered. "Lila, what are you plans for when you leave here?"

A brief frown flitted across her lips. "I haven't really thought about it, but I'll definitely spend a couple weeks with Dad and help him around the shop if it needs it, though I suspect he probably won't need much assistance in that arena. Then I guess I'll go back to work at the hospital."

"I see. Do you like your job?"

"I love it. I'm actually excited at the prospect of going back."

Hunter forced himself to get the words out for the next question. "Is there anyone special you left behind?"

"If I did, it would be over now considering what I've been up to these last couple months," she laughed. "Why?"

"Just curious. I find it hard to believe a beautiful woman like you would remain single for long."

Lila rolled her eyes. "You're not harping on looks again are you?"

"No. Just wondering." He took a deep breath. "Have you ever been in love?"

It took several moments of silence before she spoke. An unreadable expression entered her eyes he couldn't discern. Finally, she shook her head. "No. Once, I thought I was but I was wrong. Besides, I have had a knack for attracting the wrong kind of men."

Like myself, Hunter thought. Lila didn't deserve to be here with a bastard like him. She had a life to get back to and he was keeping her from it. What was the point in holding her for another month when she'd only end up leaving him anyway? It wouldn't be any less painful to let her go in four weeks than it was now. In fact each day that passed would cause him agony because he knew the day he'd have to let her go was drawing near.

Hunter stared into her lovely face, memorizing every line of her face, from the tilt of her chin to the curve of her lips. She was the definition of pure beauty. He knew what he had to do. His heart squeezed within the confines of his chest and it became difficult to breath.

Taking a deep breath, he said, "I guess you're probably wondering what's up with the twenty questions."

She grinned. "Well, it did cross my mind."

He scratched the back of his head. "Actually, I uh, didn't quite know how to broach the subject, before, but I needed assurance you had plans once you leave here. As it turns out, it'll be sooner than we both anticipated."

Her smile fell in an instant. "What do you mean?"

This was harder than he thought it would be, but he steeled himself to remain firm. "I mean go home to stay. I think it's time to bring this arrangement to an end."

Her mouth opened and her hand went to her throat. Judging from the stricken expression this wasn't good news, but surely he was misinterpreting her thoughts.

"Have you grown tired of me?"

If he wanted to do the right thing, he'd have to sever the ties right now while he still had the strength. "Don't take it personally, Lila. It's why I only asked for three months, because that's how long it normally takes for me to grow bored with the current woman in my life. I just didn't think it would happen with you so soon. Don't worry. I'll keep my end of the bargain. As a matter of fact, if you pack now, Ernest can probably get you home by dinnertime...unless you don't mind having one last quickie before you go."

Her jaw dropped. "How can you speak to me like this? You don't really mean it. I thought things were going well."

"Oh, they were. And I appreciate your company, but you knew as well as I, this would be ending. Better sooner than later, right?"

"How can you be so cold about the whole thing? I thought we were friends."

Hunter wanted to take her in his arms and kiss the hurt he saw lurking within the depths of her eyes. "We were friends...out of necessity. I would have said anything to gain your compliance."

Her lips thinned. "I don't believe you."

"Why not? Is it so hard to believe that someone could get tired of you? Now, who's the one hung up on looks? You're not as hot as you think, Lila."

"You son of a bitch," she whispered.

"I know." His lips curved to a smug grin. "But let's end things amicably."

Her hurt was then replaced by fury. Her fists clenched in front of her and for a moment he braced himself for a punch. She didn't. Instead, the fire left her as soon as it had come and she dropped her hands to her sides. "All this time...I thought you were a good person, someone I liked very much, but you were having a good laugh behind my back. I was just another bed warmer to you. All those things you've shared with me in these past weeks have meant absolutely nothing. Have they?"

It had meant the world to him, Hunter wanted to shout, but now that he'd set on this course of action there was no turning back. "They did mean something. You were a great lay and for that I thank you. But you've also showed me that if one woman isn't repulsed by this mug of mine, I'm sure I can find another who won't be either. I simply have to go out and find myself another Pollyanna type."

She gasped.

Lila, I'm sorry. "Don't look so surprised, sweetheart. We had a good thing. Now it's time to end it."

"So it's true," she whispered.

Hunter frowned. "What is?"

"You really are a beast. You had me fooled. I believed I'd finally seen the real man aside from what the media portrays you as. But they had it right all along."

"I never pretended to be anything other than I am."

"No. I was the fool. But never again. Goodbye, Hunter." She hurried past him and if he wasn't mistaken, he saw her dark eyes shining with the suspicious gleam of tears.

When he heard the door slam behind her, indicating she'd gone back inside, his shoulders slumped. To say those things to her had been the most difficult task he'd done in his life. But deep down, Hunter knew he couldn't hold her anymore. He finally knew the meaning of the word love—letting someone go, even though it was killing you inside.

Chapter Thirteen

Lila stood to clear the plates off the table, but Mrs. Perez grabbed her hand. "Let me do that for you, dear. You've cooked this delicious meal, the least I can do is take care of the cleanup."

Her father nodded. "And I'll help. Gloria and I have sort of gotten into a little routine while you were away."

Mrs. Perez winked at James. "I wash, you dry?"

"Of course." He grinned back.

Lila hadn't missed the meaning of the exchange. Those two had obviously gotten close in her absence. It seemed a lot of things had changed while she was gone. Her father was in the works of remodeling the store. His motto had been, 'If it ain't broke don't fix it, so it' so it had come as a surprise to see the beginning of the renovations.

James had said Gloria and the teenagers who worked for him had suggested a few changes. Lila had been telling her dad for years about changing things around the store, so it surprised her that he'd been so open to the suggestion of others. Then she'd learned that Mrs. Perez had been over almost every night for dinner and in fact they'd gone out on several dates.

It seemed as if her father was doing well and thriving. He was losing weight, his blood pressure was low, and he seemed happy. Even being here right now made Lila feel like an intruder.

For so long it had been her and her father, depending on and taking care of each other, but having been away for two months, she realized her father was fine on his own. In fact, he seemed to be better off without her around.

"Okay," she finally answered. "I think I'm going to turn in a little early."

James frowned. "Don't you want some apple pie? Gloria made it from scratch."

"Yes, please have dessert with us." Mrs. Perez smiled at her. Lila didn't doubt the other woman's sincerity, but she thought it best to leave the couple alone.

"I'll pass tonight, but please save me a slice."

After she left them alone, she went through the motions of getting ready for bed. When she was in the shower she let her head rest against the stall, the tears mingling with the water falling over her head. Her father was doing great, while the world around her was falling apart.

It was time she started to pick up the pieces of her life again. Perhaps she could contact the hospital and let them know she was ready to come back to work for them. Now would probably be a good time to start looking for a place of her own, especially when it was clear her father no longer needed her.

As hard as she tried not to think about him, her mind drifted to Hunter. What had started out as a sacrifice she was willing to make on behalf of her father turned into much more. She hadn't expected to like being with Hunter. Sexually, he fulfilled her as no one else had, satisfying her so thoroughly. Besides the physical however, they'd made a spiritual connection as well. Somewhere along the line, she began to care for him more than a little. He made her laugh, he engaged her mind, and she felt safe and secure in his presence. For so long she'd had to be strong, but in those weeks she'd been with him, Lila was able to relax her guard and let go of all her worries.

She realized that his words had had the power to hurt her because she had fallen in love with him. What a fool she'd been.

She should have known what they had was doomed to end terribly. Not only were they from different worlds, he had too many damned hang-ups.

Still, it had taken her by complete surprise how he'd said such cruel things to her. It was almost as if he was trying to make her hate him. But that made no sense. By now, he probably would have moved on, so it was time she did so as well.

Later that night, as she tossed and turned in bed, Lila thought about Hunter. What was he doing now? Was he thinking of her? Did he regret the things he said? *Stop it, girl, he's not worth it.* And she refused to shed any more tears over someone who didn't deserve them.

She glanced at the clock, and saw that it was nearly midnight. Maybe a couple of sleeping pills and some decaffeinated tea would do the trick. On her way to the bathroom, to get the medication, she noticed the kitchen light was still on.

Lila frowned. Her father was usually in bed by now. Or had he forgotten to turn it off? Always conscious of the electricity bill, he wasn't likely to leave them on. After getting the bottle out of the medicine cabinet, she headed for the kitchen.

Her father was sitting at the table in his robe, sipping what smelled like hot chocolate in an oversized mug. There was another steaming cup across from him and instantly, she knew he'd been waiting for her.

She took the seat reserved for her. "How did you know?"

James grinned. "The walls aren't that thick, baby. I knew it was a matter of time before you got up. I made your favorite. Hot chocolate with cinnamon, whipped cream and a giant marshmallow. Just like when you were a little girl."

She smiled. "Thanks, Daddy, but I think I've outgrown this."

"You're never too old for my special hot cocoa. Anyway, it's the least I can do, especially when I see you're hurting. Do you want to tell me what's been going on?"

She squeezed her eyes shut. It was time to come clean. "I lied to you, Daddy."

"About your private nursing assignment? Yes, I know."

"What?"

"I knew almost from the beginning. First of all, it seemed like a major coincidence that shortly after you left for this so called job, I get a letter from Ramsey's stating they were no longer interested in buying my property. And then I get a phone call from you. You know I'm an old man and I don't mess with technology like you young people do, but I'm sharp enough to know about caller ID. When I saw that the call had come from an H. Jamison's house, I began to suspect what the deal was."

She lowered her head in shame. How stupid could she have been? She'd called from Hunter's house. Lila should have known her father would pick up on it, but she hadn't been thinking clearly. "Why didn't you say anything?"

"Because by the time I realized what was going on, it was too late to do anything about it. I'd hoped I misread the situation and it wasn't what I think it was."

"It was," she whispered, wishing she could have kept the details to herself, but she began to tell him everything, glossing over the most intimate of the details, but giving him a pretty fair picture of what had happened.

When she finished telling her tale, her father pounded his fist on the table, anger entering his eyes. "Dammit!"

"I'm so sorry. I shouldn't have lied to you, but I didn't know what else to do. Please don't hate me."

"Baby, I could never ever hate you." He scooted his chair next to hers and engulfed Lila in his embrace. She had no more tears in her, but being in her father's arms was a comfort.

"I shouldn't have lied to you."

"No. You shouldn't have, but my anger was directed to myself. When you were gone, I realized how much I had depended on you. I've said this time and time again, you're young, pretty and have a beautiful soul. You deserve a life of your own, not to have your world revolve around me. The very fact that you would do something like this shows me I should have been more firm about you getting out more and pursuing your own interests."

"Dad, you haven't been a burden to me. I love you."

"And I love you. But we both have our own lives to live and it's unfair of me to expect you to give yours up for me, and I won't let you anymore."

Lila finally found the courage to meet his eyes. "Are you disappointed in me, Daddy?"

"Honestly, I'm not happy about what you did. In the future, come to me before doing something that will affect me, okay?"

"I promise."

"Like I said, I've had a lot of time to put things into perspective. I've allowed my life to become stagnant. You and the shop have been my life and I don't believe that's been healthy. Lila, while you were away, Gloria and I have gotten close and I'm thinking about asking her to marry me. I know you may think I'm rushing things, but at my age, every day is a blessing."

"That's wonderful. I think you two are cute together."

He grinned. "You're not upset?"

"Not at all. She's a very nice lady, and I know she's been crushing on you for a while. At least one positive thing has come of this whole mess after all. If you two got married, would she move in here?"

"I haven't thought that far yet, but it would make sense with the store downstairs."

"Then I should probably start looking for another place to live."

"Honey, you will always have a home here."

"I know, but if or when you and Mrs. Perez get married, I

don't think it would be a good idea for me to be around. You two will need some time to yourself. I know if I were recently married, I wouldn't want my grown daughter hanging around."

"Is there no hope for you and Hunter?"

Lila brought her head up sharply. His question took her by surprise. "What do you mean? He used me. I don't even want to talk about him."

"Are you sure? From what you've just told me, something doesn't quite add up. A man doesn't go from the way you described him to a jerk with the snap of the finger without there being a reason. Us guys aren't as complicated as you women."

"It doesn't matter. It's over."

"But you still love him," he said softly.

Lila sighed. "Dad, I don't want to talk about this anymore."

"Okay, baby, but you've always been a fighter. You always stood up for the little guy. I remember getting a call from your teacher when you were ten, and she told me you'd punched some little boy in the nose. When I came to pick you up from school and asked you why you did it, you looked me square in the eye and said, 'Because he was picking on the smaller kids'."

Lila laughed at the memory. She had been a bit of a firecracker back in the day. "What does that have to do with anything, Dad?"

"You seem ready to fight for anyone else, myself included, but when it comes down to you, you don't fight for yourself."

"Dad—"

He held up his hand. "Hear me out, baby girl. While I want to smash this Hunter character's face in for making such an indecent offer to you in the first place, I don't think he's as indifferent to you as you claimed he was. Something doesn't add up. And anyway, you still have feelings for him. Don't you think you owe it to yourself to find out the real reason behind his sudden about face?"

Her father might be on to something, but did she have the

courage to put her heart on the line?

"This is getting ridiculous. You haven't heard a word I've said have you?" Thomas spoke loud enough to bring Hunter out of his daze.

Hunter tore his gaze away from the painting on the wall. He hadn't really been paying attention to much lately because his mind randomly wandered. "Huh?"

"Exactly. You can't go on like this."

"What are you talking about?"

"I think you know. You're letting your personal life get in the way of business again and this shit is getting old fast."

"What do you expect me to do about it?"

"Find someone else."

"I don't want anyone else."

Thomas rolled his eyes. "Then go to her, stupid. Get down on your hands and knees and grovel if you have to, but make things right. I'm tired of you sleepwalking through the office like the world is about to end."

"For me it did, but there's no going back. She wanted to go home. She was missing her father and what kind of bastard would I have been to make her stay somewhere she didn't want to be?"

"Did she actually say she didn't want to be with you?"

"No. She's too nice for that, but I could see it in her eyes."

"Is it possible you might have misinterpreted what you saw? She could have been missing her home, but it doesn't necessarily mean she didn't want to be with you."

"I don't know what to think anymore, but I know I shouldn't have held her because of that stupid agreement I made. But..."

"But what?"

"I was afraid of what she'd say when I told her how I really felt. I'm not sure if I would have been able to handle the rejection if I laid my heart on the line with her. With the other women, I got over it...but Lila, she's different."

"Because you love her?" Thomas asked softly.

"More than you can know."

"Obviously not enough."

Hunter shot his friend a glare. "What do you mean? Not being with her is killing me."

"If you really loved her, you would have taken that risk. That's what love is. I made that mistake once before and now it's too late for me, but it isn't for you."

"What the hell am I supposed to do? Go to her house and demand she love me back?"

"No, but you can go to her and tell her how you feel. At least you'll know one way or the other of her feelings for you instead of dwelling on what ifs. If she rejects you, then maybe you can move on with your life. Anything is better than the way you've been lately. I think I'd prefer the angry ogre over this show of apathy on your part."

Hunter swiveled in his chair wondering at the validity of his friend's words. Could he do it? Go to Lila? In all his life, he'd never met a woman worth laying everything on the line for, but Lila was well worth the fight. It was on the tip of his tongue to say so when they heard a commotion outside of his office.

"You can't go in there!" his personal assistant cried out.

It was déjà vu. Hadn't he lived this scene already?

His office door came crashing open, and Lila stood in the doorway looking so beautiful and as pissed as the first day he'd laid eyes on her.

"Mr. Jamison, I apologize for allowing this to happen again. She walked right past me. I'll call the police right away," Ann said from behind Lila.

"Call off your guard dog, Hunter." Lila's gazed was zoned on only him.

"Ann, that won't be necessary. I'm always available to Miss Saunders."

Ann looked as if she wanted to protest, but thought better of it. She shot Lila a glare before turning on her heel.

Hunter saw the smug expression on Thomas's face and he barked, "What the hell are you standing there for? Can't you see this is a private matter?"

Thomas grinned. "Of course. I trust you'll be more yourself the next time I see you." He nodded in Lila's direction before he left the two of them alone.

"And tell Ann to take messages for the next hour or so. I don't want to be disturbed," Hunter growled.

Thomas's smile widened. "Will do." He practically skipped out of the office.

Lila closed the door behind her and strode over to his desk.

Hunter schooled his features, hoping she couldn't read the turmoil raging within him. He wanted to take her in his arms and hold her close, but held back to see what she did. "To what do I owe the pleasure of this visit?"

She cocked her head to the side, her eyes narrowing to dark brown slits. "Is my showing up a pleasure?"

"Yes," he answered honestly.

She slammed her hand on his desk. "Then why the hell did you send me away the way you did? Were you telling me the truth when you said you were bored with me?"

"Lila, if I didn't know better I would think you actually cared." Hunter groaned inwardly. Now why the hell had he said that? He didn't want to drive her away again. "Look, I didn't mean that how it must have sounded."

"Then how did you mean it?"

"I don't know. My words get all jumbled up when you're around and I don't quite know how to act."

"Is that why you said those hurtful things to me? Because I'm not leaving here until I get the truth."

This was as good time a as any to lay his heart on the line. "When I saw how happy you were at the mention of going home, I knew I couldn't keep you with me anymore. It wouldn't have been right. And because I was too much of a coward to tell you how I really felt."

"And how is that?"

"I-I love you, Lila, I think I have since the moment I laid eyes on you, but I didn't know it then. Maybe it was lust at first sight but our time spent together meant so much more to me."

"You should have told me, Hunter."

"I didn't think someone like you would love someone like me back."

She placed her hand over her chest. "Someone like me? I'm just a person and I really wish you wouldn't place me on a pedestal. I'm not perfect. And someone like me would be honored if someone like you loved her." She walked over to his desk to stand in front of him. "During our time together, I'd come to love you, too. And I've spent the last couple weeks in hell trying to figure out why you would hurt me the way you did, because the man I came to care about wouldn't have done that."

"What?" Hunter wasn't sure if he'd heard her correctly.

Lila took a deep breath. "I said I love you, too."

Unable to contain himself any longer, he gathered her in his arms and ground his lips on hers, unleashing all the hunger that had been pent up over the last several weeks without her. Finally, he lifted his head. "Say it again."

"I love you."

Hunter rested his forehead against hers. "I'm sorry for the things I said. I thought I was doing the right thing by letting you go."

She pulled back just enough to slap him on the chest.

"Don't you ever do that to me again! I will be the one to decide what's right for me."

He wrapped his arms tightly around her, not wanting to let go even if his life depended on it. "I won't ever do anything so stupid again. Please tell me this isn't a dream, my beautiful Lila."

"I hope it's not," she laughed through the tears streaming down her cheeks, "because if it is, I'm going to be pretty pissed."

Hunter grinned before burying his face against her neck, and inhaling her flowery scent. Having her in his arms again brought his body to life. His cock jumped to attention and he knew he couldn't go another second without having her. Raising his head, he looked deep into her eyes. "I need you. I can't wait."

Lila pressed her body closer, winding her arms around his neck and kissed his jaw line. "Neither can I but is it a good idea to—"

"No one would dare disturb us now." Not giving her a chance to say another word, he covered her mouth with his, relishing the way her soft welcoming lips seemed to fit so perfectly with his. Hunter had no idea how he'd managed to get through the past two weeks without her lying next to him.

He pushed his tongue past her lips to taste the heady flavor that was unique to only her. Lila returned his kiss with the enthusiasm of a woman starving. Good. That meant she wanted him just as badly as he wanted her. Too bad she was wearing so many clothes, but that could easily be remedied.

Breaking the tight seal of their lips, he fumbled with the buttons on her blouse until her top gapped open to expose her lace-covered breasts. Impatiently, Hunter pushed her bra up. Her nipples were already hard and they looked ready to be sucked. The sight of the hard blackberry-colored tips made his mouth water. "Gorgeous. I've missed doing this." Dipping his head, he took one hardened nub between his teeth and nibbled.

Holding his head to her chest, she wove her fingers into his hair. "Oh, Hunter, I missed you doing this to me."

He licked, laved and teased the taut point, making Lila moan deeply. Hunter loved how vocal she was. It told him how much she enjoyed his sensual ministrations although he wasn't sure of how much foreplay he could offer. He couldn't remember being this horny in a long time and he wanted nothing more than to fuck her bowlegged, to stave the frustration they'd both experienced the last couple weeks.

"More," she groaned.

Hunter raised his head with a smile. "You liked that?"

"Mmm, you know I do."

Chuckling lightly, he set his sights to her other nipple, giving it the same loving attention as he had the other. She tasted just as good as he remembered, but there was something he wanted more: some of that hot, tight, satisfying pussy of hers. Releasing the turgid tip with a wet pop, he moved to his knees as he dropped kisses against her belly. Hunter worked frantically to unfasten her jeans.

Lila offered him assistance, obviously as eager to get undressed as he was to undress her. Once he helped her out of her pants, her panties followed. Leaning forward, he placed a kiss against the patch of hair resting between her thighs. The scent of her arousal greeted his nostrils, making his cock harder than it already was.

Placing her hands on his shoulders to brace herself, she spread her legs in anticipation.

Hunter looked at her. "You're ready for it, aren't you?"

"You'd better believe it. I've spent too many sleepless nights fantasizing about this."

"Then I certainly hope the reality lives up to your dreams." He slipped his middle finger past her slick folds and into her tight cunt.

Lila inhaled sharply. "I have no doubt it will," she moaned, grinding her hips against his finger.

With his free hand he parted her labia before latching on to her clit. Eating Lila's pussy was such a turn on, he hoped he didn't shoot his load before he could get his cock inside of her. Hunter sucked on the engorged nubbin while sliding his finger in and out of her channel. She was so wet and ready for him, her juices rolled down the inside of her thighs.

"Hunter, I love it when you do that to me. It feels so good," she groaned.

He added another finger, shoving the digits deep into her hot hole. Lila cried out sharply, her hands gripping his shoulders tightly.

The grinding motion of her hips encouraged him to suck harder on her clit and finger her harder and faster. He loved the way she moved in rhythm with his touch and couldn't wait to be one with her again.

He continued to thrust his fingers into her until Lila began to shake. During their time together, he'd come to know her body well, and when she was about to orgasm. Slowly removing his cream-soaked fingers, Hunter began to lap at her pussy in anticipation of her climax.

When it came, Lila screamed his name. "Hunter!" Her nails dug into his shoulders and he was sure, had he not been wearing a shirt, she probably would have tore into his flesh. He licked her pussy and inner thighs, catching her juices on his tongue.

She leaned forward as if her legs were going to buckle, but Hunter was ready for her. Catching her in his arms, he eased Lila on her back.

With frantic motions, he unbuckled his belt and was out of his pants in five seconds flat. His cock strained against his boxers to the point of pain. Hunter made short order of those as well. He didn't bother to take off his shirt. The sooner he could be inside of Lila, the better.

With a smile on her face, offering wicked delight, she spread her legs, and held out her arms to him. "Hurry, Hunter."

Needing no further encouragement, he positioned himself between her thighs. Grasping his cock he guided the rock hard shaft to her pussy. He ran the tip along her slit before pushing himself into her.

Hunter gasped as he sunk balls-deep into her. "Jesus Christ," he hissed between clenched teeth. Her pussy gripped him in a vise, sucking him deeper still. She was so damned tight and it felt right as if the two of them were made for each other. Planting his hands on either side of her head so his arms could hold him braced, Hunter remained still for a moment simply to savor this moment.

What a fool he'd been to let her go. They belonged together. She was his.

He glanced down at Lila, to see her eyes closed. A smile curved her full lips and he could tell she was enjoying the sensation of being deliciously stuffed with his cock. Bending his head, he dropped a light kiss against those luscious lips of hers.

Lila opened her eyes with a smile. "I love you, Hunter, but I'd love you more if you finished what you started."

Hunter threw his head back and laughed. "What Lila wants, Lila gets."

"And don't you forget it."

He moved slowly at first to find his rhythm, and then began to pick up the pace. Lila lifted her hips to meet each thrust and clenched her muscles even tighter around his cock. Hunter knew with absolute certainly he wouldn't be able to hold out long, but he intended to revel in every moment of it.

Hunter positioned his upper body on his forearms, enabling him to kiss her more easily. Lila wrapped her lithe legs around his waist, her eyes locking with his. Cupping the back of his head, she guided it towards hers until their lips met. Their tongues dueled as they strained together in a dance as old as time.

His balls tightened signaling his climax was near. Gritting

his teeth, he tried to hold on, wanting Lila to come first. Fortunately he didn't have long to wait before her legs tightened around his waist and she cried out release. Finally he let go. With a loud grunt, he came, shooting his seed deep into her pussy.

Panting he rested his head against the curve of her shoulder. Never had he been so overwhelmed with emotion. He felt so many things for this amazing woman, love, pride, and contentment, not to mention happiness.

"I love you, Hunter Jamison," she whispered.

Hunter's heart leapt in his chest. There was no feeling in the world like loving someone and being loved back. For so long he'd scorned the emotion called love, but no longer would he doubt its existence because he found his soul mate in Lila. "I love you too. More than you can know."

Without warning she began to giggle. "Do you think they heard us outside? Your assistant's desk isn't that far from the door."

Hunter smiled. "I don't give a damn. It's no one's business what I do with my woman."

"Am I really your woman, Hunter?"

"Damn right." He kissed the tip of her nose. Hunter wanted to pinch himself to verify this wasn't a dream. "I can't believe this is happening, that you actually love me—especially when I look like this."

She ran his fingers along his scars. "All I see is a handsome prince."

The sincerity in her words could not be denied. "A prince needs a princess. I want you to be her."

Lila raised one delicately arched brow. "Are you asking me to marry you, Hunter?"

"No. I'm telling you. After making the mistake once, I'm not going to do it again. I can't take back the nasty things I said, but I can spend the rest of my life making up for them."

She threw her arms around his neck and he held her tight. Nothing ever felt so right.

The Beast had finally captured his beauty. And this time, it was forever.

About the Author

To learn more about Eve, please visit www.evevaughn.com. Send an email to Eve at eve@evevaughn.com or join her Yahoo! group to join in the fun with other readers as well as Eve! http://groups.yahoo.com/group/evevaughnsbooks

Look for these titles by
Eve Vaughn

Now Available:

The Life and Loves of April Johnson
A Night to Remember
The Reinvention of Chastity
Stranded
Broken

Head Over Heels:

A Cinderella Story

Lena Matthews

Dedication

To Leo, who made me a believer in happily ever afters.

Chapter One

If Cyn Elder had to look at another crusty heel today, she thought she might heave. Normally, helping customers find shoes wasn't such a chore, but today she felt as if she'd seen every bunion in the state of California. Was a pedicure such a novelty? And would it kill people to handle their corns before they tried on her shoes?

"Will there be anything else?" The tight smile she forced across her face must have spoken volumes to the woman, who quickly shook her head, and picked up her shoes to head to the counter.

Cyn watched her retreat with a small twinge of regret. Never would she be intentionally rude to a customer, but today had been a day from hell. The two workers her father *insisted* she hire didn't show up as scheduled, that alone was annoying, but knowing the twin sisters were kicking back in *her* apartment per her father's other order, was downright infuriating.

Trying not to dwell on the negative aspects of her life, and man were there many, Cyn grabbed the shoehorn and grimaced in pain. Standing, she stretched her aching back, feeling the tender muscles cry out in pain. Three more minutes to closing time and then she was off to do as she pleased. And it pleased her to take a long hot shower, slip in between her comfy cotton sheets and pass out.

Cyn mustered the last bit of goodwill she could find, and

made her way over to the counter to ring up the customer. After quickly seeing the lady out, Cyn sighed with relief. Her day was over. With a twist of her wrist, she flipped over the sign and then pulled down the blind, bringing her horrible day to an end. The Glass Slipper was officially closed. Seven o'clock had never looked so beautiful to her before.

Cleaning up though, especially tonight, felt like a reward after the day she'd had. If she had only been given a second or two to pop in the back and get the smell of feet out of her nose, the day might have gone a lot smoother. Or if she had any real help, real being the key word, things wouldn't have seemed as if they were piling up.

Stop it, she ordered herself. Stop dwelling on the bad. Her life wasn't horrible. In all honesty she didn't have much to complain about. The only thing she wished was for her father to wake up and realize his live-in lover was a live-in loser. Then again, if wishes were horses—

Bang! Bang! Bang!

Startled, Cyn jumped and glanced around. With her hand over her pounding heart, she made her way nervously to the front door. There was someone there, but with the blind pulled down she couldn't tell who it was.

"We're closed," she yelled out, refusing to open the door.

"Yoo hoo, girlfriend, you have to help me."

Well damn. The falsetto voice gave her customer's identity away. Sighing, Cyn pulled up the blind and tried not to blanch when her visitor's face popped into view.

MeShell was one of the ugliest women Cyn had ever seen, but that wasn't saying a lot because she was a he. A very unattractive he in fact, but that didn't stop Ms. Thang from going all out in drag. Looks aside, MeShell was a sweetheart, but nice or not, Cyn wasn't in the mood to deal with any more customers.

Shaking her head, Cyn gestured grandly to the clock on the wall behind her and shrugged her shoulders in fake sympathy.

Still MeShell persisted. "If you help me out this once, I'll be your best friend for life. It will only take five minutes, ten tops."

Cyn rolled her eyes and kept her hand firmly on the door. She'd heard this spiel from MeShell before, and the way she was going, they were going to be best friends for several lives to come.

"It's been a long day, MeShell."

"Each day is only twenty-four hours, darling, so please do me a favor and I'll do you one in return."

The only favor she could possible do Cyn would be to leave. "Thank you but no."

"Please, please. I know you've probably had a hard day, girl." Dramatic to the bone, MeShell gestured wildly as she spoke. "And you know I wouldn't dream of bothering you at closing time, but I hobbled here as fast as my little feet could carry me with a broken shoe. But I have plans, girl. Big plans that involve me looking as hot as a tamale and landing Mr. Right and by landing I mean I need him to land on me because this girl hasn't been landed on in a long while. You get my drift, sugar?"

Did she ever. Sighing, Cyn watched MeShell with guarded eyes. She was beat. Tired to the bone, but an extra fifteen minutes wouldn't make her any less tired. Besides if it helped the fellow sexually deprived, she was all in. Maybe she'd earn her wings to horny heaven for helping out and the God of all vibrators would send her an energizing toy.

Relenting, Cyn unlocked the door, much to the drag queen's delight.

"You are the living end, girl," she practically squealed, hobbling into the store on broken heels.

"Tell me about it," Cyn murmured, closing the door behind MeShell's back. Cyn locked the door firmly and pulled down the shade again. She didn't want to chance any more lost souls begging for entrance. "Just don't go telling anybody I let you in after hours."

"Girl, please. You know discreet is my middle name." MeShell fluffed her blonde wig and batted her sea green contact-lensed eyes Cyn's way. A six-foot-two drag queen who was almost so black she looked blue, with fuchsia pink lipstick and matching eye shadow was not Cyn's idea of discretion, but hey, whatever made her boat float.

Trying to find her hidden smile, Cyn thought of good things. Fuck raindrops on roses, she needed lime in tequila to cheer her up. "So which pair were you eyeing?"

"As if you have to ask." MeShell struck a pose, with her hands held highly in the air and shimmied her hips. The silver sequined after-five dress shimmered in the light. "The six-inch silver stilettos, baby."

"I'm not sure if I have them in a size thirteen, MeShell." The drag queen community had always been a big supporter of independent stores like Cyn's, so she made it a habit to carry larger sizes for such occasions. The lively nightlife of San Francisco had helped keep her family's shoe store in the game for three generations, despite the Bill Gates super malls of the world.

"I'm a size ten." She snapped her finger over her head. "Thank you."

"Girl, please." Cyn cocked her head to the side and tried her best to hold back her laughter. Even on her bad day she could tell a person's shoe size from a block away. "Those are gun boats and you know it."

"Stop it."

"You stop it. Have a seat while I go check the backroom, and keep your grubby little paws out my stocking sampler box."

"Please. As if I'd take your old raggedy pantyhose."

"Whatever, I meant what I said," Cyn tossed over her shoulder as she slipped into the stockroom. Thankfully, everything was organized and it only took her a minute or so to find the shoes. "Here you go. Let's try them on."

"Girl. Girl. Girl." Before Cyn could sit all the way down on the stool in front of MeShell, the woman had her shoes off and feet stretched out. "Put them on. Put them on."

"Step it down a notch." Exhausted or not, Cyn couldn't help but be infected by MeShell's enthusiasm as she helped her slip on the shoes. The size thirteens fit, as she knew they would. Damn she was good. "Well, what do you think?"

"I think they look divine." MeShell stood and began to sashay around the room. "I look fierce, don't I? Go ahead, don't be afraid to tell the truth."

Laughing, Cyn stood. "Too fierce, girl."

"Don't I know it."

"Let's ring you up and get you on your way. I don't want you to miss your party." The phone rang as she begun to total up the purchase. "One sec," Cyn said to MeShell, as she picked up the phone. "Hello."

"What are we doing tonight?"

Cyn smiled, feeling the first sense of real pleasure since the whole damn day had begun. But Miller Tate had the ability to cheer her up without even trying. It was a gift only a best friend possessed, and he was the best. "I don't know what we're doing tonight, but I know what I'm doing, and it involves a bed, cotton sheets, and a headscarf."

"As stimulating as that sounds, I'm afraid I'm going to have to break your heart, because you are going out tonight. Even if I have to pull your fine behind kicking and screaming all the way."

"I so don't think so." Was no one above listening? She just wanted to sleep.

"I don't hear you. As your best friend, it is my duty to save you from yourself and the two evil flying monkeys you have waiting for you back at your place."

Cyn smiled at Miller's apt description of the demonic duo. She was worn-out, but she knew, as Miller did, if she went home, she'd just end up regretting it.

"So where are we going?" *Please say movies. Please say movies. Please say movies.*

"To a party."

Damn it! At least at the movies, Cyn could have drifted off to sleep, but there seemed as if there was no chance of that happening now.

"Whose party?"

"DelRay's new club is opening tonight, and guess who is on the guest list?"

"DelRay's?"

"You're going to DelRay's too?" MeShell asked, butting into the conversation. "That's where I'm heading. Who are you talking to?"

"Miller."

MeShell grimaced at the same time Miller asked, "To whom are you talking?"

"MeShell."

Miller's snort of annoyance made Cyn bite back a smile. Miller and MeShell might both be batting for the same team, but that didn't mean they liked one another. "What does shim want?"

"MeShell is going to the same party."

"Maybe we're going to the movies after all."

Now he was talking. "Did anything come out this week worth seeing?"

"Movies? Oh no." MeShell reached across the counter and snatched the phone from Cyn's hands. "Listen, Miller. This is the party to end all parties and my girl is not going to miss it."

Cyn just shook her head and let them battle it out as she swiped the credit card. By the time the transaction was through, MeShell was handing her back the phone.

"Did the two of you get things settled?"

"Yes," Miller muttered. "I'll be by in an hour to pick you up. Don't worry about clothes. I'll pick out your outfit when I get there."

"I do know how to dress."

"Really, since when? Later." Miller hung up the phone before Cyn could get another word out, much to her amusement. With a shake of her head she clicked the phone off. Turning back to MeShell, she handed her the receipt and her bag. "I guess we'll see you later tonight."

"You know it, sweet meat. I'll be the one on stage shaking my tail feather."

"I can't wait." The hell she couldn't. This was so not how Cyn had pictured the night ending.

This was so not how Parker Maguire had pictured the night starting or being at all, for that matter. When his college buddy had called him with a business proposition, Parker'd thought, sure, a nightclub in the heart of San Fran sounded like a wonderful way to invest some money. The investment was a step away from the Hollywood scene. A way for him to branch out into something new and fun.

Good Lord, what had he been thinking? It was becoming increasingly clear he didn't have the slightest clue what partying consisted of these days. The exact moment he apparently morphed into his father wasn't exactly clear, but nevertheless, it happened.

The Hollywood night life had nothing on the Bay Area and that wasn't a compliment.

So instead of being on the crowded dance floor, groping and grinding, he was standing in the VIP balcony, feening for a cigarette, wishing he'd stayed home and merely wrote a check instead of demanding to be more than just a silent partner. Right then and there, Parker thought, silence might not have been so bad.

The crowded club and overpowering smell of desperation leaking from the pores of the half dressed girls and over dressed men reminded him why he had stopped going to meat markets such as this in the first place. That and the fact everyone he met these days wanted something from him.

His high-profile role as a wheeler-dealer in the land of make-believe ensured him a place of honor in the sexual hall of fame. In his early years in the business, Parker had caressed more pussy than a veterinarian. Surprisingly, he'd grown tired of it. The countless encounters that is, not the sex. He was bored not dead.

He was looking for more. What that entailed, he wasn't sure, but a glance at the crowded floor assured him that *more* wouldn't be found here. The only thing he'd found so far was the beginning of a headache.

Despite the balcony being enclosed, the loud music still somehow managed to seep into the room. It wasn't as deafening as on the dance floor, but the steady thump was still mind-numbing. When had he reached the point where loud music was disturbing him, not that he would describe the pounding mix playing as music? It was more like a never-ending version of the same song being played at different speeds which just further beat home the point he was just too damn old for clubbing.

He needed a drink. Then a good kick in the ass. Maybe not even in that order. With a disgusted snort, he headed out the room and almost collided with the bouncer standing on the steps leading to the dance floor. Surprisingly, the bulky man wasn't alone. He was in the midst of a face-off with a very attractive, yet tired-looking African American lady.

In spite of her club-like attire, which consisted of a black, midriff exposing halter-top and matching black short skirt, she seemed a bit different than the other women skulking around the club. For one, the man-hungry-hunter look was nowhere to be found in her hazel eyes, just a hint of boredom and annoyance. Also, even though her clothes were sexy, they weren't blatant, I-can-see-your-pubic-hair-runway-from-a-mile-away sexy. Parker couldn't speak for any other man, but he was a bit old fashioned. In his book, the one with the balls led the chase. Plain and simple.

The hallway was as insulated as the room, so it didn't take much to clearly hear the argument at hand.

"I'm not going to tell you again." Muscle guy had his arms crossed over his massive chest, in what Parker assumed was to be an intimidating pose. But from the annoyed look on the woman's face, pressure was the last thing she was feeling.

"You didn't have to tell me the first time. All you needed to do was ask. You know, just because you have a dick, doesn't mean you have to act like one."

"That's it. You're out of here."

"Eat me," she spat.

"Bitch."

"Hey," Parker shouted, angry now. He didn't know what exactly had gone down and he didn't care. There was a right way and a wrong way to talk to a lady. "Back down."

Muscle guy turned around with a scowl, but when he recognized who was speaking to him, his attitude immediately disappeared. "Sorry, sir, this lady was blocking the stairs."

"No, this *lady* was sitting on the stairs, for a moment."

"It's a fire hazard, sir."

"Yes, because if by some off the wall chance Club A Go Go caught on fire, my big ass sitting on the second to last step was going to be the reason everyone burned up and died. Yeah, right."

Apparently the bouncer didn't know when to leave well enough alone. "It's against the law, sir."

What an ass. Parker truly didn't invest half a million dollars in tittypolozza to referee grudge matches. Though, before he could speak, the fireball mouthed off again. "No, what should be against the law is the overpriced, watered-down drinks. Whoever owns this place needs their ass kicked."

"Really?" Amused now, Parker focused all his attention on

the woman. "Well, as one of the aforementioned owners, should I be worried?"

"Maybe." Her bottom lip quivered as if she was biting back a laugh. "Sorry, I didn't know I was in the company of club royalty."

Her obvious amusement made it difficult for Parker to believe her. Bored no longer, Parker leaned against the wall and smiled. "Forgiven. Now if you would—"

The spitfire raised her hands, halting his words. She in essence shushed him. A first for Parker. He was an order giving type of man, not someone to be dismissed. Yet instead of being irritated, he was intrigued. Who in the world was she?

"No need to call for reinforcements. As I was telling Schwarzenegger here, I was just resting for a moment. I'll leave."

The hell she would. "I wasn't going to say that. There's no need to hurry. In fact, if you feel the need to...rest a bit more we can go back upstairs."

"We?" She tilted her head to the side and raised an eyebrow. "And why would I go anywhere with a complete stranger? I don't know you. You could be crazy."

The bouncer snorted and shook his head, much the way Parker wanted to. A complete stranger, wow. Parker didn't want to toot his own horn, but he'd been on more magazine covers than some of the movie stars he produced films for. He was called the "Prince of Hollywood" or sometimes the "Movie Midas", because every film he produced turned to gold. Yet, from the disinterested way she was watching him, Parker was willing to bet that even if she knew all of that, she'd still be hesitant about going into the room with him.

How refreshing.

"True, but there's a couch and all the free overpriced, watered-down drinks you can drink. Plus it's going to annoy the hell out of him." This time the smile broke free, turning her pretty face beautiful. Damn. "I can promise you I'm not crazy, but then again, a crazy person would say the same."

"So true."

"Then what do you have to lose."

"Only my life."

"There is that. But I promise not to kill you." When she still didn't look convinced, Parker took his hand from his pocket and raised it in the air, with his index and middle finger pointed up. "Scout's Honor."

"When you put it that way, it's almost impossible to resist." She smiled.

"Almost?" Parker wondered what he'd have to do make the offer irresistible.

"Yes. Almost."

"Hmm..." Leaving was no longer an option for him. Parker was there to stay. "Almost means there's something I can do to convince you."

"There're two things."

Parker loved a good negotiation. "I'm listening."

"The door stays open at all times."

"Deal."

"I text my friend to let him know where I am and he's allowed to come up at anytime."

He... Parker didn't like the idea of a he, but she did say friend. "Deal."

"Just like that?"

"Just like that."

Her eyes widened as if she was surprised, then flashed with amusement. "This club may not suck so much after all."

"Great." Parker stepped away from the wall and pushed the door all the way open for her. "Maybe we'll put that on the napkins and billboards."

Laughing, she walked past him and into the room. The night was looking up already.

Chapter Two

Cyn couldn't believe she was accompanying a strange man into the private VIP room at the hottest new club in town. Although some people would have been blasé about the whole thing, for her it was borderline taboo. As silly as it sounded, Cyn wasn't as flamboyant as most of her friends. Okay, to be fair, it was hard to top her out-there friends, but then she never really tried.

Unlike everyone else, Cyn had been fed the responsibility line her whole life. She was raised to believe it was her duty to take care of her family first, then herself. So while her friends were off clubbing, she could usually be found working late or taking care of some family issues.

But tonight, oh tonight, was going to be a different story. Cyn had never considered herself much of a risk taker, but tonight she was going to do something daring. She was stepping out of the dutiful daughter role and into femme fatale. Well, maybe not femme fatale, but something akin to it.

The idea of a vixen version of herself made Cyn chuckle. The boldest thing she normally did was use one toilet seat cover instead of two. Oh yeah, Mr. VIP Man's virtue was safe. Unfortunately, because the man was hella fine.

On average, Cyn wasn't one to be attracted to men outside her race. It wasn't a prejudice, just a preference. But now she was going to have to seriously rethink white boys. When she'd been arguing with Schwarzenegger, Cyn hadn't really paid much mind to the interloper, but as soon as he interrupted, all her attention moved to him. And rightly so.

Dressed all in black, he loomed over her and the bouncer by several inches. Cyn wasn't a slouch at five eight so that meant her host was at the least six three. His light shoulder-length hair was a strong contrast to his tanned skin.

She wasn't willing to give up on a good looking guy just because he was pigmently challenged. Yes, rethinking her bias against white boys was first on her list of things to do tonight. Closely followed by flirting with said white boy.

As they entered the VIP room, Cyn looked around the posh surroundings, duly impressed. Although the thumping beat of the music reverberated from below, she could envision conversation actually taking place in this room. The leather couches looked plush and she couldn't wait to rest her tired feet. A woman who sold shoes for a living couldn't be seen rubbing her aching dogs. It just wouldn't do.

"Why don't you have a seat and I'll get us some drinks."

"Sounds heavenly. I'll have a diet soda. In an unopened can, please." Cyn collapsed onto the couch, stroking her hands over the soft as butter leather. Ever so discretely she slipped off her shoes and wiggled her toes. Nirvana.

"Unopened can?"

"Yes, I still don't know you," she reminded him smugly. Cyn might want to spread her wings, but she didn't want to spread her legs...unwillingly that was. There were a lot of crazy men out there and she refused to fall victim to one if she could help it. "No offense meant, but anyone worth their salt knows better."

"No offense taken. In fact..." his voice became muffled for a bit as he bent over to open the mini fridge, "...very wise."

When he walked back to her, he had two sodas in hand. He handed her one can, but then kept his hand extended towards her. "I'm Parker Maguire."

She took his hand in hers. "Cyn. Nice to meet you."

He eyes seemed to laugh as they shook hands. "Just Cyn?"

"Yes." Damn, she wasn't making a very good wild woman. "You know like the artist formally known as Prince."

This time the smile spread from his eyes to his lips. "Do you have a symbol too?"

"No, Cyn will do."

"So, Cyn." Parker opened his can and sat on the far side of the couch. The fact he didn't immediately plop next to her and get all in her space impressed her. "Tell me what you really think of our club?"

Before she could answer, he interjected. "I mean aside from the watered-down, overpriced drinks and the exuberant bouncer, that is."

"To be honest—"

"Were you going to lie?"

A smart ass. She was in love. "I was thinking about it."

"Then I'm glad you changed your mind."

"No problem." She smiled. "I'm probably the last person to ask such a question."

"Why is that?"

"Because I'm not much of a club goer. I know my presence here is a bit misleading on the matter."

"Actually it isn't." Parker set his drink on the floor next to him. "You seem a bit..."

"Out of place?" That was how she felt anyway. This environment just wasn't her thing.

"No," he said. "It's hard to explain."

"Try."

"It's like being in a room full of wildflowers then spotting a rare orchid, blooming at the edge." As if he was embarrassed by his wording, he added, "Then imagine the orchid making a three hundred pound bear fear for his life with a snap of her fingers."

"He wasn't scared." Parker delivered the line like a seasoned pussy pro, yet despite knowing that, Cyn found

170

herself preening anyway.

"He was minutes away from surrendering. You had him scared."

"Who's the liar now?"

"Would I lie to you?" The teasing tone to his voice was gone, replaced by a heavier, deeper pitch. The underlying sensuality of his words captivated her. Much like the man himself.

"I don't know."

"Would you like to find out?"

The cerulean blue of his eyes were like a cold wave, but Cyn felt anything but chilled. In fact, she was feeling a bit warm. It was becoming extremely evident she needed to get laid. Now the only question was, if Parker was the rain to her drought. "I haven't made up my mind yet."

"Let me know when you do."

"Do you always move this fast?"

"This seems fast to you?"

"Speed of light fast."

"Damn I'm good."

"I'll have to take your word for that."

"No, you don't."

"Really?" Cyn took a sip of her soda. She was feeling mighty parched. "You have references?"

"No. You can just judge for yourself."

"Hello. Speed of light." Cyn flexed her toes against the carpet, stretching the ligaments in her feet. She was going to pay dearly tomorrow for twenty minutes of vanity tonight. "You're bad."

He chuckled. "I was just answering your question."

"What am I going to do with you?" His smile grew wider. "That was rhetorical."

"I didn't say a word. I was being good." Parker glanced down at her feet. Then glanced back up at her with a frown.

"What?" Cyn glanced down too.

"Are your feet hurting?"

"A little. What a woman won't do to look good." Or to please their picky gay friends.

"Put your feet up here and I'll massage them for you."

"Uh, no."

"Why? And if you say it's because you don't know me, we're going to have words. I'm offering to rub them." He wiggled his fingers. "With my hands, not my tongue. It's not my kink."

"That's good to know, but still…"

"For Pete's sake, woman." Parker moved to the floor and picked up her right foot, much to her surprise. Before she could snatch her foot away, he placed the ball of his thumb against her arch and began to move it in a circular motion.

The sweet sensation took her breath and every ounce of protest she might have voiced melted away. "Oh God," she moaned, dropping her head back. It had been so long since anyone rubbed her feet.

"That's right," he teased, adding more pressure. "Who's the man?"

"You are."

"Who has the best hands in the world?"

"You do."

"And who are you going to reward with a kiss?"

Without hesitation, she answered, "You."

"Damn straight."

If the boys could see him now. The thought had Parker grinning devilishly. No one would be surprised to see him alone in a room with a sexy lady like Cyn. The shock would come from seeing him on his knees in front of her. The role was normally reversed, but something about the way she moaned under his touch told him she wasn't someone who was pampered often.

For the life of him, he couldn't tell why. From the little bit of time they'd spent together, he was ready to shower her with rose petals. If his hunch was right and she was single, Parker was going to make it his mission to get to know her better. Much better.

"Mmmm." Cyn opened her eyes and smiled down at him. She looked all kinds of relaxed. Her sable, shoulder length hair was tousled a bit from when she laid it back against the couch, giving her a sexy, tousled look. It was almost as if she had just climbed from her lover's bed. From his bed. "Can I keep you?"

Even though the remark was a teasing one, he couldn't help but be encouraged by the implication. "I should warn you, I'm not house broken."

"I know how to roll up a newspaper."

"S & M. *Nice.*"

Laughing, Cyn pulled her foot away and sat up. "You are too much."

Parker frowned. He felt the loss of her touch instantly. He'd never been affected by a woman so quickly before. This was more than attraction. It was downright obsession. Parker made his way over to the bar, uncomfortable with the direction his thoughts were taking him. He needed a drink.

A real one.

"Would you like another drink, Cyn?"

"I still have my soda."

"I meant a real drink." Turning, he flashed his most disarming smile. The one that charmed hardened nuns and suspicious mothers alike. It was a mask of the highest quality and unlucky for him, she saw right through it.

"No, thank you."

"Still don't trust me?"

"I still don't know you."

Parker turned away and made himself a bourbon and coke, all the while thinking how her words didn't sit right with him. With his drink in hand, he made his way back to the couch and

173

sat down. This time a bit closer to her.

"What would you like to know? Ask away. My life is an open book." Thanks to the paparazzi. "If you ask, I'll answer."

"Really?" The idea seemed to intrigue her. Cyn eased up on the couch and tucked her legs underneath her. The black skirt rose high on her thigh, teasing him with a sexy flash of brown flesh. His palms tingled to touch her, but he knew if she didn't trust him to pour her a drink, she wouldn't trust him to partake of the sweet chocolate flesh before him.

"Yes. What do you want to know?" He braced himself for an onslaught of questions about his job and income. When he'd given her his name earlier, she didn't respond. So either she was the best actress on the face of the earth or she didn't have a clue.

"You asked me earlier what I thought of your club, Why don't you tell me what you think of it?"

The question took him back a bit. Parker hadn't been expecting that. "Umm..."

"Is that a no-no?"

"Not at all. It was just surprising."

"Why?"

"I don't know. I was expecting something along the lines of materialistic stuff."

"Please." She rolled her very expressive hazel eyes. "I so don't care about those sorts of things. I mean it's obvious you must have some money, you do own a club."

"Part of a club and to be honest, not a very big part."

"Either way, it's your business, not mine. Besides, knowing what kind of car you drive won't tell me anything about you, except where you shop. It's not what you do that's important. It's who you are when no one is around that matters most."

She amazed him. Her insight was as refreshing as her honesty. "Who are you?"

She lightly laughed. "I'm Cyn, the lady asking the

questions."

Either his life had become overly jaded or he needed to get out more. He'd forgotten women like Cyn ever existed. Mentally shaking his head, he thought about her question. "I'm sure it's a good investment, but I'm not sure if this is what I want to do for the rest of my life."

"What do you want to do for the rest of your life?"

"I have no idea. I have a great job now but it's getting old. Or I am."

"You, old? I doubt that. How old are you, gramps?"

"Thirty-five. You?"

"Twenty-five."

"Aww...you're a baby."

"Whatever, old man." She tsked. "You seem to have accomplished a lot at such an early age. Your parents must be proud."

That was laughable. "Proud isn't exactly the word I'd use."

"Why not?"

"I could make money hand over fist, but until I deliver upon my parents' steps a dutiful wife and strapping young heir, they'll never be pleased. My father wants a namesake and my mother wants a grandchild to brag about over tea at the Country Club."

"Do they beat you?"

Her comment startled him. "No."

"Are they evil drunks who touched your little boy places when no one was looking?"

"No." She really was too much.

"Then it could be worse," she said with a smile and a shrug of her shoulders.

"Well, when you put it that way..." he laughed. "What about your parents?"

Her smiled dimmed. "My mother is dead and my father is gullible."

"Gullible?"

"Big time. He used to be normal back in the day, but now this hag he's in lust with has him on a leash. And not the hot sexy kind either."

Hot sexy leashes. A woman after his own heart. "Yes, but did he beat you or touch your little girl places?"

"Nope." She smiled. "So it's not that bad."

"Not at all." Parker took a drink from his glass. To his utter amazement, Cyn held her hand out for his glass. He handed it to her and watched as she took a dainty sip, then gave it back. Her actions spurred him on. It was definitely a step in the right direction. "Next question."

Cyn continued to barrage him with off the wall questions all the while taking sips from his drink. Parker stood to refresh the glass at least twice and each time she waited until he took a drink before partaking herself. He decided he liked the interesting little ritual they'd created.

He also liked the way she lined up the glass to match almost exactly where his lips had been with her own before drinking. It was as intimate as a kiss, sexy even, but not as fun.

For every question she asked, he would ask one of his own. They talked and laughed and spent the evening getting to know each other on a level Parker had never been to with another woman.

She'd discovered more about him in their time together than a decade worth of interviews by experienced reporters had over the course of his career. The woman could charm the birds from the trees. It was a good thing she didn't know what kind of gold mine the information was.

In the midst of a funny story about silly fears, Cyn's cell phone rang. It was the first interruption they'd experienced since entering the room. And it was a very unwelcome one. Frowning, she pulled the phone from her little black purse and gasped.

"What's wrong?" He asked worriedly.

"Do you know what time it is?" Flipping the lid open, she immediately apologized. "I'm so sorry. I know. I know."

He glanced at the watch on his arm. It was almost midnight. They'd been talking for almost two hours. Where had the time gone?

"Okay. I'm on my way." She slammed down the lid on her phone and stood.

On her way. What the hell was going on? "Everything okay?"

"No, Miller is upset and ready to go."

"Who is Miller?" Parker made it a habit to know the name of the men he planned to destroy. "Why do you care if he's upset?"

"Miller is my friend. The one I was supposed to text two hours ago. He's ready to go."

"So let him go."

"He's my ride." Cyn bent over to slip her shoes on and stumbled. Parker caught her and pulled her flush against him as he helped her stand.

"I can give you a ride." In more than one way. "You don't have to go now."

"I do. He's upset. Apparently he ran into his ex and things went south."

She pulled back and he let her. It would do him no good to try to force her to stay.

"Cyn, wait." She paused at the door and glanced over her shoulder. "I want to see you again."

His words brought a smile to her pretty brown face. "You do?"

"Yes." Thinking quickly, Parker grabbed his wallet and pulled out one of his business cards. He walked across the room and handed it to her, but didn't let go. Instead, he moved in closer and used his free hand to draw her against him once more.

Cyn leaned into him and tilted her head back, awaiting the kiss they both knew was a long time in the making. And just as he went to lower his mouth onto hers, her cell phone rang again.

Cursing, he released his hold on her and the card both. "Call me. This evening has been..."

"Yes it has." Her look of disappointment as she headed out the door was the only salve to his pride. At least she regretted the interruption as much as he did.

Parker was half way back across the room before he realized he didn't have a way to contact her. He didn't even know what her full name was. Spinning around, he rushed over to the door and looked down the stairs, but Cyn was long gone.

"Damn it," he muttered infuriated. She'd call he told himself, or he'd turn this city upside down looking for her.

Chapter Three

As far as Cyn was concerned, she'd just earned her wings to good friend heaven. Instead of spending her evening with Parker, who at this very moment could have been talking her into his bed, she was sitting on Miller's floral couch, eating ice cream out the container with MeShell as Miller ranted on and on about his ex Yancy.

Cyn had never liked Yancy, even when he and Miller were dating. As far as she was concerned Yancy had been lucky to have Miller. Not only was her friend a great guy he also happened to be very attractive. Although average height and build, he had big dark eyes, closely cropped black hair and skin the color of rich dark chocolate. Looks and personality. The perfect package to anyone with a brain, which of course left Yancy out, who proved his lack of intelligence by cheating on Miller. She'd been more than happy when Miller dumped his ass. But now that Yancy was the reason she wasn't getting any tonight, she really hated him. The things a girl gave up in the name of friendship.

"I don't know why I let him do this to me," Miller fumed in mid-pace. From the way he was wearing a path in his living room, he was going to have to re-carpet his apartment soon.

"Because you're a drama queen with a massive self-destructive streak and lousy taste," MeShell offered, snaring the cookies and cream container from Cyn.

Friendship dictated that even though Cyn secretly agreed

with a couple of MeShell's comments, she didn't concur out loud. "I think it was a rhetorical comment."

"My momma always said, tell the truth, shame the devil, girl." MeShell passed the ice cream back.

"No one asked you or your momma," Miller snapped. "What are you doing here anyway?"

"Enjoying your meltdown. It's practically Oscar worthy." MeShell brought her spoon in front of her like a microphone. "The award for best dramatic actress in a very gay role goes to..."

Miller shot MeShell an aggravated look and the finger, much to Cyn's amusement.

Cyn had her own theory on why MeShell had joined them, and it had nothing to do with cattiness. When she had come downstairs, Miller had been barely holding it together, while MeShell appeared as if she was seconds away from taking off her wig and throwing down. Cyn was beginning to think there was more behind their Sonny and Cher routine than met the eye.

"Great, my pain is your pleasure," Miller lamented.

"Honey, all pain is my pleasure." MeShell smirked. "That's just the way I get down."

That was far more than Cyn wanted to know. Ever. Also, thinking of getting down was getting her down. She could have been getting laid with a capital L.

Parker was too yummy. Why oh why did she let her stupid little morals get in the way? Though, to be honest, she had really enjoyed simply talking with him. They'd talked about stupid things, such as their favorite color and foods, and even a few deep things such as their views on religion and politics.

It was the best non-date she'd ever been on. Hell, those two hours were better than some real dates she'd been on. How sad.

Miller interrupted her selfish thoughts with one of his own. "God, I hate him."

"No, you don't," Cyn felt compelled to say. "If you did, we wouldn't be having this *Waiting to Exhale* moment."

"I'm exhaling. I'm exhaling all over the damn place. I'm over him."

"Take a deep breath in and get over yourself. We have more important things to discuss." MeShell scratched her head, her blonde wig moving with each motion. "Like me, or better yet, like Ms. Cyn over there."

"Me?" Cyn looked up from the ice cream with spoon in hand. She'd known this moment was coming. "What did I do?"

"You disappeared."

Before Cyn could scoop out a spoonful of yummy gooey calories, Miller snatched the ice cream and spoon away. "Yeah, where did you go?"

"To the VIP room." The look of utter surprise on their faces made her laugh. "You two aren't the only people I know."

"Who do you know?" MeShell's artistically drawn-on eyebrows arched as if in surprise.

"Lots of people."

"Like?" Miller asked, joining the nosey bandwagon. He sat on the coffee table, his drama apparently forgotten.

"Like one of the owners." Cyn reached for the ice cream but Miller moved it out of the way.

"We all know DelRay," MeShell said, noting the obvious. "And if you tell me he gave you a pass to the VIP room, when I had to blow the bastard to get in the club, I'm going to be highly irritated."

Miller and Cyn both turned to MeShell, who was looking fit to be tied. "You blew him?" Miller asked, his disgust more than evident in his tone.

"Could you please move your high horse, his shit is stinking up the room?" With an annoyed sigh, MeShell removed her wig and dropped it on the table next to Miller who was digging into the ice cream with gusto. "Do you think a fairy godmother was behind our invitations? Did I miss the pumpkin coach outside the club?"

"Our?" Cyn questioned, confused.

"Yes, our." MeShell ran her hand over her dark bald scalp then stood up and stretched. "I didn't want to hear Miller here crying because he didn't get to go."

"That was nice of you," Miller said warily. "What do you want?"

"Oh please. I don't want anything from you." MeShell looked over at Cyn and grinned. "But you, I do want something from."

"What?"

"Information." MeShell sat back down next to her on the couch and leaned back against the cushions. "Why did DelRay let you get into the VIP room?"

"He didn't."

"Then who did?" MeShell was as tenacious as a dog with a bone.

"Parker." Just saying his name made Cyn smile. She was such a goner.

"Parker who?"

"Could you be more in my business?" Moving quickly, Cyn grabbed the container from Miller. Her joy in her conquest was short lived when she saw it was empty. *Damn it.*

"Yes, I could. Now talk. Don't make me get ugly." Miller opened his mouth to say something, but was stopped by MeShell, who held her hand up to silence him. "No comments from the peanut gallery."

"What do you want to know?"

"Everything you know," MeShell answered just as quickly.

Miller moved MeShell's hand from in front of his face. "We don't need to know everything, but something. Let's start with what he looks like."

"He looks like your average white guy, except there wasn't

anything average about him."

"You with a white guy?" Miller's eyes were open almost as wide as MeShell's mouth.

"What? I can like a white guy."

"You can," he agreed, nodding his head as if he was speaking to someone a bit dimwitted. "But you never have before."

"So what's wrong with trying something new," MeShell interjected, as if her own disbelief hadn't been evident just moments ago. "If Cyn wants to try the other *other* white meat, I say go for it."

"You would."

"I am in the room." She was going to send them to separate corners soon. "And it's not a big deal. All we did was talk."

"For two hours—"

"In the VIP room—" MeShell cut in.

"Alone," Miller finished, his voice as disbelieving as MeShell's.

"Yes." Was it so hard to believe?

"Damn." Miller looked anything but pleased. "What a waste of a good hair day."

"It wasn't wasted. I looked hot, thank you very much. Hot enough to hang out in the VIP room while you were fighting on the dance floor as if you were in some cheesy eighties break dancing movie."

"She has you there," MeShell said.

"Moving on, what did you guys talk about?"

MeShell snorted, as she sat up. "More important, are you going to see him again?"

To appease them both, Cyn decided to answer each question. The first answer was easy. It was the second she was unsure about. "We talked about everything." She closed her eyes for a few seconds and smiled at the memory, before opening them once more. "He's so funny. Not just the things he says, but the way he says them. He has this little crinkle thing that happens in the corner of his eyes when he's thinking."

"Nothing a little botox can't cure." MeShell waved her hand as if dismissing Cyn's comment. "So you like him."

That was a no brainer. "Yes. I think I do."

"Then you're going to see him again?" MeShell asked.

"Maybe."

Cyn's answer obviously wasn't good enough for MeShell. "Did you give him your number?"

"And have him call when the gruesome twosome are around? I don't think so."

"Email?" MeShell persisted.

"No. There wasn't time. Someone had me on redial."

"No time? You were up there for two hours," Miller said. "All that talking and you couldn't rattle off an address."

"Apparently not." When he put it that way, it seemed a bit silly. But there was a saving grace. "He did give me his business card."

"He did." MeShell smiled. "Hand it over. You know you can tell a lot about a man by his business card."

"Really?" Cyn picked her purse off the floor and opened it. After shuffling through her bag for a few seconds, she pulled out his card and handed it over to MeShell. "So, what does this say about him?"

MeShell took the card, glanced down and screamed.

"What?" Cyn jumped up, startled to hell and back. What in the world was up with her?

"Oh my God! Oh my God!" MeShell stood as well, waving the card about. "Do you know...of course you don't. Oh my God!"

"What the hell is going on?" Miller demanded. Snatching the card from her hand, he read the name, and then he too screamed, "Oh my God!"

"What the hell." Cyn was confused as all get out. Then a

thought raced through her mind. "Do you guys know him or something? Is he married? Or gay?"

"He's not gay, girl." Miller raced over to his bookstand and grabbed the periodical lying on top. He made his way quickly over to Cyn and thrust the cover of the magazine in her face. Annoyed, Cyn pulled the weekly gossip rag from Miller's hand and held it a bit away from her so she could see whatever it was he was trying to show her. To her utter surprise, Parker was staring back at her from the cover.

"Oh my God!" she echoed, slumping back down on the couch. Parker wasn't gay. He was famous.

"Is it him?" MeShell demanded. "Is this the same guy you were with?"

In the photo, Parker's hair was shorter and his eyes didn't have the same glow to them as they did earlier this evening, but there was no denying who he was. "One and the same."

"Parker Maguire and my best friend. Oh my." Miller seemed as dazed as she felt.

"It's him, but I still don't know who he is. Should I?" This only proved it. She needed to get out more.

"Yes," MeShell and Miller parroted.

"Is he an actor or something?"

"No, honey, he's the Prince." MeShell retorted, as if she should've known what that meant.

"He's a prince?" Now she was even more confused.

"No, girl. That's what they call him. The Prince. He's Hollywood royalty. His dad is a director, his mother was on one of those nighttime soaps, and he's a movie producer." MeShell placed her hand over her chest and took a deep breath. She was more frazzled than Cyn. "Did you really have no idea?"

"Not a clue." Cyn felt like the world's biggest idiot. "I mean, I knew he wasn't eating Top Ramen for dinner every night, but I had no idea he was Richie Rich."

"He could kick Richie Rich's ass, girl."

Unlike MeShell, Miller focused on what mattered the most. "Are you going to call him?"

Now that was the million dollar question. "I have no idea."

Parker was not a happy camper. Standing at his office window, he scowled at the Hollywood sign in the far distance, and pondered, not for the first time, why Cyn had yet to contact him. The question plagued him like no other.

They'd had a good time. Or so he thought. Parker could only speak for himself, but the short time he'd spent with her Saturday left him hungry for more. And not just in a sexual way. Sure there was that, but Parker wanted to get to know Cyn better. He wanted to see her smile again, to hear her laugh. Hell, right now he'd be happy just to find out her last name. Parker didn't think he was asking for much.

The way she'd rushed off Saturday left a lot of questions unanswered in his mind. He could kick himself for letting Cyn leave without getting her phone number. The worst part was the not knowing. And man was there a lot he didn't know. From her last name to her phone number to the down low on the man she left him to be with. Who was this Miller and how important was he to Cyn?

Damn it all to hell! Parker ran his hand through his hair in frustration. If he had to take San Francisco apart with his bare hands, he would find Cyn. No matter how long it took.

"I take it from your frown your new venture in Frisco isn't going as well as you hoped."

Parker glanced toward the open doorway of his office at his friend and partner, Solomon Carnell, and frowned at the intruding brunet. He was already in a bad mood and the last thing he needed was to be poked at by his well-meaning friend. Solomon had been against the club investment from the beginning, now he was just waiting for the opportune moment to supply the requisite "I told you so".

"When did you get back?" Parker asked, ignoring his friend's question for the moment.

"This morning." Solomon strolled into the room, and headed straight for the mini fridge in the corner. After extracting a beer, he sat in the black leather chair across from Parker's own and kicked his feet up on the polished marble desk. Even though Solomon had an office of his own just a few doors down, he spent most of his time in Parker's. It was easier for him to annoy Parker that way. "But you digress. This meeting isn't about me in all my splendor, but about you, and the shitty little look on your face. Did DelRay screw you over?"

Knowing Solomon as he did, Parker was well aware the persistent man wouldn't leave until he dragged every last detail from him. Solomon was annoying like that.

"No." Solomon's grin dimmed a bit. *It served him right.* "The opening went off without a hitch. The club was packed all weekend long. I'm sure I'll see a nice return for my investment."

"Wonderful."

"Yeah." Parker smirked. "I can see you're overjoyed for me."

"I think the guy is a loser."

"Yes, I know, but you don't have to worry. I still like you best," Parker mocked.

Solomon snorted. "As if I care. I'm just looking out for my boy and his bank account."

"I know, and trust me, I appreciate it." And he did. Theirs was an equal partnership. Where Parker brought in the Hollywood connections and the movie know-how, Solomon was the brains behind their ventures. He made sure the I's were dotted, the T's were crossed and everyone was paid on time. "But everything went smoothly."

"Then what's with the frown?"

"I have some stuff on my mind."

"Like?"

"Like stuff," Parker repeated. They were men, for Christ's

sake, they didn't talk about their feelings. "Let it go."

Saying that to Solomon was akin to waving a scab in front of the fingers of a seven year old. It just encouraged the man to pick. "Then this has to be about a woman."

"Why do you say that?"

"If it was about anything else you would have already spilled the beans. For some annoying reason you have an outdated moral code when it comes to chicks."

"Horrible isn't it?" Parker dryly said.

"Yes, it is." Solomon agreed, missing the sarcasm all together. "Come on, I tell you about the girls I screw."

"Much to my delight."

"Exactly. Besides this—" Parker's ringing cell phone halted Solomon's inquisition. Parker answered it without glancing at the number, happy for the interruption. "Speak."

There was a brief pause followed by a rapid, "Arf, Arf."

"Hello?"

"Ahh, much better." Cyn's amused voice filled the line. "I was afraid you were going to have me roll over and play dead next."

Parker went from annoyed to extremely pleased in the space of a heartbeat. "Can you hold on for a sec?"

"If this is a bad time, I can call you back."

"This isn't a bad time at all." As if he was going to give her a chance to run again. Parker placed his hand over the mouthpiece and lowered the phone. Addressing Solomon, Parker gestured with his head to the door. "Get out."

Solomon grinned evilly and scooted further down in the chair, as if making himself more comfortable. "Don't mind me, I'll wait."

"You have one choice. You either walk out or I'll throw you out. Head first." Even though Solomon was a few inches taller and more muscular, Parker would have followed through on his threat.

Instead of infuriating Solomon, Parker's words seemed to have amused him. "It's like that, is it?"

"Yes."

"Then I'll go, but only because you asked so nicely." Solomon stood and set his beer on the desk. "But I'll be back for the goods."

"Yeah. Yeah. Yeah." Parker didn't care why he went, as long as he did. "Shut the door behind you."

"Don't do anything I wouldn't do," Solomon teased, closing the door as Parker requested.

Annoying prick. Parker sat down and took his hand away from the phone. "Playing hard to get, were you?"

"Me?"

"Yes, you. Why did you wait so long to call?"

"To be honest, I wasn't sure if I should call or not."

"Why?"

"I wasn't sure exactly how I was supposed to go about addressing royalty."

"Ahhh." Parker smiled. So much for anonymity. "I see you found out."

Cyn didn't say anything for a few seconds, but when she did, her voice was far less friendly. "You should have told me who you were."

Parker's smile slid away. He hadn't expected Cyn to be excited he was a semi-celebrity, but he didn't expect her to be upset either. "I did."

"I think I would have remembered if you did."

"I told you my name, Cyn."

"Come on," she said impatiently. "You knew I had no idea who you were."

"I did," he admitted, unashamed. "And let me tell you how refreshing it was. How refreshing it is. Besides, Cyn, you said it yourself. It isn't what I do that matters. It's who I am. Or at least I thought it didn't matter to you."

"It shouldn't."

"But it does."

"A little," she said softly.

That was not what he wanted to hear. "Why?"

"For many reasons."

"Give me one." Parker wasn't going to walk away without a damn good fight.

"We don't have anything in common."

"We did the other night," he reminded her.

"That was before I knew who you were."

Sighing, Parker stood and walked over to the window. This is why he didn't press the issue of his identity the other night. He knew, to the core of him, if he told her who he was and what he did, she would have bailed. "I'm the same person."

"No, you're the Prince."

"It's a stupid trumped up name." One he'd never hated as much as he did right now. "All of that stuff, Cyn, it's all fake. The glitz. The glamour. The people. You never know who really likes you for you."

"Poor little rich boy syndrome."

"Something like that." Parker turned his back to the Hollywood sign and leaned against the window. It was a telling gesture, in more ways than one. "Come on, one date. You and me. Just like before. No titles, no interruptions, no bullshit."

"That's a lot of nos."

"I was hoping if we get all the nos out of the way now, there wouldn't be any tomorrow night."

"Are you that used to getting your way?" The laughter was back in her voice, just the way he preferred it.

"Yes."

"I can tell."

"One date." Parker didn't know when to quit. "Tomorrow night."

"I have to work."

"Then Saturday night," he persisted.

"I shouldn't say yes."

He had her. "But you're going to."

"Aren't you worried I might be going out with you now because I know who you are?"

"No." The very idea made him want to laugh.

"Why?"

"Because you wanted me the first night. Not the Prince, but me."

"Just a tad bit cocky."

"Do me a favor, Cyn. Never put tad bit and cock in the same sentence again. I have a reputation to live up to."

"Or down."

Parker walked back to his desk and sat back in his chair. He fumbled around his desk until he found an ink pen and his address book. "Give me your address. I'll pick you up."

"No, I'll meet you somewhere."

"Meet me?"

"Yes. I don't know you well enough to give you my address."

Parker dropped his pen and leaned back in his chair. At first he was impressed with how cautious she was. Now that it was working against him, he was annoyed. "That excuse is going to get old fast."

"But it's not old now, so it's good enough for me."

"We'll play it your way. For now."

"I'm willing to accept those terms."

"Where do you want to meet?" If Cyn still felt as if she needed a safety net, he was happy to provide it. But whether she admitted it to herself or not, Cyn had nothing to be afraid of when it came to him. Yes, Parker meant to have her, but at the same time, he wasn't planning on letting her go.

Chapter Four

"You have to open the store for me today."

"I don't have to do anything but stay black and die." Cyn continued loading the dishwasher, not bothering to looking up. Drew Truman, the eldest sister of the gruesome twosome, wasn't worthy of the respect or the time and energy it would have taken to glance up.

"Fine." Drew's long suffering sigh was as dramatic as the want to be thespian could utter. It was a noise Cyn was unfortunately well acquainted with since Drew and her equally annoying sister, Staci, moved into her townhouse. "You don't have to, but I need you to open the store for me today."

"Sorry, I can't. I have other plans."

"Liar."

"You're right. I am lying." Cyn closed the dishwasher's door and straightened. "I'm not sorry at all. In fact, this is this least sorry I've felt all day."

Of course that wasn't saying a lot. The Elder Saturday family breakfast, a tradition begun long before Cyn had even began to eat solids, had lost its thrill for her. Thanks in large part to her father Walt's live-in girlfriend, Franny, and her twin daughters.

"What is that suppose to mean?"

"You're a smart girl," she lied. "You figure out."

"I can't believe you're acting like this. What's so important you can't open the store?"

"I could ask you the same thing, but you know what, I'm not. Because I don't care. You don't want to work today. Fine. Take it up with my dad, but don't expect me to cover for you this time." Or ever again.

Cyn was done working shifts she hadn't been scheduled to work. She was tired of putting up with the three ungrateful women who made her life miserable for the sheer fun of it. For the last two years she'd bitten her tongue and held back, just because she wanted to please her father, but she could no longer do that.

She didn't have a life. Last Saturday was an eye opening experience. This thing with Parker might very well go nowhere, but it wouldn't be because she didn't try. She'd been ten types of fools to let him slip away. It wasn't everyday a girl went out with a Prince and even if tonight was the only time she saw him again, she was going to enjoy herself. She deserved it.

"You're just being selfish." Drew's face turned up in anger as she spoke. The sad thing was, she and Staci both would have been very pretty girls if it weren't for their very ugly attitudes. They both had shoulder-length ebony hair, coffee-tinged skin, and slender yet feminine bodies, but their bitchy personalities made all those features pale in comparison. It really was a waste. "Mean spirited even."

"You would know." Cyn turned around and began to wipe down the counters. As soon as she was done cleaning her father's kitchen she was leaving. The longer she stood around arguing, the longer it would take for her to finish.

"I'm going to tell your father."

"Okay." Cyn loved her father, truly she did, but she wasn't going to work on her day off just to prove it.

"Fine." Drew huffed out of the room, leaving Cyn alone in the peaceful silence. With Drew and her sister for roommates, it wasn't a state she had the liberty of enjoying much any more, so she tried her best to relish the brief moments when they came.

"What's this I hear about the store not opening today?" Walt's booming voice startled Cyn out of her silent reverie. Damn, talk about brief. She didn't even get to fully zone out yet.

Turning around, she eyed her father who was standing in the kitchen doorway with Franny, Staci and a grinning Drew at his heels. Despite the deep pitch of his voice, the robust sixty-three-year-old man was the least intimidating man in the world. Even though he stood over six feet tall and possessed a voice that could shake the leaves from the trees, he was as kind as they came, a fact Franny used to her advantage for the last two years.

Smiling, as she usually did when her father was in her presences, Cyn leaned back and rested against the sink. "Sorry, Daddy, you'll have to ask Drew about that. It's her turn to open the store."

"Is it now?" Walt turned his level stare to Drew, who scrambled into the middle of the room to quickly answer him.

"Yes, but I have an audition today at twelve," she whined, much to Cyn's annoyance.

Cyn didn't believe her for a moment, but then again, she didn't care. Audition or no audition, she wasn't going to open the store. "The schedule has been posted on the board for over two weeks. She could have switched with any of us at any time. Did she really have to wait until an hour before the shop opened to do so?"

"But I just found out about it."

"Just now? Five minutes ago?" Cyn questioned, one eyebrow raised.

"Well, no."

"Exactly. I'm not switching. I covered for you the last two weekends in a row. I'm not going to do it again."

"You worked the last two weekends for her?" The surprise in her father's voice made Cyn almost reluctant to continue, but she knew if she didn't speak up now she'd spend the rest of her life being their lap dog.

"Yes." Cyn nodded her head to emphasize her words. "And I have plans tonight that I'm not going to break."

"Well, I don't blame you," Walt sympathized.

"But, darling." Franny stepped up and leaned against Walt's arm, resting her head on his shoulder. The twins had inherited their mother's looks as well as her devious ways. In the most manipulative move Cyn had seen in a while, Franny lovingly caressed his chest as she spoke in a soft girlie voice. "It's not as if Drew is asking Cyn to cover for her so she can go to the mall. This audition could be important for her career."

"What career?" Cyn asked. An extra in a straight to video horror film did not constitute a profession.

"Everyone has to start off somewhere, Cynthia. Besides, my girls weren't as lucky as you are to have such a kind and generous father."

Here we go again. "Be that as it may, I have plans today, so I can't work."

"What type of plans?" Franny eyes narrowed with annoyance as she crossed her hands over her breasts, as if she was put off by the whole discussion.

"I have a date."

"A lunch date?" Franny questioned with a faint of hint of disapproval.

"No." Not that it mattered. "A dinner date."

"Then I don't see why you can't open up just this once."

"Just this once?" Had her words fallen on deaf ears? "Did you miss the part where I said I worked the last two weekends for her?"

"Family pitches in at times like these."

Family my ass. "Fine then. Let Staci work today."

"Me?" Staci squeaked. "Why do I have to work? It's not my day."

"You're preaching to the choir, sister." Cyn smirked.

"I have one question." Walt chimed in. Cyn could already hear father's next words. She took a deep breath and prepared herself for the disappointment of his capitulation. "Who's this young fella you're going out with?"

Okay, she hadn't been expecting that. "No one you know."

"Well, I hope not, seeing as how every man I know is either gay or not good enough for you." Walt stepped away from Franny and walked over to Cyn with a large grin on his handsome face. "Are you going to bring him by the house so I can meet him?"

"No, Dad, this isn't the gun over the fireplace type of date."

"Aww...come on. I haven't dusted my rifle off in years."

"Dad." Cyn buried her face in his shirt, breathing in the familiar scent of his Old Spice cologne. "I haven't known him long enough for you to scare him off yet."

"You never let me have any fun," he teased.

"That's because—"

"Walt, honey," Franny called out, interrupting as she always did when they were talking. "What about the store? Who's going to open it?"

"I will." Walt offered, much to everyone's surprise. These days her father was more of a behind-the-scenes kind of man, leaving the day to day running of the store in Cyn's capable hands.

She knew one of the main reasons he'd wanted her to hire the girls was because he was trying to help relieve some of the stress on her shoulders, unknowingly giving her more than she had in the beginning. And Cyn, forever the peacemaker, worked hard to make sure he didn't have to know.

"You?" Fran stiffened, the fake smile she wore like fur, frozen on her face.

"Yes, it is my store after all."

"But we had plans," Franny whined in almost the same pitch as Drew. Like mother like daughter.

"Plans change. As you said, dear heart, family pitches in at times like these. But, Drew, I expect you at the shop no later than three, plus you'll take one of Cyn's closing shifts this week to make up for the weekends she covered for you."

"But..." Walt raised a brow and he stared at Drew until she caved. "Yes, sir."

"Wonderful." Walt's face relaxed. He was a pushover the majority of the time, but he never failed to step up to the plate when necessary. "Now, Cyn, I want all the details of this young man."

With his hand around Cyn's shoulder he led her from the room, but not before she saw Franny shoot her a hostile glare as if it were Cyn's fault her father was working today. With a heavy sigh, Cyn shook her head. She knew without a doubt this wouldn't be the last time she was going to hear about this.

This was ridiculous. Parker released a heavy sigh and for what seemed to be the millionth time, walked to the door of the restaurant and peered into the dimly lit street. It was five minutes past the hour. Where was she? Better question, what the hell was wrong with him? Anyone would think from the way he was acting he'd never been on a date before.

For the life of him, he couldn't figure out why he was so anxious. On the same note though, what drew him to Cyn was just as baffling. She wasn't the most beautiful woman he'd ever seen, he lived in Hollywood for Pete's sake. But there was just something about her he couldn't get out of his mind.

There were no two ways about it, she was haunting him. Even though they lived over three hundred miles apart, Parker found himself damn near breaking his neck doing a double take when a woman who even slightly resembled her walked by.

He needed a drink. He needed a smoke. Hell, he needed to get laid. He needed her under him, writhing beneath him, meeting him stroke for stroke. Her heated flesh, her breathy cries, just her.

"Christ." Frustrated, he turned his back on the door and ran his fingers through his hair. He needed to get a hold of himself before he attacked her the second she entered the restaurant.

It was just a date. A simple little da—

"Hello, stranger."

And just like that, his tension eased. His mouth curved in an unconscious smile as he turned around. "Hello."

She'd been worth the wait. In a word, she was beautiful. No wonder he'd been obsessing all week long. His gaze raked boldly over her as he took in her enticing appearance. She was wearing a simple yet elegant black knee length dress, that showcased her legs and ample curves to a T. Sexy and sophisticated, two of his favorite qualities in one tempting little package. Life didn't get any better.

With an apologetic smile, she walked to his side. "Sorry I'm late. Traffic was heavier than usual. Were you waiting long?"

"No. I just arrived a bit ago," he lied huskily. "You look lovely."

"Thank you." The sweet coco butter scented fragrance she wore danced through his head, as she ran her gaze down his body and her brushed finger across his lapel. "You look wonderful as well."

"Thank you." Unable to help himself, Parker brought his hand up and covered her own, connecting her to him once and for all.

Startled, Cyn raised her head and her heated gaze met with his. The rest of the world seemingly fell away as they stared into one another's eyes. Why were they here? He didn't want to break bread with her; he wanted her to be his meal so he could feast on her tender flesh.

Enough was enough. "Come here," he ordered, sliding his hand down her arm and around her back. With a gentle pull he brought her into his arms and lowered his mouth upon hers.

Her lips parted and he drank in the sweetness of her kiss. To his delight, she kissed him back with a fierce hunger that matched his own fevered pitch. His hands explored her thinly covered back as he devoured her mouth with his. Their bodies melded into one.

If it wasn't for the sound of someone clearing their throat loudly, Parker would have been content to never stop. Reluctantly he pulled back and stared into her passion filled eyes. Her breathing was rough and halting, much like his own.

It was gratifying to know she reacted to him just as strongly as he did to her. This woman was completely under his skin. And damn it, he still didn't know her last name, but that was going to change, here and now. Parker took a step away from her and held out his hand. "Hello."

"Hi." Her brows furrowed as if in confusion.

"I'm Parker McGuire. Movie producer, nightclub owner, also known as 'The Prince of Hollywood'." He didn't want her to say he was holding anything back again. "And you are?"

With an understanding smile, she took his hand into hers. "Cynthia Elder, manager of The Glass Slipper, shoe seller, also known as Cyn, to my friends."

"Are we friends?" he asked, her hand still clasped in his.

She gave a shaky little laugh before replying, "I hope so."

"So do I."

"Sir," a voice called from behind him. "Your table is ready."

"Nice to meet you, Cyn Elder." Parker released her hand and placed his on her lower back. With a nod of his head, he called for the maître d, who led them to their table. The restaurant was dimly lit, the perfect place for a romantic dinner. The ambience was perfect for seduction, but exactly who would be the seducer he wasn't sure. For he'd been seduced from the moment they first met. If Cyn felt half the desire for him he felt for her, they were in for a night neither would forget.

When they arrived at their table, Parker waved the waiter

away from her seat and held out her chair for her. After she took her seat he went around the table to his own chair. But instead of sitting across from her, Parker moved it next to hers and sat by her side. "Much better."

"I agree."

After receiving her permission, he ordered for both of them and requested a bottle of chardonnay before sending their waiter on his way. The waiter quickly returned with the chilled bottle, pouring them each a glass. When the man finally scurried off, Parker turned his attention back to Cyn who was watching him with a look akin to amusement on her pretty face.

"Well, well, well." Cyn swirled her wine around her glass slowly. "Do you always command service like this?"

"Usually."

"Then you need to come with me to the dry cleaners. I can't get any respect there."

"Say the word and I'm there." At this point he was willing to do whatever she wanted, leap tall buildings with a single bound even.

"Really, are you just going to hop in your car and race up here to fix my problem?"

"If you'd like."

"Hmmm..." She nodded thoughtfully, as if weighing his words. "I might have to take you up on that."

"You go right ahead."

"I will."

Parker felt like a gauche schoolboy, making small talk with Cyn. He never had problems letting a woman know when he was interested, but tonight he seemed like a fumbling idiot.

"Have I told you how lovely you look?"

"Yes, right before you kissed me."

"Are you complaining?"

"Just answering your question." She smiled seductively.

"Well, here's another question for you. Is your cell phone

off?"

She frowned in confusion. "No, why?"

"Because I don't want to chance you running off again. I let you escape once. I won't make that mistake again."

"I'm here aren't I?" She took a sip of her wine, a coy smile hovering over her lips.

"Yes, but just think where you could have been if you hadn't left." Taking her free hand in his, he rubbed his thumb over the soft flesh of her wrist. He could hear her breath catch at the caress.

"And where is that?"

"My bed." Just saying the words made the image pop into his brain. Cyn, nude, lying across his bed, with her arms spread wide and welcoming.

"The night is still young."

"Is that a promise?" He certainly hoped so.

"No," she laughed. "I don't make promises I can't keep."

"Then keep it." His fingers glided along her arm and he watched as her body reacted to his touch. He could tell she was just as attuned to him as he was to her.

"What am I going to do with you?"

"I can think of many things."

"Feel free to share?"

"I don't think you're ready for that just yet."

"Then think again." Her teasing words had an arousing effect on him. Suddenly, she was no longer a passive party in his subtle game of flirtation. She was a full-out accomplice.

Last Saturday hadn't been a fluke. There was something between them, so much stronger than simple desire.

Chapter Five

After dinner, Parker suggested they drive over to Delilah's Jook Joint, a local jazz club off the Bay. It was a stark contrast to the restaurant where they'd just eaten. Where Agua was a four star crème de la crème eatery, Delilah's wasn't on any tourist maps. It was a local club with dark, seedy music that spoke to the soul. Definitely not the type of place Cyn would have imagined Parker would haunt.

Since she'd driven to the restaurant, she followed him over to the club in her car, using the time alone to think back over the evening. Just like the first time she met him, Parker blew her away. He was cute as hell and twice as charming. She couldn't remember the last time she'd been so drawn to anyone. From the first moment she laid eyes on him in the restaurant, she'd known without a doubt where the night would lead.

It was very easy to see why he was sought after by the media and women. He had a way of looking a person directly in the eyes when he talked to them, making them feel as if they were the only one in the room. Even Cyn, who considered herself jaded and schooled, felt a tingle after talking to him for mere minutes.

Noticing the time, Cyn reached across the center divide to the passenger seat and wrestled her purse open. As she wove through traffic she pulled out her cell phone and turned it on. Using the speed dial she called Miller. The phone rang only twice before it was promptly answered.

"Do you know what time it is?" Miller her protector tore into her as she knew he would. He was her safety call, something she was supposed to have done over an hour ago.

"My bad. The time completely ran away from me."

"No excuses. I've called your cell phone three times."

"I had it off," she meekly said. The sad thing was Cyn knew better. Lord knows she'd chewed Miller's ear off for the same offense so many times before. The way the world was today, a person had to be careful.

"Off," he bellowed. "What in the world for?"

"Because I'm on a date and I didn't want to be disturbed."

"Of all the irresponsible things to do—"

"Oh, pipe down," a voice called out from the background.

"Is that..." *No, it couldn't be. Could it?* "Is that MeShell?"

"Yes." And from the sound of Miller's voice he was none too pleased about his visitor. "I can't get him to leave."

Him. For as long as Cyn could remember Miller had referred to MeShell as shim. Interesting. Very interesting. "What is she doing there in the first place?"

"I have no idea why *he's* here," he stressed the pronoun, "but he needs to leave."

"I'll go when I'm good and ready." MeShell's voice rang out loud and clear.

Apparently she wasn't the only one on a date tonight. "I won't keep you. I just called to check in. Everything is going good. Dinner was fine now we're off to Delilah's."

"Delilah's? His idea or yours?"

"His," she said as she pulled into the semi-crowded parking lot and parked next to Parker's Porsche. Her Mazda looked tacky next to his ride, but then again, he made movies and she slung shoes.

"Well, well then. Cute and good taste. You go ahead then."

"I think I will."

"Really..."

"Yes, but I have to go now. We're here. I'll call you afterwards to let you know I'm heading home."

"You better not be going there alone."

"I doubt either one of us will be going to bed alone."

"Bite your tongue," he argued, much to her amusement.

Cyn would have given just about anything to be a fly on the wall of Miller's apartment. Something was definitely going on between him and MeShell, and Cyn couldn't wait to find out all the juicy details. But that would have to wait for tomorrow. Tonight, she was going to concentrate on her own social life for a change. "Love you."

"You too, doll. Have fun."

By the time Cyn hung up, Parker had exited his car and was waiting patiently for her. When she unlocked the door, he opened it and held his hand out for her to take. "My lady."

"My, my. You princes and your manners."

"It's all due to charm school."

"I bet." After locking and alarming her car, they set off for the club. "I have to say, I'm very impressed with your taste. First Aqua, now Delilah's. How does an L.A. brat like you know of all these cool places?"

"Google.com."

"Now why don't I believe you?"

He brought his hand to the corner of his upper lip and pretended to twist a mustache. "Because keeping you on your toes is part of my *evil* plan."

"Tell more about this nefarious plan of yours."

"First I fill your tummy with wonderful food, and then I feed your soul with equally wonderful music."

"Are my soul and tummy the only things you plan to fill tonight?" The words slipped out before she could stop them and from the grin on his face, he was glad they did.

"Lord, I hope not," he murmured as he held open the door for her to enter.

Delilah's was one of her favorite places in the Bay Area. Unfortunately, Cyn didn't often have the opportunity to come here. She was looking forward to showing Parker around the place, but to her utter amazement he didn't just know of Delilah's he knew Delilah. When they walked into the club, the dark-skinned, heavyset woman greeted him as if he were a long lost son. She came from around the bar and crushed him to her in a bone-breaking hug.

After a few back-cracking slaps, she pushed him from her and stared up into his face. "Damn, boy, when was the last time you brought your pretty ass in here?"

"It's been awhile."

"I'd say." The loud woman cackled as she stepped away. When she glanced over Parker's shoulder and spotted Cyn, her smile widened. "Although last time you were here, your date wasn't as lovely. Who's this cute little thing?"

Grinning, he placed his arm around her and brought her forth for introductions. "Cyn, this is Delilah, my godmother."

"Nice to meet you." She held out her hand but it was swiftly cast aside as Delilah wrapped her arms around Cyn, hugging her almost as fiercely as she'd hugged Parker.

"We don't stand on ceremony around here, girl."

Nor did they understand the meaning of personal space. "I see."

"Ya'll go over there and have a seat. I'll send Geanie over to get you a drink. And, boy, don't you think of leaving here without saying goodbye."

"I wouldn't dream of it. Can you go ahead and send Geanie upstairs?"

"Sure can."

As they made their way up the stairs, Cyn couldn't help but tease him. "Bring all your dates here, do you?"

"You'd be the first."

"Then what did she mean when she said I was prettier than

the last date you brought here?"

A slow smile spread across his lips, making him look even yummier than usual. "She's talking about my best friend, Solomon. He's as in love with Delilah as I am. Whenever he's in town he bugs me to bring him here so he can, as he says, woo her."

Cyn glanced over her shoulder at the woman in question behind the bar, laughing it up with her customers and found it easy to believe how his friend could become enamored with the vivacious woman. "She seems as if she's a wonderful lady."

"She is," he agreed. "She's my mother's best friend. Back in the day, Delilah used to be a make-up artist and she worked on one of the shows my mother was cast on. They've been friends since the moment they met."

"So now that you have me here, whatever shall you do with me?"

"You mentioned over dinner you enjoyed playing pool."

"I play a little," she lied.

"You want to play a few games?"

"Most definitely."

The upper area was less crowded and more relaxed, which was just the atmosphere Cyn preferred. The three pool tables were filled with players and smokers, smashing the balls to the heavy beat of the music. Parker slapped down seventy-five cents on the corner of the table, signaling he wanted to play next and pulled out a bar stool for her.

Easing up on the stool, she leaned back against the bar and watched the men in front of her clearing the table.

"What would you like to drink?"

"A soda would be great."

"What, no more alcohol?"

"No, I have to get up early. I have to meet my trainer at the gym."

Placing his hand over his heart, he let out a moan of

despair. "Say it isn't so, pretty lady. Tell me you're not trying to slim down this lush body."

Lush. She rolled her eyes. Man was he full of it. "I'm actually very happy with my body. I work out to stay healthy, not to get skinny. There is a difference you know."

"Marry me."

She couldn't help herself, she had to smile. Something she'd been doing a lot since meeting him. "Now what would you say if I said yes?"

"Thank you, Lord, comes to mind." Parker's face was devoid of humor and if she didn't know better, she might have thought he was serious.

"Whatever, smooth talker."

"I know you won't believe me, but it's only around you."

"My drink," she commanded, giving him a little nudge towards the waitress making her way in their direction. There was plenty of time for him to talk her out of her panties. Right now she wanted to play some pool.

He racked up the balls, centering them as perfectly in the triangle as he could, trying to make sure everything evened out. This was the official tie breaking game and he had absolutely no intention of letting her win because she was a girl. Female or not, the woman was ruthless.

He should have known he was in for it when she offered to break. No one offered to break if they "played just a little" as she'd claimed. Not only had she made sure the balls scattered around the table, she'd also knocked three solid ones in with the first stroke of her stick. The damnedest part was the vixen had the nerve to give him a little smile and say "beginner's luck", as if he would buy that.

But it wasn't just luck kicking his ass all over the green felt table; it was also her body, which always seemed to be in his peripheral vision whenever it was his turn to make a shot. Cyn did everything from passing behind him and accidentally stroking his ass, to leaning down to check out his shot and pressing her full breasts against his arms. She was a cheat. A dirty rotten, sexy-as-all-hell cheat and Parker was loving every second of it.

She came up behind him and breathed on his neck. "Here let me help you line that."

Parker stifled a grin. She just wasn't going to play fair. "Get your little sweet ass on the other side of the table."

"I'm just trying to be helpful." She pouted, making her lips look even more kissable than he could have imagined. Not that he needed any help in the imagination part. All night long he'd been thinking of things to do with and to her, and half of them involved tying her naughty body to the very table he was using to hide his erection.

Parker steadied the shot and forced himself to concentrate on the white ball in front of him instead of the blue balls in his pants. He brought the stick back and sent it barreling towards the ball, giving himself a little mental high five as the balls scattered in every direction, sinking three stripped ones at the same time. Standing, he eyed the table, calculating his next shot, before looking over at Cyn, who was frowning at the table. "For some reason, I'm not believing the whole you trying to be helpful thing."

"Now why is that?"

"Corner pocket," Parker called, as he lined up his next shot. "Hmm, could it be you're a hustler."

"Now, now, Parker, if I was trying to hustle you, I would have made a wager."

"It's not too late." He could think of several things he'd be willing to bet on. "I'm willing."

"So I see."

He froze on the down stroke and looked up into her twinkling eyes. If he had any doubts before that she wasn't aware of his attraction to her, those were now laid to rest. He was certain she missed very little. "What do you mean?" he questioned as he took his shot, cursing to himself as he missed. She was getting to him.

"I just meant you look like a betting man." Taking the stick out of his hand, she nudged him with her hip and leaned over to take her shot. She looked up before she thrust her stick between her long brown fingers and cocked a brow, "What did you think I meant?"

She executed her shot perfectly, winking at him as she stood. *Fuck this*, Parker thought, as he watched her bend over again. Her dress rose a bit in the back, flashing smooth, groin-tightening chocolate thighs at him, forcing a savage growl from his throat as he noticed he wasn't the only one looking.

A couple of guys at the next table were watching her intently, *too* intently for his peace of mind. He didn't mind she was teasing him, but the thought of anyone else enjoying the view was enough to piss him off. Glaring at the men in question, he walked behind her, blocking her ass from their sight.

"Aww," one complained, earning a scowl from him as he twisted around to see who said it.

"What did you say?" she asked when she stood once again.

"Nothing," he replied as he turned back to face her. "Did you make it?"

"Weren't you watching?"

"No."

"Then yes." The laughter in her voice told him another story.

"Cheat." He reached for the stick, brushing his hands against her. All the laughter froze as the touch forced them to make eye contact, real contact for the first time, and he really liked what he saw. He wasn't the only one feeling the pull between them. He was just the only one not fighting it. "You know you worried me there for a moment."

"*Moi*?" she asked, pressing her hand flush to her chest. Once again his mind went back to the pool table, and her on top, arms spread wide gripping the pool stick as he feasted on her body. "How did I do that?"

"I wasn't sure if you were going to show tonight."

"And stand up the Prince? Never." Her pretty brown face was relaxed in a smile. Never had he been turned on before by just simple foreplay. And that was what it was. They hadn't touched, not really, but he was just as aroused as if they had.

It was something about her—no—it was everything about her that was a turn on from her smooth, chocolate skin, to the sexy sway of her ass. He was intoxicated on her beauty and enraptured by her charm. "So does this mean I get your phone number this time?"

"If you're a good boy."

"Oh, baby, I promise you. I'm good."

"I bet." Glancing down at his outfit, she looked him over in a way that made him feel it as if it were her fingers instead of just her gaze. "I like you in black."

He was willing to bet he'd like himself in black as well. "Thank you."

She looked at him with a twinkle in her eyes as she picked up her drink. "I have this theory."

"Do tell."

"All men look good in black. Black clothes, black cars..." she toyed with the straw in her glass, with a soft demure smile across her lips as she continued, "...black women."

Damn! He went from intrigued to aroused in two seconds flat. Leaning in closer so there was no chance she would miss his words, he teased back, "I'm a man of science you know, and I'm a big believer in theories. The *'big bang'* is one of my personal favorites."

She coughed on her drink, bringing her hand quickly to her mouth to stifle the soda that was surely about to fly out. Sputtering, she reached behind her on the table and grabbed a napkin to wipe up her mess. "Boy..." she chuckled, in between coughs, "...you are too much."

"Just enough I'd say." He could tell she was used to having the upper hand in relationships. She was in for a mighty fall if she thought he was going to roll over and play lap dog for her. "Are you a betting woman?"

"Could be. Depends on the bet I guess."

"I win this game, you come home with me."

"Hollywood?" She quirked her eyebrow questioningly.

"No, I have a townhouse here, as well."

"Okay, and if I win..." Her voice trailed away as she waited for his response.

"We'll go out for coffee instead," he offered nonchalantly.

She pondered the comment for a moment, before setting her drink back on the table. "Sounds like a great bet."

Bending, he took aim. It was a win-win situation as far as he saw it. Yes, he wanted to go to bed with her, but half an hour spent in her presence was a great consolation prize. As he pulled the stick back, she chimed in, "I want to change the bet a bit."

Damn, he knew things were too good to be true. "You want me to change my wager?"

"No." Walking around to where he was, Cyn ran her hands down his stick suggestively. "If you win, I go home with you. If I win, you go home with me."

Chapter Six

There had been no sweeter victory for Cyn as when she sank the black ball in the corner pocket. Although the winner of the game held no real importance, seeing as how they both had the same end goal in mind.

She'd made some rash decisions in her time, but taking Parker to her bed, only a week after she met him, made all the sense in the world to her. Everything about him worked for her. Playing coy just seemed silly and false. She wanted him. He wanted her. What else was there to say about the matter?

They barely made it into her house before they began to merge into one another. His lips teased her neck as he pushed her gently back against the wall, his greedy hands moving under her dress to pull at the soaked silk clinging between her legs.

"Tell me something." Parker's fingers slipped beneath her panties and slid teasingly across her curl-covered mound.

"Hmmm...anything."

"How attached are you to these?"

"The panties?"

"Yes."

"Not at all."

"Wonderful." That was the only warning she received before he pulled his fingers from out of her moist sex and with each hand took a hold of the fabric on her hips. With a deft pull, he ripped the silk sides in two. The tattered remains fell to the floor like scraps of unwanted material. "Much, much better."

He moved his hand between her thighs and slid two fingers into her damp, snug box. "Much." He groaned again.

"Ohhh." Cyn tilted her head, exposing the length of her neck to his teasing lips as his fingers pumped inside her. She wanted nothing more than to surrender to him and come screaming his name, but there was a little matter of her unwanted houseguests hopefully sleeping just a few rooms away. She stole a quick glance down the hall and lowered her voice to a whisper. "We have to keep it down."

Parker moved his mouth from her lips and took his hand from between her legs. He brought his damp fingers to his mouth and closed his eyes as his licked his fingers clean, moaning aloud as if she was made of the finest chocolate. When he opened his eyes again, they were filled with passion. "Not going to happen, honey. He's up and raring to go."

She laughed softly. "That's not what I meant, pervert."

"Why so silent?"

"Roommates."

"And?" he said in a lowered voice.

"And I won the game, so that means my house, my rules."

"I still say you cheated."

She hadn't, but if it made his fragile ego feel better... "Does it really matter?"

"Yes, I have a king size bed and a headboard you can hold onto."

His words sent shivers down her overheated body. "I have silk scarves."

"Damn," he groaned. "You win."

Hooking her fingers in his belt loop, she gave a teasing tug, forcing him to follow her into her bedroom. "I think you're mistaken, handsome. The scarves are going on you."

"Me, you. Either way I'm game."

Not bothering with the main light, she pulled him into her bedroom, releasing his belt loop long enough to lock her door and put on her bedside light. Turning back to him, she felt her womb clench with desire.

Cyn felt an almost desperate need to have him inside her. Never before had she been so overwhelmed with passion as she was with him. She was willing to bet though, he was more than capable of feeding her frenzy.

"I want to drive for now." He didn't say a word, merely raising a brow as she walked back towards him, debating what to run her fingers over first. He was like one big temptation and she had no idea where to begin.

Standing in front of him she studied him for a moment. Of her twenty-odd years on this earth she'd come into contact with many beautiful men in many different colors, but this man and this color, held her fascinated.

She reached out without thinking and lightly brushed her fingers across his mouth, feeling the subtle difference of his body versus hers. He stayed still and silent the whole time, allowing her the moment of exploration.

It was almost as if he was a fragile work of art. Every nick and scrape a memento of another time and place that had marred him, yet in a good way. The scars proved he was fallible, mortal. This beautiful man who she held at arm's length as she gawked like a silly schoolgirl at his beauty and grace.

"I never knew a man could be so pretty."

"And I never knew it could hurt to stand so still next to you, dying for a touch."

Tilting her head to the side, she pondered his answer. "Why are you waiting so patiently?"

"Because I'll have plenty of time to worship your beauty later. Now I'm just here at your command."

Oh, my. She loved the sound of that. Cyn walked around him and sat on her bed. She kicked her heels off and crossed her legs. "Undress for me."

He grabbed the bottom of his shirt and brought it over his head. His muscular chest was a bit tanner than she would have expected, but just as nice as she hoped. As quickly as he disposed of his shirt, he kicked off his shoes then moved his agile fingers to the button of his pants. As he slid his pants down, she took in a deep breath to calm her racing heart. There were no two ways about it. The man was an Adonis.

Stock still, dressed in black boxers and a thin gold chain holding a saint medallion, he looked as if he was just waiting for her next instruction. But all rhyme and reason slipped from her mind the minute his pants hit the floor. All she wanted now was him.

"Don't stop there." Her words were a whispered plea. One he answered promptly and with no question.

He moved his hands to his sides and pushed his boxers past his lean hips until they pooled on the floor next to his discarded pants. His hard cock was long and thick and just what she needed to quench her hunger.

Licking her lips, she stood and pulled her dress off. She reached behind her back and undid her bra. His eyes lit up as her breasts were bared, but unlike Cyn, he apparently wasn't in the mood for visual foreplay.

"Come here," he ordered huskily.

Going to him was harder than sitting still and watching him undress, but from the intense look in his eyes, she would have to say he felt the exact same way. They met half way, lips crushing into lips, fingers touching and teasing. It was as if everything before this moment had been a long, torturous version of foreplay, and now they both wanted to get to the heart of the matter.

They fed off one another's hunger. Kissing, touching, moving against each other as their passion rose. As if they were of like minds, they began to make their way back to her bed, all without breaking free of their embrace.

Big mistake. Cyn's desire was no match for her

equilibrium. In their haste to be with one another, they didn't take mind of her shoes lying aimlessly on the floor and tripped.

The force was great enough to tear her mouth from his as they tumbled backwards. Luckily the bed was right behind them, leaving them a soft place to fall.

"Fuck," Parker muttered as he braced his hands to cushion his collapse on top of her.

Holding himself so as not to crush her with his weight, he smiled down at Cyn, who was having a hard time trying to keep it together. This wasn't romantic, erotic or sexy. But it was fun. And sometimes being able to have fun with a man in bed was more important than being able to have an orgasm with one.

Hopefully, though, that wouldn't be the case tonight, because the undercurrent of sexual energy he was creating was enough to warm her on the coldest of nights.

Leaning more to the left, he used his right hand to brush away strands of hair cascading into her face. "I imagined it going a lot smoother than that."

"A bit more cool, I suppose."

"Not necessarily cool...just not so bumbling."

"Oh, I don't know." She slithered underneath him until her pelvis was directly lined up with the large mass stretching out to greet her. Comfortable with him over her, she wrapped her legs around his hips, loving the full feel of him inside the confines of her thighs. "I think you hit your mark."

He pressed his hips forward forcefully. "I met my mark for sure, but this isn't the way I wanted to be introduced to her. I think she and I now deserve a little verbal time. To communicate that is."

Cyn laughed, as she ran her hands through his soft, silky hair. "Let the peace treaties begin."

"If you hear me shouting 'thank you, God' while I'm down here, feel free not to send for reinforcements. This is definitely a one man job," he teased, as he lowered himself between her thighs.

He let out an appreciative groan as he parted her folds with his thumbs. It was she who groaned next as the touch of his tongue swiped over her engorged clit. As if feeding off of her response, he indulged and feasted on her moist flesh. His tongue teased and tormented her pussy, bringing forth guttural groans from deep within her.

She tried hard to keep her moans quiet, but it was a losing battle. Parker was an orally talented man. It had been so long since she'd made love with someone other than herself. So long since she'd found anyone worthy of giving herself to, it was almost impossible for her to just lay back and enjoy the pleasure he gave her.

After just a few seconds of his masterful kisses she was ready to come. Her body felt as brittle as shattered glass. She wanted to orgasm. She needed it. But he was deliberately withholding the firmer touch she desperately required.

"Please." She wasn't above begging to get what she needed. Her body arched toward his as Parker's tongue lathed her pussy. "Please."

"I will, baby. You can count on it." Pulling back, he slipped his fingers inside her tight channel. The tips brushed against her G-spot sending waves of pleasure racing throughout her body. "Is that what you want, sexy? You want to come for me?"

"Yes. God. Yes," she cried, pumping her body onto his tortuous fingers.

"Then do it, Cyn. Fly for me." Parker took her clit between his lips and sucked. The suction combined with his thrusting fingers was just what she needed to send her cascading into ecstasy.

Quiet be damned, Cyn screamed out her release as she came, flooding his fingers with her juices.

He took an instant to savor the moment before he rose to his knees. He ran his heated gaze over her body, taking in every inch of brown flesh, the fullness of her breasts, the sexy length of her legs and the sweet valley between her thighs. He was going to fuck the hell out of her.

"Like what you see?" she asked in a sultry tone that set his blood ablaze.

"God, yes." He ran his finger down her thigh to her knee then circled back and headed for the paradise awaiting him. "I've wanted you this way since the first day we met. Gorgeous, naked and beneath me."

"I'm not beneath you yet."

"That's just a matter of semantics." He moved forward until he was kneeling between her thighs with his body draped over hers, bringing them eye to eye. "Is this better?"

"Much."

"I'm here to please."

"I like the way you think."

"And I love the way you taste." Parker glanced at her breasts, so tempting they should have been a sin. "Let me see if you taste this good everywhere."

He bent and took her nipple into his mouth, rolling his tongue over the dark bud. He bit gently, adding just enough pressure to heighten her senses. Her moan was the only sign of approval he needed before he transferred his attention to her other breast, to tease the same way.

Her fingers entangled in his hair and tugged, pulling him away from her tasty morsels. "Stop teasing me and fuck me."

"Say please."

"Are you kidding me?"

Parker moved down again to recapture her nipple and prove beyond a shadow of a doubt he was far from kidding. He wanted her to beg him. To plead for her pleasure as if only he held the key to her release.

"Damn you." She tugged harder on his hair, but still he wasn't budging.

"Say it." He blew his warm breath over her pebbled nipple. "Say it and I will."

"Fuck me, you bastard. Please!"

He smiled at her turn of phrase, loving the fact he had her so worked up. Parker reached over the side of the bed, grabbed his discarded pants and pulled out his wallet. He retrieved one of the two condoms he'd stashed there earlier in the evening before tossing the slacks back to the floor.

After sheathing his erection for their protection he leaned forward once more. He bore his weight on one arm as he used his other hand to position his cock at her entrance. She wasn't the only one he was torturing. He ached to pierce her flesh and sink deep within the warmth of her body, but he held back. He needed to know she wanted this just as badly as he did. "Now say pretty please."

"Pretty fucking please." Wrapping her legs around his hips, she pulled him toward her, apparently tired of waiting.

But so was he. "Close enough." He pushed forward, sinking inch by excruciating inch into her tight, wet pussy. From the death grip her inner walls had on his cock, it had been awhile since she'd made love. That pleased him in a caveman-like way.

She enveloped him with her heat, damn near searing the condom to his shaft. How was it possible for her to be this hot and this tight? She had the perfect pussy, which shouldn't have surprised him. She was the perfect woman after all.

"Yes. Yes. Yes." The words tumbled from her lips as he drove inside her. So much for not being too loud.

"What happened...to being...quiet?"

"Fuck them."

"No, Cyn. Fuck me," His need to posses her was brought on by animalistic hunger, but he didn't just want her body, he wanted her soul. Loving had never felt so right before. She fit him like a glove, as if she was the Eve to his Adam, made from his very own rib. As maddening as it was, the only thing he could think was *mine*. So he said it.

His woman. His pussy. His everything.

She thrust back against him, angling her hips so he was

scraping against her clit with every downward stroke. The tight sheath of her pussy cradled his cock like a closed hand, bringing him nearer to the precipice of his release.

But he wasn't ready for this to end just yet. Pushing her legs up, he hooked them over his shoulders, driving into her with deep, long strokes. The change in angle had Cyn gasping and he watched as she threw out her hands to find something, anything to hold on to. Parker wanted to see her wild and out of control, as out of control as he felt.

"Come for me, baby. Flood my cock with your sweet juices."

His words appeared to be her catalyst. Crying out, she sobbed his name as she came, milking his cock with her sweet pussy. Her orgasm trigged his. Unable to help himself, Parker ground his hips and thrust deeper inside her.

"Damn, baby…so fucking good," he groaned as he spilled his seed inside the latex covering. "So good."

Limp and sated, she dropped her arms to the bed and unwrapped her legs from around his waist. "Damn."

He couldn't agree more. Parker lingered inside her for a minute more, before he could gather the strength to pull out. He dropped lifelessly on the bed next to her, exhausted and satisfied…for now.

Their harsh breathing was the only sound in the room but it spoke volumes. Their loving hadn't been soft and gentle. It was fierce and earth shattering, not something to bounce back from quickly.

When his body began to chill from the cool breeze wafting in from the window, Parker roused himself and stumbled toward what he hoped was a bathroom. To his delight, it was, and he made quick work of disposing of the filled condom and cleaning himself up.

He took a few minutes to soap a warm washcloth for Cyn and traipsed back into the room. She was just as he left her. Lying limply in the bed with a tiny smile on her face.

He brushed the damp cloth against her skin, cleansing

away all evidence of their loving from her body. After he was done, he returned the cloth to the bathroom. He went back into the bedroom and climbed in bed beside her.

Content, he gazed at her once more, taking in everything. She was an ebony goddess. Her supple brown skin was an exotic contrast next to his paler skin. She was lovelier than words alone could express. And she was also falling asleep.

"Wait," he whispered softly to her. "Don't drift off on me just yet."

"Why?" Opening an eye she peered at him warily. "If you're thinking of round two already, you're going to have to give a sista a minute. I need to recoup."

"How about you recoup at my place? Come home with me."

"Your townhouse?"

"No. Hollywood. Actually Bel Air to be exact."

She snickered, a sound so enduring it brought a smile to his face.

"What?"

"You're the prince of Bel Air."

"And I haven't heard that one before," he replied in a dry tone.

She closed her eyes again and gave a fake yawn. "That's a long drive."

He could tell she was trying to dismiss him, but it wasn't going to work. Not now. Not ever. "Not to the airport. I have a private plane waiting on standby."

That got her attention. Her eyes popped open once more and she stared at him, shock written clearly on her face. "You didn't drive up here?"

"No."

"What about your car?"

"I leave it here at my place for when I'm in town."

"You leave a Boxster Porsche just sitting around?"

He wouldn't say just sitting. It was parked in a secured,

221

maintained garage. He doubted that was the point though. "Yes."

"That must be nice."

"It has its moments." Even though he could tell his wealth bothered her, he wasn't going to downplay his finances just to give her a false sense of comfort. This was who he was. Good. Bad. Indifferent. And if she was going to be part of his life, she needed to get used to it, because God willing, his money wasn't going anywhere. "So what do you say?"

"Can I think about it?"

"Sure." Parker eased from the bed and reached for his boxers. "You have five minutes."

Cyn sat straight up. "Five minutes!"

"That's right."

"I can't make a decision like that so quickly."

"Fine, let me make it for you." Parker pulled on his pants but left them unbuttoned. "You want to. I want you to. What's the problem?"

"I have a job."

"You have two days off. You said so yourself."

"I have responsibilities."

"To yourself. Come with me. Let me show you my...palace," he added with a wink.

"Why are you so hell bent on getting me to say yes in such a hurry?"

"Because I'm going to make love to you again tonight. And again in the morning, and in the afternoon, and so on and so on, but I refuse to do so quietly. I want your release to echo in my ears and stay with me forever. We can't do that here. So for the last time, Cyn, come with me. I'll make it worth your while."

She bit her lip nervously and glanced from him to the door. Her indecision was as evident as her desire. He could only hope the latter won out. "I need to be back no later than Tuesday afternoon."

"That I can do." Standing, he held his hand out to her in a grand gesture. "Come, princess, your pumpkin awaits."

Chapter Seven

The city lights overpowered the sky, allowing only a few faint stars to illuminate the dark night. Thankfully, the pool and spa were equipped with their own ambient lighting that switched on the moment she opened the door.

After undressing, she laid her clothes on the lounge chair next to the pool. She switched on the spa with the remote control from the table before making her way over to the hot tub. She'd been eying that bad boy since the first day she'd come to Parker's house, but this was the first time she'd an opportunity to use it. In fact, this was the last chance she would have to use it before returning home tomorrow and she wanted to enjoy the moment to this fullest.

Cyn moaned in appreciation as she sank into the bubbling water. Her eyes closed briefly as she reveled in the luxurious moment, but quickly reopened. She didn't want to miss a minute of this. This was paradise. The only way it could possibly be better was if Parker was able to join her, but he had some last minute business to take care of, leaving her to herself for the first time that weekend.

It was okay though because she was in nirvana. Enjoying life the way it was meant to be enjoyed, completely worry and stress free. The shop was the farthest thing from her mind. She was too busy concentrating on Parker and the overwhelming, mind-numbing feeling she was falling in love with him.

It was probably a big mistake. She'd only known him for a

short time, yet he felt as if he was a part of her soul. When this little fairy tale was over, as she expected it soon to be, she would have to pick up the many pieces of her shattered heart. But until that day came, she was going to enjoy every second she had with him, as if it was her last. Prince Charming only came around once in a girl's lifetime.

"There you are."

Parker's voice startled her and woke her from her daydream. Turning her head, she spotted him standing in the doorway and smiled. "Done with work already?"

"Mostly." He began to undress, but unlike her, he dropped his clothes carelessly on the ground. A sure sign of a man used to others picking up after him.

"Slob," she teased, something she'd been doing a lot of this weekend. His lifestyle was so lavish, so gaudy, so unlike anything she'd ever seen before, yet he still had an air of humility about him that made it all seem so surreal. He had money, but he wasn't all about money.

"I wasn't going to leave them there."

"Sure you weren't." To her amusement he did pick his clothes up, but then dropped them just as carelessly on the chair. She was sure his pants alone cost more than her entire wardrobe, yet it didn't seem to faze him that they lay in a wrinkled pile next to her faded jeans.

"Why so quiet?" He stepped into the spa, hissing as the hot water scalded him. "So much for having children."

"I'm sure your swimmers can stand a little heat."

"I hope so." He eased onto a seat across from her and leaned back against the backrest. "How did I know you would be out here?"

"Because it's the only place in your palace I can find without a map." To say his house was big would be the understatement of the year. It was three stories high with the pool and spa on the top floor, along with an elevator. *An elevator.* She'd seen apartment complexes that were smaller.

"It's not a palace," he argued.

"Mausoleum?" she teasingly shot back.

He grimaced slightly. "Definitely not that."

"Mansion?"

"I prefer home."

She almost laughed at the pained expression on his face. "I had to stop and ask for directions to the bathroom."

"You did not." Parker reached out and pulled her from her seat and onto his lap. "You do realize your nose grows when you lie, don't you?"

Something was growing under the water, and it had nothing to do with a lie. Wiggling her hips, Cyn brushed her mound against his rising cock. "You're like a sixteen-year-old boy."

"How so?"

"You're constantly hard."

"You say that as if it's a bad thing," he teased. He pulled back her shoulders so she was leaning away from him, and bent forward and took her nipple in his mouth. He alternated between teasing nibbles and long licks, keeping her on the edge of reason with his sweet torture. There was no doubt about it. He was trying to drive her insane with pleasure.

"Oh no." She gripped his hair in her hands and pulled him away from her breasts. "Just merely pointing out the obvious. It's probably a good thing I'm going home tomorrow."

"Why?" He grasped her hips in his hands and worked her back and forth over his shaft. The movements played havoc with her body. Her clit was pulsing and her pussy drenched from desire.

"Because my pussy needs a break."

"But you're not home yet, so no break for you." Parker slid his hand between them and ran his fingers across her clit. "This pussy belongs to me for twelve more hours."

"Then you better use it wisely." She rose to her knees and

grasped his cock in her hand, lining him up to her opening.

"Oh, I plan to." He pulled her down as he pushed his hips up, plunging his shaft deep within her.

Their moans came out as one, both of them groaning in unison from the pleasure of their joining. He filled her as no other had before and stretched her flesh to accommodate his cock. Her tender pussy was a bit sore from the constant action it had received for the last few days, but she refused to halt their loving.

She wanted him. Even if she was forced to walk bowlegged for the rest of the week, Cyn was going to ride him as if he wore a saddle.

"I don't know what's hotter, baby," he groaned, rocking into her. "Your pussy or this spa, but I know for sure which one I like best."

"The spa right?" She began to move on top of him, slowly sinking on his throbbing cock then rising once more. It was an erotic tango of moves and dips, which had them both panting for more.

"Oh, yeah..." He groaned, digging his nails into her hips. "Definitely the spa...fuck...hmmm."

Biting her lip to stifle her moan, she gripped his shoulders and used him for support as she rode him. Taking him over and over into her warm center. He reached up, filling his palms with her breasts again, stroking and teasing her. The warm night and hot water was no match for the heat building between the two of them. Their breaths quickened with every plunge, becoming as gritty and raw as the city itself.

The water, already wild from the jets, splashed about them even higher, thanks to the tidal wave they created with their thrusts. Not one to give up control, Parker held on to her hips, controlling her movements. When she tried to speed up, he'd slow her down, letting her know in a no uncertain terms, who was in charge. "In a rush?"

"To come, yes."

"When I say so."

"Bastard." She whimpered, unable to do anything but concede to his command.

"Tell me you don't love it and I'll stop." He thrust his hips upward as he pulled her down on him, causing her to groan in ecstasy.

"You're evil," she gasped as he drove the breath from her body.

"I know." He began to rock her faster and harder. Cyn dug her fingernails in his shoulders.

"Oh, oh, oh," she moaned. Her head was spinning. Her vision clouded over as her body surrendered to the pleasure overtaking it. "Parker...yes...oh..."

"Fuck, baby. Hold on." Parker quickly stood and moved them until her back was against the wall of the spa.

He gripped her to him tightly and tilted her hips as he powered into her fiercely. Cyn wrapped her legs around his hips and held on to him for all she was worth.

"Oh, oh, oh." Her gasps were barely audible over the roar of the jets, but it didn't stop her from making them. Nor did it stop her from coming. Throwing her head back, she let the sensations of him powering into her come crashing down, driving her over the edge into orgasmic bliss.

"That's right. Come for me."

Instead of immediately finding his own release he continued to drive his cock into her, pulling her back to the brink once again. Her second climax, although not as powerful, ripped through her.

Just as she thought he would never come, he pushed at her thighs and pulled out of her pussy. Gripping his cock, he fisted his shaft a few times, spilling his milky seed into the hot water.

"Fuck," he groaned, trembling above her. "Too good. Too fucking good."

He was right. It was.

"If you look at your phone one more time, I'm going to throw it to the ground and run it over with the golf cart."

Parker glanced up from his iPhone and over to his mother, Olivia Maguire. Despite her warning, the petite blonde never wavered from her putting stance.

"I'm expecting a call."

"We're in the middle of a game."

"We're not even on the green yet," he felt compelled to remind her. "We have to wait until Dad gets here to tee off."

"That's beside the point." Her piercing blue eyes bore straight into him and for a second he was transported back to childhood. But as quickly as her maternal powers appeared they disappeared. Not even on her worst day had Olivia been much of a disciplinarian.

"Uh huh."

"Parker, you know the rules. No business today. It's family time." When Olivia noticed her stern expression hadn't gotten her the results she craved, she tilted her head to the side and smiled, trying charm instead.

It was a move that had worked for the beauty countless times in the past. Olivia was a stunning woman. She always had been. And unlike other women her age, her classic good looks hadn't withered with time. She'd been a television icon in the seventies. And thanks to Nick at Nite and nostalgia, her popularity was coming back strong.

But Parker was her son, not a fan and he wasn't easily swayed. It was almost a week since he'd heard from Cyn and he was not pleased. He thought they'd had a great time this weekend, so her disappearing act made no sense whatsoever. He'd left over thirty messages on her cell phone and twice as many with one of her roommates, all to no avail. If it wasn't for work, he'd have flown there days ago. Being the boss sometimes meant having to put in the extra hours, even if he didn't want to.

Ignoring his mother, Parker returned his attention to his cell and began to dial Cyn's number by heart. Before he keyed in the second number, the phone was snatched from his hand and went sailing through the air.

"Mother!" To his everlasting relief, his father, with his perfect timing, caught it in midair as he came up on them.

"Whoa." Abraham Maguire glanced at the gadget then tossed it to Parker without missing a step. Stopping in front of Olivia, he pulled her into his embrace and dipped her. It was a move Parker had seen his father make over a million times, and it never failed to make his mother giggle like a teenage girl. "Gather the kids, honey, it's raining iPhones, one of the seven signs of the Apocalypse."

"Abraham, talk to your son."

"Okay." Abraham straightened and released Olivia. Frowning, he turned to Parker with a stern expression that immediately melted away and held out his hand. "Hi, son."

"Hey, Dad." Parker gripped his father's hand in his and smiled.

The older man's eyes twinkled with merriment. Parker was the carbon copy of his father in looks and deeds. If it wasn't for the graying hair they might have passed for brothers. A fact his mother loved to point out. "What's new?"

"Nothing and everything."

"Splendid." Abraham clapped his hands together and rubbed them gleefully. "Let's play."

"After I make a call."

"See." Olivia pouted, this time turning her charms on her husband. "He's breaking the golden rule."

"Just because everyone in the world you want to speak to is standing right in front of you, doesn't mean it's the same for the rest of us."

"Oh, really?" She questioned inquisitively. "Whom do you wish was here?"

Fuck! He walked right into that one. "No one. Now excuse me."

This time his mother offered no arguments. Unfortunately his luck ended there. Once again he was directed straight to Cyn's voicemail. Irritated he ended the call, refusing to leave a message. He'd heard of playing hard to get but this was freaking ridiculous.

Turning around, he headed back to his parents who from the way their heads were bent together, meant only one thing. They were conspiring. *Would he ever learn?* "Are you two ready?"

"Yes," Olivia answered. With a wave of her hand she gestured for their caddy and hooked her arm under his. "Abraham, why don't you drive the cart and I'll walk with Parker."

"Walk." Stunned, he turned questioning eyes his father's way, but the traitor quickly looked away and did as he was bid. "Mother, you hate walking the green."

"A little stroll will do me some good. Besides this way we can talk."

Oh, joy. "About?"

"The phone call for one."

"Or we can not talk about it."

"Then let's talk about the costume ball."

Was it that time of year again? "Okay." Where was she going with this? Every October his parents hosted a costume ball benefiting the Make a Wish Foundation. Not only was it an annual event it was also a family event. Something he wouldn't be able to get out of no matter how justified the excuse was.

"I received the invites in the mail the other day and they're to die for."

Parker nodded and continued to walk to the first tee, refusing to comment until he knew exactly where this was leading.

"I'd be more than happy to send one to someone for you," she offered.

"You would?"

"Yes." Her eyes glittered with amusement. "Is there anyone in particular you want me to invite?"

Parker paused and turned to face her. "You know, Mother, there is someone you can invite for me."

"Really?" He could practically hear her mental wheels turning as he spoke.

"Yes. Solomon. He was beside himself last year because he didn't get one."

"Parker." His mother slapped him on his arm in mock rage. "You know I wasn't referring to Solomon."

Abraham slid out of the cart and joined them. He wrapped his arm around Olivia's waist and pulled her to him. His parents were an affectionate couple, and even though it was slightly sickening, it was also sweet. "Are you done pumping him for information?"

"No," Olivia answered at the same time Parker said, "Yes."

Laughing, Abraham shook his head. "If you just let her fix you up with someone, she wouldn't pester you as much."

"As much. What do I have to do to get not at all?"

"Get married and give me grandchildren," she volleyed back.

"All in due time."

"Time is a-wasting. Your father isn't getting any younger."

"Right." Parker was smart enough not to mention the fact his mother was two years older than his father. "I can pull an Angelina and adopt one for you."

"Kids aren't puppies. You don't swing by the pound and pick one up," she grumbled. "I want a little boy with your father's eyes and your spirit. Or better yet, a little girl who's the spitting image of her grandmother."

"Would you settle for a little girl with big brown eyes and caramel-colored skin?"

Olivia's eyes widened. "Is there one on the way?"

"No." And for some reason the idea of that bothered him. "But anything is possible."

"So you're seeing someone."

"Maybe." He hedged. It was hard to put a handle on what Cyn and he were. They were more than lovers, at least he felt as if they were.

"And she's Latino?"

"No. She's black."

"So you are seeing someone." Ever the hound dog, she pounced. "Wonderful."

His father's rich vivacious laughter burst free. "You just don't learn do you, boy?"

If Parker were limber enough he would kick his own ass. "Apparently not."

"Send me her address and I'll fire off an invitation to the ball ASAP." Turning to her husband, she grinned. "Did you hear, Abraham? He's seeing someone."

"Yes, dear."

"Mixed couples make the most beautiful children," she continued to gush.

"Hold on." If he didn't put a stop to this now, she'd be out buying cradles before the day was over. "Things haven't progressed that far yet."

"What do you mean?"

"We're in the beginning stages of dating."

"What's her name? Do we know her?" A quick frown marred her perfect brow. "She's not an actress is she?"

Olivia had never been shy about her feelings about the new breed of women taking over Hollywood. Race and gender was never her Achilles' heel, but she'd made it very clear if Parker brought home an actress, she would disown him. His mother was so weird. "No. She runs a shop."

"On Rodeo?"

"No. Somewhere in San Francisco."

"San Fransi—" She sighed. "Never mind. Just get me her address."

"I'll ask her if she—"

"Of course she wants to go. Now go through your little computer and get me her address and number."

"She'll never let us play if you don't," his father solemnly told him.

"Fine," he grumbled, much to his mother's delight.

First she bitched he had the phone, now she was ordering him to use it. He should have just left the damn thing in the car.

Chapter Eight

Baahhrrinnnnggg.

"Damn it." Cyn juggled the grocery bags in one arm as she tried to dig her keys out of her pocket. She was in a race to answer the phone. Since losing her cell phone the other day she'd been tied to the one in her house, hoping against hope Parker would call.

She hadn't heard from him in almost a week. Thanks to her lack of Gingko she was unable to call him. Not only had she lost her phone, she lost his business card as well. If she didn't hear from him by the following Saturday she was going to go down to the club and pester DelRay for his number. It was embarrassing, but for Parker she'd be willing to swallow her pride.

After unlocking the door, she dropped the bags on the floor and dashed into the kitchen. She could hear the television blasting in the living room, which had her seeing red. Drew and Staci were home, and yet they didn't bother to answer the phone. God she hated them.

Out of breath, she grabbed the phone off the charge. "'Lo."

"So, you are alive."

"Parker." She pumped her fist in excitement. "Hey you."

"Hey you. Is that all I get after all this time?" Even grumpy she was glad to hear from him. "I've been calling you all week."

"You have?"

"Yes, damn it. Would it have been too much effort for you to return my call?"

Under normal circumstances Cyn wouldn't bother to dignify so much attitude with a response, but she was willing to make an exception this time. Besides he sounded really cute when he pouted. "I lost my freaking cell and your business card. Arrgg. The fates are plotting against me."

"And my messages?"

"I wasn't able to check my phone mess—"

"Not those. The ones I left with your roommates."

"You left...messages?" Cyn closed her eyes and took in a deep breath. She was going to kill those bitches if it was the last thing she did. Because of them, she'd been working non-stop at the shop. They were *supposedly* sick. Supposedly being the key word and between her father and herself, they been covering the store since the moment she landed in town. Normally, it wouldn't have bothered her to be at work, but now there was someone special in her life she wanted to spend time with, it wasn't so easy to roll over and play dead. "They never gave them to me."

"None of them?"

"No." She exhaled and opened her eyes. "None of them."

"Fucking bitches."

She couldn't agree more. "I'm sorry."

"You don't have to apologize for their forgetfulness."

"Yeah...forgetfulness." She didn't buy that for a second. "I'll take care of it."

"Are you okay?" His concern came over the line loud and clear. It was enough to make her want to smile again.

"Just tired."

"Do you want me to send the plane for you? I can't take off just now or else I'd come there and get you myself."

Send the plane. This time the smile did appear. "As much as I'd love to run away with you, I can't. I have to work this weekend."

"How about the weekend of the seventeenth?"

"Is that when you'll be free again?" The very idea of not seeing him until next month was painful.

"Lord, no. We'll see each other before then. There's a ball that Saturday that I would like you to accompany me to."

"A ball?" Was he serious?

"Yes, costume. It's cheesy I know, but it's for a good cause."

"Will I see you?"

"Yes."

"Then that's all the cause I need."

Parker's voice lowered to a seductive pitch. "Would it be forward of me to tell you I've missed the hell out of you?"

"It wouldn't be forward enough."

"This long distance thing is for the birds. I want to see you."

His words warmed her heart. Sinking to the floor, Cyn rested her back against the cupboard and stretched her legs out in front of herself. "I want to see you too."

"It's turning into a need. I'm not sure how I feel about that."

He wasn't the only one. "Let me know when you do."

"I will. Take down my number again. This time I'm going to give you my house, my cell and my private line. And don't put them on the same paper. I don't want to take the chance you can't reach me."

"Needy much?"

"Where you're concerned? Hell, yes."

Grinning, she stood and pulled out a pen from the junk drawer. She wrote his numbers, making sure she copied each number on more than one paper. What had once seemed like merely a run of bad luck regarding the cell and business card, now seemed a bit more sinister.

"When is your next day off?" he asked, once she was finished jotting down his information.

Day off. What was that? "I have Thursday off, but I have a million errands to run. I'm also in the process of hiring new people." Or she would be once she finally convinced her father to let the demonic duo go. "So I'll be swamped at the store until the training is over. But no matter what, I'll make sure to get that Saturday off."

"Swamped, huh?"

He sounded like a lost little boy. "Unfortunately. What about the week after next?"

"Let me see what I can arrange on my end. I'm not willing to let this fade away."

His words brought a smile to her lips. "Neither am I."

"Good. I have to go. Call me tonight."

"I will."

"Bye, love."

Love? "Bye."

As soon as she hung up, her smile slid away.

She ripped the paper off the notepad and stuffed it into her pants pocket before storming into the living room, hell bent on vengeance. It was bad enough she was forced to share her home, her job and her father with Drew and Staci. She could even live with the fact they borrowed her clothes and never returned them, but she be damned if she was going to let them ruin the one ray of sunlight in her otherwise drab existence.

The evil duo was where she'd expected them to be, sitting on their asses watching her television. Irritated, Cyn walked over to the entertainment center and turned it off. When Drew raised the remote to turn it back on, she bent over and pulled the plug from the wall.

"What the hell is your problem?" Drew bellowed.

"You and your sidekick." Cyn crossed her arms over her breasts. "Which one of you bitches has been keeping my messages from me?"

The twin sisters shared a guilty look, letting Cyn know it

wasn't a one-man act. Drew was the first to meet her eyes but instead of appearing the slightest bit guilty, she looked pleased. "All of this over a few missed messages?"

"Three is a few, Drew. I believe there were more than three." Cyn turned her heated stare to Staci who had the grace to look ashamed. "Isn't that right, Staci?"

"Maybe one or two more."

"Right." She didn't buy that for a second. "After everything I've done for you, my father has done for you, you'll still act like a bunch of—"

Drew rolled her eyes as if she was bored. "Get over yourself, Cyn. The world doesn't revolve around you."

"My world does and from now on, you're not welcome in it." She'd tried. Lord knows she had, but she wasn't a saint nor was she a doormat. "The two of you have a month to find another place to live." Cyn wanted to say a week, but she knew if she did they would be on her father's doorstep by sundown.

Her words apparently caught their attention. "What?"

"You...you can't do that," Staci whined, rising to her feet. "Where will we go?"

"Not my problem." And man did it feel good to say those words. Satisfied for the first time in a long time, Cyn moved from in front of the television and headed back to the kitchen.

She was headed off in her path though by Drew, who was no longer looking so pleased. "This isn't over. Not by a long shot."

"Oh, but it is." Cyn brushed past the angry woman. She would no longer let her family obligations deprive her of those things she wanted in life. And Parker was number one on her priority list. Her father was just going to have to understand. As for Drew, Staci and their mother, she didn't really care if they understood or not. It was her time now.

No matter how many times Parker saw Cyn, it was always as if he was looking at her for the first time. Standing outside The Glass Slipper, he peered through the window and watched her work. Not that she was working. With the exception of Cyn and an older African American man, the shop was empty. Not that it seemed to bother Cyn. She was sitting on top of the counter as she talked to the gentlemen, smiling and laughing with him as if he was an old friend.

Just watching her smile brought a smile to his lips. She looked as lovely as he remembered. She was dressed in a mauve, short sleeve shirt and a matching floral skirt that showcased her sexy legs in the hottest of ways. It seemed as if it had been years since he'd last seen her, not merely a couple of weeks. With his work schedule and hers, they hadn't been able to get together. They talked every day, several times a day on the phone, but it wasn't the same.

Despite being horny as hell, he'd purposely made sure all of their phone calls were as non-erotic as possible. That was until last night. Thanks to a little breathless moan on her part and a willing cock on his, their goodnight call turned into a *good night* phone call.

Dirty words merged into heady moans, which were soon over taken by guttural groans as they came together. Although the orgasm was much needed and long overdue, it paled in comparison to the real deal. Parker didn't want his hand. He wanted Cyn. So much so he blew off his meetings today to come see her.

And it was well worth the headache he'd have when he flew home tomorrow afternoon. She didn't know he was there, in fact she didn't even know he was coming to town, which allowed him to view her in an entirely different way, unguarded. Parker sometimes felt she erected a wall around herself to keep him at a distance. It wasn't going to work though. He was too stubborn and falling too deeply in love with her to allow that to happen.

Unable to wait a moment longer to have her in his arms, Parker opened the door and walked into the shop. When the bell above dinged, two sets of similar eyes turned in his direction, but he was only interested in one.

A soft gasp escaped Cyn before she jumped off the counter and ran full force into his arms. Pleasure like none other filled Parker as he swept her up into his arms and swung her around. God, he'd missed this woman. He'd been wrong earlier. He wasn't falling in love with her. He was already there.

As they stood staring into each others' eyes, Parker realized it was more than just the few nights apart that were getting to him. It was her presence in his day to day life he was missing, although he'd only had it for a short time. She wasn't around when he wanted to share some news. She wasn't the last person he saw before he drifted off to sleep. Nor was she the first person he saw when he woke. Cyn wasn't there. And he didn't like it one bit.

"Hello, stranger," she said in her standard greeting. Her warm brown eyes seemed to smile as she stared up at him.

"Hey." Parker stared at her, wishing he could come up with some clever line, but it had been too long and he needed her, right now, if only in a small way. Bending his head, he kissed her. The feel of her soft, full lips under his was good, but still not enough. His tongue swept inside her mouth, relishing the taste of her as he pulled her body tight against his.

The sound of a clearing throat finally penetrated the haze in his brain, forcing him to remember where they were and reminding him that they were not alone. Begrudgingly, he broke their kiss and stared down into her eyes as he tried to communicate all his feelings in that one look. He loved her and he wanted her to be able to tell with every touch, every look, and every caress of his hand.

"I take it you missed me." Her voice was husky

"I'd say," said a deep voice from behind them. "I was about to break out the fire hose."

"Dad."

Dad! Parker immediately dropped his arms, released Cyn

and turned to face the father of the woman he'd been seconds away from molesting. Not exactly the first impression he wanted to make. "So would this be a good time to let you know that I do know your daughter and that I'm not some random freak with a foot fetish who likes to accost women in shoe stores?"

"Yes. Now would be the time."

"Oh, stop it. He knows exactly who you are," Cyn said with exasperation. "Parker Maguire, this is my father Walter Elder. Dad, this Parker."

She'd told her father about him. *Interesting.* "Nice to meet you, sir."

"Call me Walt." Her father offered Parker his hand. "So you're the young man who has captured my daughter's heart."

"Dad!" Although her response was indignant, she didn't correct her father's assumptions.

"Only as much as she's captured my own." Parker was more than willing to let this man know just how he felt about his daughter. He didn't want there to be any misunderstandings. Cyn turned with a frown marring her lovely face and Parker realized he'd just declared himself to her father, although he hadn't actually told her of his feelings.

"I'm glad to hear it. She deserves only the best."

"I agree." *Whole-heartedly.*

Cyn cleared her throat loudly, turning the attention of both men toward her. "*She's* in the room. Can I be included in this conversation?"

"This is man-talk, woman." Her father's eyes twinkled with unsuppressed amusement.

"That's right. I need to find out what your bride price is." He turned his attention back to Walt. "Now are we talking ten goats or twenty?"

Walt brought his hand up to his chin and rubbed it as if he was contemplating Parker's question. "It depends on the goats."

"Great." She groaned good-naturedly. "Two wise asses."

"For the price of one." Parker teased and pulled her in tight to him. She felt so good in his arms he didn't want to ever let her go. "Aren't you the lucky one?"

"That's me. The lucky one," she said with a roll of her eyes. But even her sarcasm was welcomed, especially when she snuggled up to him as she gave him hell. "I still can't believe you're here. I didn't think I was going to get to see you before the ball."

"What kind of ball are we talking about here?" Walter asked.

"A charity costume ball my mother hosts every year. It benefits the Make a Wish Foundation." An idea struck him. "If you like I'd be more than happy to get an extra invitation for you and yo..." Cyn pulled away from him and discreetly shook her head as his offer slipped out, forcing him to trail his words off weakly. "Urrr..."

Thankfully, Walt was shaking his head at the same time. "Thank you anyway, but I have to pass. My days of dancing till midnight are long past." Walt glanced over at his daughter with love in his eyes. "Have you picked a costume yet, honey?"

"No. I haven't had time to look for anything." Cyn turned to him and eyed him speculatively. "What are you going as?"

"Prince Charming." He watched her lips twist in grin. "Shut up."

"Oh, I don't think so." She teased. "And tell me, Prince Parker, did you come up with this idea all by yourself?"

"I'm not that vain. My mother had the costume made. She's big on themes. This year she wants us to dress up like characters from a fairy tale. Lame I know."

"It's not lame. I think it's sexy you still do what your mommy wants."

"Brat." Cyn was lucky her father was in the room or he might show her what he really thought of her comment, with his hand against her upturned bare bottom.

Cyn blew him a kiss in lieu of a response. Their childish

antics seemed to amuse her father who discreetly interrupted them. "If you pardon an old man's foolishness, I think I might have an idea."

"What?" she asked.

"It's a surprise." Walt walked back around the counter and picked up his car keys. "I'll be back."

"A surprise. Dad!"

"Twenty minutes tops." Walt grinned as he hurried out of the shop, leaving Parker and Cyn staring after him.

Cyn glanced from her father's retreating back to Parker and took his hand into hers. "I can't believe you're here."

He couldn't believe it took him that long to make the trip. "I couldn't stand to be away from you any longer."

"Really?"

"Really."

She glanced at the door then back to him with a wicked little grin. "You know a lot can happen in twenty minutes."

"Do tell."

She put her finger to her lips before winking at him. Then with a spring in her step, she walked over to the door. She turned her head toward him and waggled her brows. He knew she was up to something nefarious when she flipped the lock and the closed sign and then pulled down the shade.

"What's going on?"

Rejoining him, she took his hand and began to pull him toward the back of the store. "There's a little something back here I think you need to see."

"What's that?"

"Me."

Chapter Nine

The second they stepped in the storage room, they were all over one another. There was no time for finesse. They were on a time crunch. Although there was a lot they could do in twenty minutes, Cyn was only interested in one.

Fucking.

Cyn wasn't sure who initiated the kiss, but she didn't care. All she cared about was being in Parker's arms once more. His tongue swept across hers as he ran his hands over her back, as if familiarizing himself with her body once more. It was a sentiment with which Cyn could definitely relate as she wrapped her arms around his neck and held on to him with all her might.

A low growl sounded deep in his throat as she pressed her breasts up against the massive wall of his chest. She could feel the evidence of his desire touching her belly, pressing hard and thick in all its glory. She felt as if she was on fire, and Parker was the only one who could quench her flame.

Their mouths were fused, as if they were attempting to make up for all their time apart in this one moment. Yet it still wasn't enough.

Parker broke their kiss as he nudged her back against the wall and shoved his hand under her skirt. He brushed his fingers against her cloth-covered mound, before taking the silk material in his hand and tugging lightly. "I want this off. Now."

Cyn considered herself a very independent, head strong,

Sojourner Truth type woman, yet the second Parker's voice took on that commanding tone, her knees weakened, her pulse sped up, and she instantly became wet. "Bossy."

"The clock's ticking, Cyn." He took a step back, giving her enough room to do as he bid, but nothing else. "Don't have me tell you again."

Oh God, she was going to combust into a million particles. But it was going to be well worth it. Licking her lips, she moved her hands to her waist and pushed the red silk past her hips.

He watched her intently as her panties dropped to the floor. His heat-filled gaze practically devoured her whole. With a simple look, Parker made her feel as if she was everything, the most beautiful and desirable woman alive. And he was all hers.

She couldn't wait to take him into her body again. The second she stepped out of her panties she reached for him. She wasn't in the mood for foreplay. She wanted him to take her and take her now. "Fuck me."

"You should know better than that. Spread your legs. Now." Parker dropped to the floor in front of her, wound his hand in her skirt, and held it up and to the side. He moved her left leg over his shoulder and pulled her hips forward before inhaling deeply. Leaning back he looked up at her with a heat-filled gaze. "God, I missed the scent of you."

"Is that all you missed?"

"No. I missed the way you taste as well. I missed waking up with you in the morning." Parker spread Cyn's nether lips wide and lightly brushed his finger over her clit, dragging a moan from the depths of her. "And I really missed the way you cry my name when you come."

"I don't cry your name."

"Yes, you do." He blew lightly on her overheated bundle of nerves, before caressing her once more. "Should I remind you?"

"Please do." Cyn whimpered as she leaned weakly against the wall. She didn't know if she had the strength to stand while he pleasured her, but she was going to do her damndest and try.

"I think I will." And that was all that he said. The smooth flesh of his finger was replaced by the warm heat of his mouth. His tongue stroked over her sensitive clit, lashing her engorged bud as she leaned back against the wall and held on for dear life.

"Parker," she moaned, as she buried her hands in his thick hair and held him to her pussy. She didn't want him to ever stop. The touch of his mouth was like heaven on earth, and it'd had been way too long since she'd been to heaven.

His tongue lathed the sensitive bundle of nerves as he slid two fingers deep within her moist depths. There was nothing gentle about the way he finger fucked her, which was good because she wasn't in a gentle state of mind. She wanted to be taken, ravished, fucked until she couldn't think straight, and Parker was just the man to do it.

"Oh, God. Don't stop," she begged. "So close."

His mouth teased and tormented her as his fingers plunged into her hot, wet sex, fucking her over and over until she thought she'd go mad from the pleasure of his touch alone.

Her body trembled as the climax, seemingly out of reach, rushed upon her.

She screamed his name as she came. Her orgasm tore through her at lightening speed. One second she was on the brink and the next she was falling head over heels into the abyss. Her release was so fast it was painful, but well worth the wait.

Her spasm had barely slowed before he pushed her leg to the ground. Her hand fell limply from his hair as he stood. All of her energy was spent in keeping her on her feet. He made quick work of his pants, pushing them down past his knees. The sound of foil ripping was the only warning she received before he lifted her hips, anchored her to the wall and centered his cock at the apex of her sex.

"Still in denial about the crying?" he asked, as brushed his crown against her moist tender flesh.

"I didn't cry." Her voice was rough and shaky. As light-headed as she felt, Cyn was surprised she was able to form words into sentences. "I screamed."

"Even better." Without saying another word, Parker began his slow penetration into her body. He pushed into her steadily, not stopping until he was buried balls deep inside her. "Damn, I missed you," he groaned. "I can already tell, baby, this is going to be a fast and bumpy ride."

Cyn cried out as her body stretched around his thick cock. It had been so long, so fucking long since she'd felt him inside her. "Do you hear me...complaining?"

"No." Parker dug his fingers into her hips and pulled back until only the head of his cock remained, before plunging forward once more. "The only thing I want to hear you do is moan."

That was something she could do with absolutely no problem. Cyn dug her nails in to his shoulder as he powered into her. If it weren't for his shirt, she was sure she would have scarred him for life.

Normally she loved to be naked with him, to feel their skin sliding against each other. But their need was so powerful, so urgent, there was no time for all the niceties. Removing clothing was something that would take too much time. She needed him now.

"You're so fucking tight." He murmured between thrusts. "So tight and hot. How did I go so long without my fix of you?"

"Don't know. Don't care." Talking could come later. "Just don't stop."

"I wouldn't dream of it." He pushed into her again and caused her to gasp with the force of his thrust. "But meet me halfway there. Fuck my cock, baby, as I fuck your pussy."

She had no problem acceding to his demands.

They worked in tandem with one another. As Parker thrust up, Cyn bore down. She took every inch of his cock into her aching pussy, loving the feel of his hard flesh inside her tender sheath. Tightening her arms around his neck, she leaned back into the wall and arched her hips, enabling him to drive deeper inside her. Her orgasm was so fresh, her body felt sensitive to the touch, but she didn't care. Cyn would take every second of pain to have one moment of pleasure with him.

He kept her on the edge, teasing her with fast thrusts then slowing down when she began to peak only to start the whole process again. She struggled to hold him tight, to force him to give her what she wanted, but he proved far stronger than her at controlling his passions. She could see on his face though his own effort to resist her urgings.

"Parker...please," she whimpered, begging for what she needed.

"There's that cry I'm talking about." Her words were apparently the catalyst he needed to acquiesce to her demands. His cock jack-hammered in and out of her pussy, causing his pelvis to brush against her clit with every thrust. All she could do was hold on and enjoy the rough, wild ride. So much for working together. His loving was fierce and all consuming as the man himself. He took without asking and gave without quarter.

"Don't stop. Don't stop," she begged. "I'm so close."

"Then come for me, baby. Come all over my cock."

He powered into her at backbreaking speeds, pounding her to orgasm with every push. The pressure continued to build with his every thrust until her climax rushed over her, shaking her body from the strength of her release. As she shuddered in his arms, his control vanished, and he sped up, reaching for his own climax as she trembled around him.

Her spasms had barely slowed when his began. Cyn's eyes fluttered open just in time to see Parker's release. Never before had she witnessed something as sensual, so erotic or beautiful in her life as her man giving in to his pleasure. His head fell back, baring his tightly coiled neck to her gaze as he let out a deep guttural groan and came.

Even though she was sure he came, he continued to pump inside her, but at a slower, less rushed pace. "Jesus...Jesus..." he groaned. His body shook with the force of his release as he finally came to a stop. "Ohh. Damn, woman. You're going to be the death of me."

"I do believe..." she said weakly, "I was the poundee and you were the pounder."

His hold on her loosened, but he kept her pinned to the wall. He leaned forward and pressed his damp forehead against her shoulder. She could feel his body racked with aftershocks as his cock was forced to move every few seconds inside her in the most delicious of ways.

"Are you complaining?"

"No. Bragging."

"That's my girl." With a tortured groan, Parker pulled out of her and took a step back, slowly lowering her to the ground. "Bathroom?"

"Down the hall." She gestured with her head, too tired to move her arm. Closing her eyes she leaned her head back against the wall, inhaled deeply and smiled. The room smelled like leather and sex. Not a bad combination, but without a doubt, Cyn knew she'd never be able to come in here again without thinking of this moment. Parker made a mark on her life. In more ways than one.

"If you stay like that, I might be forced to fuck you again." His smooth words were followed by a cool cloth against her sex.

"Damn that's cold." She opened her eyes and stared into Parker's laughing visage.

"It's not cold, baby, you're just so damn hot."

"Smooth talker."

"Just one of the many reasons you love me." His gaze grew serious. "Isn't it?"

Love. Suddenly her mouth felt extremely dry. The woman

who normally had so much to say was speechless. There was no doubt in Cyn's mind she was in love with him, she just didn't know if she wanted to be the one who said it first. It was so cliché. Regular girl falls for famous rich guy. That was the stuff story books were made of. Hell, Parker had even made movies along those same lines. But this wasn't a movie and this wasn't a fairy tale. This was her life. And she was too afraid to ruin it by speaking out of turn.

"Well..."

"I..." Cyn was thrown for a loop, but apparently Parker wasn't.

"Listen, woman," he barreled on. "Don't try to pretend you're not as crazy for me as I am for you."

"I'm crazy alright. Crazy for falling in love with someone like you."

"Someone like me?" Parker cocked a brow. "What's wrong with someone like me?"

"Nothing." She tossed her hands up in the air in resignation. "That's my whole point. From the moment you swept into my life, you've done everything right."

"And that's wrong?"

"Yes!"

"Oookay." He dragged the word out as he regarded her with an amused expression on his face. "You know that makes no sense, right?"

What did that have to do with anything? "Does it have to?"

"You're not like anyone I've ever known. You know that, right?"

"And that's why you love me."

"One of the many reasons." He gave her a lazy cocky smile. "So we both just admitted we're in love with one another, right?"

Damn it! Would she ever learn to just leave well enough alone? She sighed heavily before admitting what he already knew. "Right."

"Then we should do what people do when they're in love."

She dropped her gaze to his zipper then looked back into his eyes. "Again?"

"That's not what I meant. But don't lose that idea." His expression became serious for a moment. "This long distance stuff is for the birds."

That was no lie. "I know it's terrible."

"Then do something about it. Move in with me."

Well, that sounded all well and good until logic weighed in on the matter. She adored Parker, but she just couldn't uproot everything. Or could she? Then again, maybe he wasn't asking her to. Cyn tilted her head to the side and studied him. "Are you considering moving to San Francisco?"

"No."

"Then we have a little problem. My life is here. My job. My home."

"Have you thought about branching out? I'm sure there are drag queens in L.A. that need shoes. Just think of it. The Glass Slipper II."

Cyn felt as if she were on a roller coaster. First seeing him, then their frantic love making in the back room, quickly followed by their declarations of love for one another, only to have him spring this announcement on her. She didn't know up from down.

The idea of a long distance relationship was a daunting one, but so was moving to a new city. Her family and friends were here. It was all she'd ever known. But then seeing Parker earnestly standing before her, she knew she didn't want to lose him. There had to be a way to make this work. "Parker...I..."

He silenced her by placing a finger gently across her lips. "Don't respond now. Give me your answer at the ball."

Cyn moved his hand away from her mouth and locked their fingers together. "The ball?"

"Yes. Meet me at nine o'clock in the center of the dance

floor."

"Cinderella had until midnight."

"Yeah, well, Prince Charming's heart wasn't on the line."

Damn him. Did he have to make this harder? Before she could respond to his heartfelt comment, the bell over the front door rang. "Shit. It's my dad."

Talk about being saved by the bell. Cyn didn't know if she'd rather answer Parker's question or face her father after making love in his store.

"It hasn't been twenty minutes," he whispered, stepping out of her way.

"Tell that to him. " Cyn grabbed her underwear from the ground and slipped them back on. She smoothed her skirt down and ran her fingers through her hair. "How do I look?"

"Like you've just been made love to against the wall."

"Ha, ha, ha," she grumbled, brushing past him as she entered the storefront once more, with Parker right on her heels "Back alrea—"

"Well, isn't this cozy?" Cyn paused in mid-step and looked into the knowing eyes of Franny, flanked by the twins on either side of her. "Tell me, Cynthia dear, whatever were the two of you doing back there?"

Well, fuck!

From the look on Cyn's face, Parker surmised their visitors weren't welcome ones. He hadn't relished being caught by her father making love in the back room, but he was willing to bet Cyn would have rather dealt with her dad than the people smirking at her now.

He could tell from the tense set of her shoulders something was up. Her ire sent his protective gene into overdrive, forcing him to step up from behind her to stand next to her and show a united front. "I thought you locked the door," he said softly out the side of his mouth.

"I did."

Lena Matthews

Which could only mean one thing. These was Cyn's wicked almost step-mother and her evil daughters. From the way she'd described them, Parker half expected the older one to have a slightly green complexion with a furry wart on her chin, and the two younger ones to sprout horns, but they didn't. In fact, the three ladies were very attractive, despite the snarky grins they wore like press-on nails.

"What are you guys doing here?" Cyn crossed her arms over chest and stared at the three women, unyielding. He could tell from her stance she wasn't going to allow them to intimidate her and it made him smile. His woman was a feisty little thing and he wouldn't have her any other way.

"I think the question is what were you guys doing?" The question came from the mother.

"Whatever I want. At last check, I'm grown."

"And at work," the woman fired back.

Cyn lifted her chin, meeting the icy woman's gaze straight on. "Funny, I didn't think you knew what the word work meant."

"I'll have to see if your father finds this situation as amusing as you obviously do."

"You're going to tattle to my dad." Cyn's smirk fed into the other lady's wrath.

"You're such a smart ass."

"Do you really want to resort to name calling, because I can think of a few choice words to sling your way."

"Hey, you better not insult Mama." One of the younger ones piped up. Of course she blanched when Cyn turned her attention toward the girl. Parker felt as if he was in the middle of a ping pong match. There was no doubt in his mind who was going to win though. Cyn was more than holding her own.

"*Excuse me.* One, you don't tell me what to do because I don't answer to you. Two, isn't your mother old enough to defend herself?" This comment elicited a gasp from all three women. "And three, you shouldn't have brought attention to

254

yourself, because I can find insults for you as well, if you think you can take them."

Parker had to control the laughter threatening to bubble up at Cyn's words. His woman obviously didn't need anyone to defend her. She was a force to be reckoned with. The other sister, obviously too stupid for words to learn the lesson Cyn just imparted, jumped into the fray.

"You think you're so smart. But you're not."

Cyn leaned forward as if waiting for more, but then laughed. "Is that it? Damn, Drew, you can't insult someone to save your life."

"Listen here, young lady, when your father hears about this he won't be happy. In fact, I look forward to seeing him taking you down a peg or two. You are too spoiled for words. And don't think you're just going to get away with kicking my girls out."

"There's nothing to get away with. It's already done. And you can tell my father whatever you want. I have nothing to hide. Just make sure it's the truth." She stared pointedly at the two younger girls and they actually had the audacity to blink their eyes in confusion, as if they had no idea to what she was referring to. If he hadn't been aware of their duplicitous nature, he might have bought into the innocent act. But, unfortunately, Parker had been a victim of one of their schemes and he was more than happy to see them get their comeuppance.

Cyn shook her head in disgust as she turned toward him, obviously dismissing them from her thoughts. "Just ignore the—"

Her words were interrupted by the arrival of her father bearing an oversized white box.

The three Cruellas immediately turned toward him and all began speaking at once. Although speaking was a relative term. To Parker it sounded as if they were squawking. Their complaints were varied, but all came down to one common factor, Cyn.

Much to his surprise though, while they bitched and

moaned about her, Cyn didn't utter a word in her defense. It wasn't what he'd come to expect of his little hellion and it took him aback.

"Enough," Walt said sharply. When the noise continued he roared it. "Enough."

As quickly as the braying had began, it ending, coming to a stuttering stop at Walt's harsh command. The room grew so hushed Parker could hear the clock ticking in the background.

In the wake of the silence, Walt set the parcel he'd been carrying on the counter and turned back around, crossing his arms over his massive chest. The easy going man Parker had been introduced to less than an hour ago was gone, and in his place was this formidable giant. "I can't leave you all together for five minutes without War World War Three starting. Without yelling will someone tell me what the hell is going on here? Cyn? Franny?"

Cyn opened her mouth to speak but was drowned out by Franny who barreled on full steam ahead. "This is about your daughter disrespecting me for the last time."

"I wouldn't count on it," Cyn murmured under her breath, much to Parker's amusement.

"Disrespecting you?" Brows furrowed, Walt glanced over at Cyn. "Explain yourself."

"Dad, there's nothing to explain or to get upset about."

"I disagree. Did you know—" Franny's eyes welled with tears, "—she gave the girls a month to move out?"

A month too long as far as Parker was concerned. Cyn was being far too nice. When Walt turned back to look at Cyn in disbelief, Parker could tell he was the only one who thought that. "Is this true, Cynthia?"

"Yes."

"See..." Fanny's smug pleasure made her crocodile tears from earlier ring false.

"Why don't you tell him why, Franny? Or did the girls even

bother to explain it to you?"

"Staci and I have nothing to hide," said Drew in a snotty little tone.

"Do you really want to get into this right now?" Everything in Cyn's stance indicated she was ready to do battle. "Huh, do you?"

Walt glanced over at Parker, and then nodded his head sharply. "No, we'll discuss this at home at a later date."

Not to be put off, Franny added an extra dig. "Another thing you might want to add to your list of 'later' conversations is why the shop was closed when we arrived."

"Closed?"

"Yes, locked tight. They," Franny pointed to Cyn and Parker as if they were some sort of criminals, "were in the backroom doing God knows what."

Could this get any worse? Walt's gaze collided with Parker's, but Parker didn't flinch. He met the surprised man's gaze head on, refusing to cower or feel embarrassed for spending time alone with his woman.

"Oh, please," Cyn muttered, crossing her arms over her breasts. "He *is* my man. Hello."

He was her man. Parker couldn't hold back his grin. *Take that, bitches.*

"And this is your place of work," Franny shot back.

"What makes you think I wasn't showing him around?"

"I'm sure he's been around, all right." Drew sniffed as if her shit didn't stink. "Lord knows you have."

"Watch yourself, Drew." Walt warned as he turned back around to face the other women. His voice had gone ice cold, and his posture stiff as a board. "What they were doing back there is none of our business. Nor is it anything that hasn't been done in this store before."

"Eww, Dad." Cyn grimaced. "I could have gone the rest of my life without knowing that."

"I assure you, honey, the feeling is mutual," he said with a wink.

Parker's esteem for the man was growing by leaps and bounds. There wasn't a doubt in his mind where Cyn got her sense of humor or fortitude from.

"But, Walt—"

"I said later, Francine." Walt's tone brooked no further argument and the older woman seemed deflated for a moment. Parker didn't miss the snide look she shot Cyn however. He had a feeling this incident wasn't over as far as Francine was concerned.

"Now for your surprise, Cyn."

Walt had turned his attention back to the large box he'd carried in. Gently lifting the lid, he revealed a swath of tissue paper. Parker noted a sheen in the older man's eyes, as if he were on the verge of tears.

"Cyn, baby, come on over here. I have something very special I want you to see."

Cyn joined her father at the counter and snuggled into his embrace when Walt wrapped his arm around her shoulders.

"When you told me about this ball—"

"Ball, what ball?" Franny exclaimed.

"Cyn's been invited to a fancy charity masquerade party." The pride in Walt's voice was more than evident.

"Is it for the whole family?"

Parker blanched at the thought of having Franny and her daughters at the event, although he'd almost invited the bitter woman. Thankfully Cyn had stopped him, but it had been a close call.

Walt frowned at Franny's interruption and she actually looked a bit worried. "No, of course not. This is a special occasion, just for my girl."

Everyone in the room could hear the love emanating from his words. But Parker could tell it didn't help to endear Cyn to the other three women. In fact, Parker could practically hear their teeth grinding.

"And for such a wonderful night, you need a wonderful dress." Walt spread open the tissue paper to reveal the dress.

"Is that Mom's...?" Cyn's voice broke and she was unable to finish her question.

"Yes." Walt's own voice sounded a bit thick with emotion and he cleared his throat before continuing. "I figure if you were going to a ball with a prince, you should have a dress fit for a princess."

Chapter Ten

"You're going to die when you see my dress." Cyn excitedly ushered Miller into her apartment. "My father found it in the attic and pulled it out for me."

Words alone couldn't express the high she was on. Not only was she going to a ball with her personal Prince Charming, she would be wearing her mother's Cotillion dress.

The ivory gown was similar to the princess dresses she'd read about in stories when she was younger. As a child she used to sit and stare for hours at her mother's photo albums. The one that held her attention and captured her imagination though, was the one with pictures of her mother wearing the pretty white dress at the formal dance.

Cyn had never had a Cotillion of her own. Her mother passed before she turned fifteen and the dreams she had were laid to rest alongside her mother. But now, she'd have a chance to be a princess, just as her mother was.

"Is this your month or what?"

"Definitely." Cyn was blessed in so many different ways. "The gruesome twosome are now officially my father's problem not mine. I'm dating the man of my dreams and I have a private plane waiting on me as we speak to whisk me away to a ball where said man is waiting for me. Could my life be more of a fairy tale?"

"It really couldn't," Miller agreed happily. "Speaking of your man, is he waiting at the airport?"

"No, I haven't seen him since last week."

"You mean when you were busted by your dad doing it in the backroom."

"Shut up." She was never going to live that down.

"No can do. As your best friend it's my job to tease you unmercifully about this to the day we die."

"Tell me something I didn't know," she said with a roll of her eyes.

"No, how about you tell me something I don't know. Are you going to take him up on his proposition?"

This was a question that had plagued Cyn like nothing else before. She weighed her pros and cons, asked her family and friends for advice and even took stock of her life circumstances, but when it came down to it, she realized she had to go with her heart. And her heart was with Parker. "Yes, I am. I'm not sure of the hows and whys right now, but I want to be with him. My dad and I talked about it and he wants me to make the move."

"He wants you gone?"

"No, he wants me to be happy and he knows Parker makes me happy. So I'm going to do it."

"Wow." Miller seemed surprised by her admission.

"I know." She smiled. She hadn't told Parker, but Cyn was pretty sure he was going to think the news was wow worthy as well. "But we can discuss all of that later. Right now, let's talk about my beautiful dress."

"When did you take it out of the cleaners?"

"Today. My dad picked it up for me and he was going to drop—" The words died in her throat as they rounded the corner and spotted Drew and Staci standing in the living room. After the little showdown at the store they'd moved out, much to her delight. So it was a bit shocking to see the two of them standing bold as day in her place again. "What are you two doing here?"

"We just came by to get a few things we left."

"Good." Cyn took off her purse and set it on the side table. "Now leave."

"We will, but first..." Staci glanced quickly at Drew then back to Cyn. She took a hesitant step back and a little to right, as if she was trying to stand behind Drew. "We need to talk to you."

"About what?" Cyn didn't really care what Staci had to say. They weren't moving back in. Not today. Not ever. The last three nights were the most peaceful of her life and she planned to keep it that way.

"There was an accident," Staci said softly.

Cyn frowned. "What type of accident?"

"Well...Walt asked us to pick up your dress."

"Oh, no." Miller caught on before she did. He stepped up behind her and placed his hands comfortingly on her shoulders. "Cyn stay calm."

"What?" Confused she glanced back at him, then to Drew who was watching her intently.

"It was an accident," Staci repeated. "You know how clumsy I am."

"What was an acc—" Sudden realization hit her squarely. "Not the dress."

"I didn't mean to."

"What did you do?" Miller questioned, his voice filled with rage.

"It's just a little wine."

"Wine." Cyn glanced wildly around the room looking for any evidence of the supposed accident. "Where's my dress?"

"I'm sorry," Staci cried.

"Where?" She was going to kill them.

"In the kitchen. I tried to clean it."

Cyn tore away from Miller and raced into the kitchen. Lying on the counter was her mother's gown. There was a large plate sized crimson stain over the bodice with several mini dots along the side.

"Fuck." Miller's outrage was no match for her own.

Deep inside, she known kicking the two of them out would have some repercussions, especially when her father had sided with her over them, but in no way did she ever imagine they would do something so malicious and cold. They didn't just ruin her dress for tonight. They ruined one of the last tangible links she had to her mother. "You...you...bitch."

The words came out stilted and without heat. Her heart was breaking. She didn't have the energy it would take to kill them and bury their bodies.

"It was an accident." The lack of remorse in Drew's voice was the final nail in her coffin.

"Get out."

"I have to get the rest of my st—"

Cyn grabbed the knife off of the cutting board and pointed it at Drew. Maybe she had the energy after all. "Get out now!"

"Cyn, give me the knife." Miller took a step towards her with his hand held out.

"She did it on purpose." Cyn took a step as well, but in the direction of Drew and Staci, who was cowering behind Drew.

"I didn't," Staci squealed.

"Liar! You're a hateful person and you're going to burn in hell. Both of you."

"Yes, they will." Miller came from behind her and grabbed her hand, pulling it to her side. "But not today, and not by your hands."

"They're evil." Tears ran unchecked down her cheeks.

"Yes, and apparently very stupid because they're still here." He tightened his hold on her wrist and pulled her back against him. "If I were the two of you I'd get out."

"But what about..." Staci began to ask.

"I'm going to count to three then I'm going to let her loose."

"But..." Drew tried to argue.

"Three." Miller made as if he was about to release her, which caused the girls to dash from the kitchen, screaming as if it their very lives depended on it.

Cyn let the knife drop to the floor and sank to her knees in front of the ruined dress. The red wine was never going to come out.

"Maybe we can soak it in vinegar."

They could soak it until the cows came home and it still wouldn't change a damn thing. "It doesn't matter."

"Don't say that."

"If this were truly an accident they would have soaked it the minute it happened. This is dried on. I wouldn't put it past them to have used my blow dryer to help it along."

"What are you going to do?"

There was only one thing she could do. "I'm going to call Parker and tell him I can't make it."

"The hell you are."

"You have a better suggestion?" Because Lord knew she didn't.

"I hate to say this, but..." he sighed as if his words pained him, "...we have to call MeShell."

"Why?"

"Because he can help."

"I don't think his magical fairy powers can help now." She hiccupped and wiped at her nose. "But if you just feel the need to see your man, don't let me stand in your way."

"Okay, first of all, shut up." He brushed a stray strand of hair behind her ear. "Secondly, you're in need of a ball gown. Who else is going to have a fabulous dress just lying around?"

He had a point. "Do you think she'll have something we can use?"

"More than sure." Standing, he reached into his pocket and pulled out his cell phone. "I'll call him."

Even as depressed as she was, she couldn't let this

opportunity pass her by. Clearing her throat, she fought hard to keep her smile at bay. "You have his number memorized."

"No." He glanced away, embarrassment staining his cheeks. "It's programmed in there."

"Uh huh."

"He did it. To annoy me."

"Right. And I guess you just never took the time to delete it."

Miller's brow rose. "Do you want my help or what?"

"I do." She stood, resolve in place. If she had to go to the ball in a dress made by mice she was going. "You make your phone call. And I'll make mine."

"Who are you calling?"

"My father."

By the time she finished her phone call with her father she was feeling marginally better. Nothing could ever replace her mother's dress, but something was being done to repair the wrong that was committed. Her father's voice broke when she told him what happened and by the time she explained everything he'd grown eerily quiet. He calmly told her to have a great time and not to worry, he was going to clean house. Somehow she seriously doubted he was talking about vacuuming and dusting.

"We better go if you're going to make your flight."

"What about—?"

Miller took her suitcase in one hand, grabbed her with the other and pulled her towards the front door. "MeShell is going to meet us in the parking lot."

When they pulled into the parking lot of the private airstrip, MeShell's car was already there. Miller parked next to the other man's vehicle and turned off the engine. By the time they stepped out of the car, MeShell was waiting for them next to his trunk. But not the MeShell Cyn was used to seeing.

Instead of the normally glamorous cross-dresser she was

familiar with, MeShell was sans makeup and wig and dressed in a black suit. Despite how rude she knew it was, Cyn couldn't help but stare. He was an ugly woman all right, but he was a very handsome man. "Wow."

She wasn't the only person who was flabbergasted. Miller's mouth was practically hitting the floor, much to MeShell's obvious delight. "What?" he asked, unable to keep his grin at bay.

"You're not wearing..." She paused, unsure of how to continue without hurting his feelings. "You're wearing a suit."

"I do have a day job, you know."

It was sad to say, but despite knowing MeShell for over three years she had no idea what he did when he wasn't in drag. Of course he had a job. She just didn't have the foggiest idea what it was. "Doing what?"

"Shelton Hughes at your service, commodity trader extraordinaire."

"Shel...Shelton," Miller stuttered. "You have to be fucking kidding me."

MeShell grimaced and glanced at Cyn. "Painful isn't it?"

She didn't want to be mean but she wasn't going to lie. "Just a bit."

"I think it's hilarious." Miller snickered. "Shelton the day trader. What a riot."

"You know what's really funny. I'm not only prettier than you. I make more money."

That wiped the smile right off of Miller's face. "You can take the bitch out of the ball gown but you can't take—"

"Miller," Cyn snapped. "MeShell is here to do me a favor or did you forget."

"You can call me Shelton. MeShell just doesn't work without the wig."

"Okay." That was going to take some getting used to. "Sorry about him. He's in a mood."

"Please, doll, I'm not even thinking of little blue boy over there. I came here to help you."

"And I really appreciate it."

"That's what friends are for. I picked out three of my fiercest numbers."

"You're too good to me."

"Yes, too good," Miller spoke up. His I-could-care-less persona was in place and at full blast. Cyn wanted to hit him. It was more than obvious there was something between him and MeShell...Shelton but Miller was too stubborn to admit it. "So are you going let us see them?"

"When we're in the air."

Miller glanced from Shelton to her. "The air?"

"Yes, we're going with her."

"You are?" Now she was confused.

"Yes. I have to make sure it fits." Shelton turned and unlocked his luggage-filled trunk. "I packed a few accessories and my sewing kit. I'm going to have to take one of the dresses in, but I can do that as you get ready."

"Don't you think you should have asked?" Miller inquired.

"No." Shelton turned to Miller and cocked a brow. "Because it wasn't an option. If she wants to look good we're going to have to go."

"Why we?" Miller crossed his arms over his chest in an obvious sign of stubbornness.

"Because you're going too."

"Says who?" His eyebrows skyrocketed to the tip of his hairline.

"Me." Shelton could be just as stubborn it seemed.

Cyn felt as if she was watching a tennis match and she knew without a doubt who she was rooting for. "Shelton's right."

"Thank you."

"He is?" Miller turned and stared at her in abject disbelief.

"Yes. He'll have to fix anything he loans me and we don't have the time to do it here. Looks as if we're going to a ball."

"I didn't have time to pack anything." Miller was grasping at straws now and they all knew it.

"Don't worry I packed some things for you to wear too. I think you'll look fabulous in gold lamé."

"Oh, God." Miller paled.

Cyn could barely hold back her laughter. It looked as if she wasn't the only one who was going to be playing dress up tonight.

For what seemed like the hundredth time tonight, Parker glanced at the antique clock over the large fireplace at one end of the ballroom. He had no idea what was keeping Cyn, but he was becoming antsy. His driver had picked them up over an hour ago from her friend's hotel room. There was no reason she shouldn't have been here by now.

Damn it. He knew he should have picked her up. He wanted to see her. No, he needed to see her. It had been a week since they were last together and he felt as if he was going through withdrawal. And now that stupid deadline was looming ahead and he was no surer of what her response would be now than he had been a week ago.

Maybe he was a fool for trying to convince her to move in with him so soon. Maybe he should have told her he was thinking long term and not just a roommate with benefits. In fact, he'd already spoken to Cyn's father about his intentions. Perhaps he should have just spoken with her instead.

"Tell me something, Prince Brooding," Solomon said as he walked up to Parker. "This mysterious woman of yours doesn't really exist, does she? Come on, you can tell me. You made her up, right?"

Parker glanced over at his grinning friend and frowned. "Not now, Solomon, I'm not in the mood."

As usual, his words had no effect on Solomon. "Moodiness.

Isn't that a symptom of mental illness?"

"Do. Not. Push. Me." Parker enunciated each word clearly and succinctly.

"Or what?" questioned his self-appointed pain in the ass.

"Or I'll signal my mother to come over here. Then whisper in her ear nine simple words."

"Which are?"

Parked grinned devilishly. "Solomon is looking a tad lonely, don't you think?"

"That's just mean." Solomon held up his hands in mock surrender. "I thought we were boys."

"Oh, look," Parker glanced over Solomon's shoulder into the far distance, raised his hand over his head and waved wildly. "There she is."

"Shit." Solomon didn't even bother to look over his shoulder to see if Parker was lying or not before he hurried away from him.

Laughing to himself, Parker lowered his hand and resumed his uncontested dual with time. It was five minutes to nine, and Cyn was nowhere in sight. With a disgruntled grumble he turned his back to the clock and shoved his hand into the pocket of the stiff burgundy slacks. The pants were extremely uncomfortable as was the rest of his cheesy outfit. Whoever thought burgundy slacks with a yellow stripe and a powder blue jacket with gold fringe was a good idea should be shot. He seriously expected some old scary chick to pop out of the corner at any time and shout bippity boppity boo at him.

His fingers brushing against the cool metal of his phone reminded him even more of their lack of communication. He debated with himself for several long seconds on whether or not he would give into his stalker-like urges and call her again, when he noticed his signal bars, or lack thereof.

"Fuck," he muttered to himself. He didn't even have a smidgen of a signal. What if Cyn had been trying to call him? Cursing under his breath, he headed for the stairs leading to the upper floor and the doors to the outside.

As he bounded up the wide staircase near the railing he noticed Cyn rushing down on the far side. With the throng of people between them he wasn't able to capture her attention, but as he pushed his way toward her he noticed one of her slim, jeweled heels had slipped off in her haste. Surprisingly she didn't stop to pick it up and instead just continued on her way through the crowd.

Parker turned and headed toward the area he'd seen Cyn lose her shoe, stooping to pick it up before trudging into the crowd after her. The dance floor had filled during his moment of morose woolgathering and it took him a few seconds to find the hobbling beauty. When he neared her, he grabbed her arm, startling her to the point she lost her balance. Her eyes widened and a smile wreathed her face when she realized who had a hold of her.

"Oh, Parker, Thank God. I thought I missed the deadline." She threw her arms around his neck and hugged him tightly.

His heart swelled, knowing she was rushing to see him to the point she would leave her shoe behind.

"That's okay, baby. For you, I would have extended it."

She pulled back and smacked him lightly on the shoulder. "Don't tell me that now. I gave up a very precious shoe to get here on time."

"I know, I found it." He pulled the jeweled slipper from his pocket and presented it to her.

Cyn gasped, her hand covering her mouth. "Oh my God, you really are my Prince Charming."

"No, just the man in love with you." Parker went to his knees in front of her. Cyn used his shoulder as a way to steady herself as she raised her dainty foot so he could help her with her shoe.

Once the slipper was on, Parker stood. He took her hand in his and stepped back to look her over. She was wearing a beautiful pale blue dress, with short cap sleeves, a full hoop skirt and a plunging neckline. Unfortunately, thanks to the swaying couples he didn't get to stare long. People began to run into them, forcing him to pull her into his arms to join the dancing. As they began to dance around the room, he noted, "This isn't the same dress."

"No." She smiled a sad smile and shrugged her shoulder. "It's a long story. A story for another time."

He was curious about what had happened but he didn't want her thinking sad thoughts. Especially not tonight. "Another time it is. You look lovely. Beyond lovely. Where did you find such a beautiful gown on such short notice?"

"My fairy godfather hooked me up." There was a twinkle in her eyes as she spoke.

Did he hear her right? "Fairy *godfather?*"

"Yes, my friend Shelton had an extra dress. He even took it in for me on the plane."

"Remind me to thank him."

"You'll get the chance to do it later. I hope you don't mind but I had to bring them along as well."

"Them?"

"Miller too. Shelton insisted, and well..."

"I don't mind at all." As long as she was here, all was right with his world. He pulled her in tighter to him and let the music do the talking for a few seconds as he relished in the moment. All around them there were various couples dancing in their fable costumes. He could see some laughing and others just swaying together. But in his mind, none could be as happy as he was at this very moment. She was in his arms once more, where she belonged. After a minute or so of silence he leaned forward and spoke softly into her ear, "Can I assume from your rush to be here on time that you have an answer for me?"

Cyn pulled back a bit until she was peering into his eyes. "Yes." She smiled. "I want to live with you in your palace. I think it's time to give Southern California an opportunity to try on a glass slipper."

Lena Matthews

Parker's heart swelled with love and happiness. "I couldn't agree more."

She gave a slight wry smile. "You do realize though, the press is going to have a field day with this. The Prince of Hollywood and the shop girl."

He spun her out smiling in delight at the pure joy on her face. "They're only going to say one thing about us."

She laughed as he gathered her back into his arms. "What's that?"

"And they lived happily ever after."

Epilogue

"If I didn't know better I'd swear you were teary eyed."

Miller shot MeShe—Shelton an unfriendly look. One of many he'd been sending the man since Shelton came up with the bright idea of the two of them joining Cyn on her little adventure. Now instead of cuddling up with a good book, he was stuck in Renaissance hell, with his former arch foe. His life was one step away from a cheesy sitcom. "I'm not going to cry."

"Aww...it's okay. You can let a tear slide. Hell, I don't blame you. I've always been a sucker for a happy ending."

"You really think they're going to have a happy ending?"

"Of course they are. Look at them." From where they stood on the balcony, Shelton pointed to Cyn and Parker slow dancing on the semi crowded ballroom floor. The party was apparently a rousing success. The ballroom was crowded with attendees and the two of them had escaped to the balcony to get a little air. "Have you ever seen a couple more in love?"

Miller watched the couple swing around on the dance floor with a smile on his face. He had to admit Shelton was right. Cyn and Parker looked as if they were made for one another. The dress Shelton selected for her to wear tonight was the perfect complement to Parker's royal garb. Tonight Cyn was definitely Parker's Cinderella and he was truly her Prince Charming.

"Was that a sigh?" The amusement in Shelton's voice wiped all traces of Miller's smile away.

"No. I was just breathing heavy."

"Sure you were." Shelton snorted, his disbelief more than evident. "She looks just divine in that dress, doesn't she? I, of course, look better in it. And out of it."

Miller was willing to bet he did, although he'd never admit it aloud. "She looks lovely." Unwilling to let an opportunity to bust Shelton's chops pass him by, he turned back and gave the man a once over. "I have to say that I'm surprised you didn't pick one of the other dresses to wear yourself."

Shelton cocked a brow. "Why would I wear a dress when you so obviously prefer me in pants? Besides..." Shelton ran his hands over his emerald velvet jacket, "...I look good no matter what."

Once again, Miller found himself silently agreeing with Shelton. The emerald jacket with tiny gold beading and matching cape and pants looked spectacular on the dark skinned man. He looked every inch the regal monarch he was pretending to be, which made Miller once again question his own outfit, a royal blue tunic, black pants and knee length boots. "Who are we again?"

"I'm the prince, you're the pauper."

"Right, and explain to me why I have to be the pauper and you get to be the prince."

"Some things don't need explaining."

"And you just so happen to have these costumes lying about."

"I enjoy playing dress up, Miller. I'm surprised you haven't noticed."

Miller snorted in lieu of a reply, as he turned his attention back to the dancers. He stood next to Shelton in comfortable silence as he pondered over something the other man said. "Tell me something."

"Okay." Shelton responded without hesitation.

"Since when did you care what I prefer?" Despite the fact

he was very interested in Shelton's answer, Miller feigned indifference.

"Since when haven't I?"

Miller was momentarily speechless in his surprise. No matter how much he might like to pretend differently, there was no way in the world he could deny his attraction to Shelton. Even when the other man pretended to be a she. Miller didn't get it, he didn't necessarily like it, but no matter what the over-exuberant man did, Miller couldn't stop thinking about him. It was something that annoyed him to no end, yet there it was. They were Here. Together. The only question was, what did he want to do about it.

"Stop thinking so hard, old man, and dance with me."

"Dance. Here?" Miller glanced around the balcony in surprised. Though this was Hollyweird, he wasn't exactly comfortable putting his business on display.

Apparently though, Shelton didn't have such qualms. "Can you think of a better place?"

Was he really going to see any of these people again except on the silver screen? No, he wouldn't. Without another second of hesitation, Miller stepped to the other man. Unwilling to allow Shelton to have the final word though, Miller placed his hand on the low of Shelton's back and pulled him in close to him as he tightened his hold on his hand. "I'm leading though."

"In your dreams."

Well, if Cyn's dreams could come true, why not his. "Shut up and dance, Shelton."

Shelton grinned and fell in line. "Whatever you say, Miller."

Miller smiled. He could get used to this.

About the Author

Lena Matthews spends her days dreaming about handsome heroes and her nights with her own personal hero. Married to her college sweetheart, she is the proud mother of two beautiful daughters, three evil dogs, and a mess of ants that she can't seem to get rid of.

When not writing she can be found reading, watching movies, lifting up the cushions on the couch to look for batteries for the remote control and plotting different ways to bring Buffy back on the air.

You can contact Lena through her website: www.lenamatthews.com.

Look for these titles by
Lena Matthews

Now Available:

Joker's Wild: Call Me
Joker's Wild: Three Nights
Joker's Wild: Stripped Bare
Something Borrowed, Something Blue
You Can Leave Your Hat On

He's hot. He's young—way too young. But he's playing for real.

Querida
© 2008 Jamie Craig

Maddy Terrell is forty years old with an adult son and a time-consuming career. The last thing she is looking for is a relationship. In fact, all she wants is a ride—from Los Angeles to San Francisco so she can attend her niece's wedding. But the ride she was counting on has just stood her up, and her only choice is to accept a lift from Tonio Herrera.

He's Latino. He's hot. He's also twenty-four, just too much of a stretch for Maddy to even contemplate, no matter how attracted she is to him.

Tonio's not driving Maddy to San Francisco out of the kindness of his heart. In fact, he has a very specific ulterior motive. Maddy is the most attractive woman he has ever met. After months of flirting, he's determined that this weekend in San Francisco will finally get her attention.

Then comes the hard part—convincing Maddy he wants more than just a weekend fling.

Warning: Shameless flirting, public sex on the San Francisco Bay, road trip fun, and a May/December love affair.

Available now in ebook from Samhain Publishing.

One weekend. His rules. Inhibitions left at the door.

Trust and Dare
© *2007 Shelli Stevens*

Angry that yet another military man has done her family wrong, Abby Cook plots sweet revenge. But when her plan goes awry, she discovers that she's targeted the wrong military man.

Mason Tyler is not used to being disobeyed. Yet the curvy blonde has rejected his advances at every turn. When he catches her in the middle of a very destructive—not to mention illegal—prank, he offers her a deal. A deal that will keep her out of jail. And let him exact a little revenge of his own.

One weekend in his bed…no inhibitions, no refusals. But when the weekend is up, will Mason be ready to let Abby go?

Available now in ebook from Samhain Publishing.

GREAT
CHEAP
FUN

Discover eBooks!

THE FASTEST WAY TO GET THE HOTTEST NAMES

Get your favorite authors on your favorite reader, long before they're
out in print! Ebooks from Samhain go wherever you go, and work with
whatever you carry—Palm, PDF, Mobi, and more.

Samhain
Publishing
LTD

WWW.SAMHAINPUBLISHING.COM

LaVergne, TN USA
25 March 2010
177194LV00002B/10/P